25 TO LIFE

A JACK BERTOLINO NOVEL

JOHN LANSING

WHITE STREET PRESS

This book is a work of fiction. Any references to historical events, real people, or real places are used fictitiously. Other names, characters, places, and events are products of the author's imagination, and any resemblance to actual events or places or persons, living or dead, is entirely coincidental.

First White Street Press trade paperback edition, June 2023

Copyright © 2023 by John Lansing. All rights reserved.

ISBN (Print): 979-8-9885166-1-3

ISBN (Ebook): 979-8-9885166-0-6

Cover design by Karen Phillips

No part of this book may be reproduced in any form or by any electronic or mechanical means, including information storage and retrieval systems, without written permission from the author, except for the use of brief quotations in a book review.

ALSO BY JOHN LANSING

The Jack Bertolino Series:

The Devil's Necktie

Blond Cargo

Dead is Dead

The Fourth Gunman

Good Cop Bad Money (with Glenn Morisano)

The Test

For beautiful Vida who takes me higher.

CHAPTER 1

Gloria was embarrassingly beautiful first thing in the morning. Her lively intelligent eyes were the color of cocoa. Her perfect skin was a shade darker. She blew steam over the rim of her coffee cup, steeling herself for the day. Gloria mentally repeated the bullet points she wanted to make with her next group of interviewees.

Mug shots of Carl Forbes, a teenage African American boy, were taped to her mirror. A daily reminder of her life's work. She quickly gathered her overflowing briefcase and iPad, and locked the apartment door behind her.

Gloria slid behind the wheel of her Fiat, the color of a pistachio, and headed for her first appointment with Councilman Mark Corcoran.

Gloria's interview with the councilman wasn't going well. Saying she worked with Project for the Innocent did her no good. Corcoran had agreed to give her ten minutes of his time, but the officious man had already checked his watch twice.

Corcoran had grown up in the Mar Vista area. Back in the day, it was a lower-middle-class neighborhood filled with modest bungalows set on half-lots, blue-collar workers, immigrants and a mix of street gangs. He was a self-made man. A success story. A working-class kid who had risen so high, he had political aspirations beyond his tenure with the City Council.

"I'm a big fan of your program," Corcoran said. His unblinking eyes used to intimidate had no effect on Gloria. "But I believe your client is a guilty man. I followed the case—hell, we all knew the kid. Quiet type, lived a few blocks over, didn't run with our set. Hard to believe him capable of such brutality, but an eyewitness saw him in the general area around the time of the murder. More important, the man confessed to the crime."

Gloria was prepared for this. "Carl says the arresting officers tortured the confession out of him. He was seventeen years old. Thirty-six hours without food or bathroom facilities. And look at the photograph, it's clear he'd been beaten."

The councilman glanced at the photo and handed it back. "He was picked out of a lineup."

"Eyewitnesses are notoriously undependable. If the cops coerced the confession, it's not a stretch to think they might have manipulated the lineup. And none of his DNA, his semen, was found on, or in the victim's body. Shelley Goldstein had been sexually assaulted before she was murdered. I believe Carl was set up. He's already served twenty-three years of his life sentence for a murder he didn't commit."

Corcoran wasn't moved. He accepted the jury's verdict, and wouldn't be swayed. He looked down at her overflowing briefcase before continuing. "Shelley was a lovely girl, and she was rich. None of the boys in our neighborhood stood a chance in hell with her. I'm sorry, but there's nothing more I can add."

"One of your friends told me you had a big crush on her."

"We all had crushes on her. Who were you talking to?" he said with attitude now.

"I don't reveal sources."

Corcoran rose from his power desk, "Good luck with the case. I respect what you're doing."

Gloria understood an exit line when she heard one. She nodded, and walked out.

Gloria had some time to kill. A couple of hours before her next interview. She picked up a latte and a croissant from her favorite coffee house, and took a window seat. She called Professor Ted Andrews who ran Project for the Innocent and filled him in on her less than stellar performance. Her mentor wasn't pleased.

"It's a little early in the game to be burning bridges," Ted said to a contrite Gloria.

"I know, you're right. I get it, I get it. But he was so arrogant," she said, shaking her head in frustration.

"Don't beat yourself up. You're doing a good job." Ted counseled her to take a few days, consolidate her notes, and then they'd revisit the case. Not what Gloria wanted to hear. And then as an afterthought, "I think I'm being followed."

That caught the professor's attention. Gloria explained it was an SUV with tinted windows. She'd picked up a strange vibe. She made a few off-the-wall turns, and he was gone. She started questioning herself, said it was probably nothing. The professor reminded her when they exonerate one of their clients, someone else's career and reputation sustains damage. It's a dangerous business they're in. He told her to trust her instincts. Gloria took that to heart and signed off.

As Gloria drove into Del Rey, a wildly diverse neighborhood in West Los Angeles, she thought of Carl's photographs taped to her bedroom mirror. Around the photos were his multiple handwritten letters, carefully constructed, flawless penmanship, scotch-taped and all but covering the glass.

Carl Forbes deserved justice.

Gloria pulled to the curb, and gave herself the once over in the rearview mirror. Pleased her eyes showed no stress from her interview with the councilman, she exited her car.

Hanna Cook was standing on the postage-sized porch of a tired California bungalow. She was pushing fifty but giving sixty a run for its money. She had the wrinkled skin and puckered lips of a smoker.

"So, what can I tell you about the bastard?" Hanna asked, droll.

Gloria shared a conspiratorial grin. Put the subject at ease, she'd been taught, and they might share their secrets.

"Do you remember the case? It was back in 2000. The sexual assault and brutal murder of a young co-ed." Gloria reached into her briefcase, "This is a picture of Carl when he was seventeen." She handed Hanna the photo and gave the woman a moment to study the image.

"What did Kevin have to do with it?"

"I was hoping you could tell me. He's on record as being part of the team who arrested the young man."

"No," she said wistfully, handing the photo back. She saw Gloria glance at the nicotine stains between her index and middle fingers and reflexively covered them with her other hand. "The less I knew, the better off I was. Kevin was an angry man who never should've been a cop. Went to his head. That, and the rye whiskey. Only thing that made him feel good ... then it made him mean. When he wasn't getting his kicks arresting dirt-bags, he'd start in on me."

"Was he ever cited for physical violence?"

"Once or twice. It wasn't like it is now. People with their cell phones, and cameras. And just try to arrest a cop back then for slapping around his wife..."

"I'm sorry to hear that," Gloria said, and decided to drop the hammer. "Carl claims your ex, and his partner, beat him into giving a false confession."

Hanna considered that. "I almost shot Kevin one night. Had his gun. He woke up staring down the barrel. I started to cry and he slapped the thing out of my hands and gave me something to cry about. First call I made after they unwired my jaw was to a lawyer. I still can't chew on the left side. I ordered a five-pound lobster the night I heard he passed."

The conversation was going nowhere. Nothing but conjecture to corroborate her inmate's story.

"But you know what?" Hanna said. And then not waiting for a reply, "As bad as my ex was, his partner was worse."

Gloria perked up. "Terry Brannigan?"

"That's the one."

"He's a big wig. I interviewed him last week. He's still on the force."

"With their closure rate, no surprise. I heard him brag he could beat a confession out of a dead man. Sweet guy," she said, dripping with sarcasm. "What's he doing now?"

"He's the commanding officer of the Metro Division. He leads five field platoons. SWAT teams."

"Makes sense. Men and their toys. The two of them thought they were Starsky and Hutch. My ex died of cancer. My theory, it was the whiskey mixed with a healthy dose of guilt. But Brannigan, I don't think he ever looked back. Get the stats, move up a pay grade."

"Really? It must have worked for him because he's one of the men being considered to replace the police chief."

Hanna's eyes narrowed, trying to make sense out of Brannigan's success. "Well, sorry I couldn't be more helpful. If you have anything else, feel free to run it by me. Might shake something loose. Who knows?"

"I'll do that."

"But if it ends with my word against Brannigan's, I won't testify."

Brannigan hadn't been defensive when Gloria laid out the allegation against him. It was more of a world-weary reaction. "Look, Carl's accusation of police brutality was a lie. It was the cost of doing business if you were an active player on the force. Nothing more, nothing less."

Gloria didn't believe Brannigan for a second. Hanna's story of her ex-husband and Brannigan's violence seemed to support Carl's version of his arrest and confession. She would keep Brannigan at the top of her list while applying for the writ of habeas corpus. It would allow the team to reopen the case against Carl Forbes. The first step in gaining his freedom.

Gloria jumped into her car, grabbed the iPad from her briefcase and entered a few salient points from the interview. Feeling vindicated from the morning debacle, she buckled up, and sped off.

It was dusk as she made her way toward Twin Dragon Restaurant. She glanced in the rearview mirror and saw a gray Ford Expedition several lengths behind her. Was it the same SUV she saw before? She wasn't sure. There were lots of SUVs in LA. When she checked again, it was gone.

Twin Dragon had been a mainstay in Los Angeles since 1962. She'd meet her father there for a quick lunch when he could break away from work at his law firm in Century City. Modest prices, great food, just what her rumbling stomach demanded. Shrimp with black bean sauce, Kung Pao chicken, braised string beans, and then, what the heck, an order of pork and vegetable dumplings. It wasn't a great day, but at least dinner in the comfort of her apartment was going to be a winner.

Gloria pulled her car onto the side street next to the restaurant. All was quiet, and she'd only be gone a few minutes. She draped a sweater over her briefcase in the rear compartment, locked up, and hoofed it around to the front entrance to pick up her order.

Five minutes in and out. When Gloria emerged, her hands were full and the smell was incredible. She rounded the corner—and had to look twice to make sense out of what she was seeing. Broken shards of glass fanned out around the back of her car. She took another tentative step forward and could clearly see the shattered rear window of her Fiat.

Her heart pounded, and her breath came in fits and starts. She prayed she was wrong. Yet as she neared her car, her worst fears were realized.

Her briefcase was gone.

Her throat went dry, and she stifled tears. She set the bag of food on top of her car and took in the scene. She looked around her car, checked the traffic on Pico, and the quiet side street for anything out of the ordinary.

Nothing. No one who could have witnessed the break-in. No one who cared that she was caught in a nightmare.

Gloria did a quick mental inventory of everything in her briefcase and came to the sickening realization her iPad and four months of hard work had been stolen. In some instances, information and notes of interviews that took hours to create, and hadn't been copied. The flood gates opened and tears streamed down her cheeks. Light-headed, she had to lean against the car to keep her balance.

The doors were still locked. She grabbed her keys and dropped them on the glass-strewn street before picking them up with shaky hands. She keyed the door and searched her car. Nothing else had been taken. The glove box was undisturbed. Broken glass inundated the rear compartment and the sweater her mother gave her for her birthday.

Was it an opportunistic crime? The thief saw an object, did a smash and grab, and disappeared. Could it have been that simple?

What else could it have been? The SUV? Gloria knew she was paranoid now. Scared silly. She chastised herself for overreacting. She could reconstruct most of the notes, most of the interviews from her handwritten pile of yellow pads. Some were duplicates, and the original files were stacked on her dining table.

She did another full-around scan of the adjacent area. No suspicious movement. She spied no cameras on nearby buildings, so no good would come from calling the police.

Gloria grabbed a few napkins out of her takeout order and whisked the shards of glass that had landed on her front seats onto the curb. She turned on her headlights and pulled out, driving toward home.

Her head was still swimming. Gloria pulled to a stop, grabbed her cell phone and called her father.

After she told him what had happened, he quickly replied:

"Look, darling, don't go home to an empty apartment," he said with a tenderness that belied his courtroom reputation. "I don't want you to be alone. Drive over the hill and spend the night. We can file a police report in the morning and set you up with a rental car."

"I've got Chinese."

"Shrimp with black bean sauce?"

"And Kung Pao."

"I'll chill the chardonnay. I don't want you to worry. Drive safely, honey."

"Okay, Dad. Thank you."

Gloria clicked off, feeling loved, and headed for the Las Virgenes exit off the 101 and her favorite route from Calabasas to the beach.

Malibu Canyon Road was two lanes of pure driving pleasure. Winding blacktop cutting through deep canyons and steep cliffs with sandstone outcroppings. It came to a dramatic end, revealing the Pacific Ocean and Malibu.

She took a deep breath and exhaled slowly. The missing rear window of her Fiat created a strange whistle as she powered the small car around the curves at forty-five miles an hour. Her rumbling stomach got the better of her, and Gloria rummaged around the bag with one hand and plucked out a dumpling. She smiled, took a bite, and glanced at the rearview mirror.

A large SUV appeared around one rocky turn, moving fast, and she hoped the driver wasn't going to be a pain, and force her to pick up the pace.

Gloria made short work of the dumpling and used two hands to maneuver around a tight curve. Her discomfort swelled as she realized the SUV was closing the distance. Headlights on high beam. It was just an irritant at first. Her body tensed as she realized the vehicle bearing down on her was a gray Ford Expedition.

Gloria wondered if she was going mad. It looked like the same car she'd seen before. No, it was impossible, she thought, but picked up her pace. Fifty miles an hour was pushing it around the tight curves, and as fast as she was willing to go. Screw the driver.

The SUV was tracking her now. Tight on her fender. Headlights blinding. She grabbed her cell phone and hit her father's number with one hand. Gloria slid around the next turn, and the phone dropped out of her hand. She prayed there was a turnout ahead, but no such luck.

"Back off!" she shouted over the whine of air thundering through the broken rear window as her speedometer hit sixty miles an hour. The gray SUV loomed in her rearview and she instinctively pushed the car to sixty-five, white-knuckling the steering wheel.

Gloria drifted over the broken white line as a car blasted by from the opposite direction, horn blaring, scaring the crap out of her. She came dangerously close to skidding onto the narrow gravel shoulder and colliding with the sheer cliff face.

And then, oh Christ, she felt the SUV nudge the back of her car.

Gloria stomped pedal-to-metal. Her small sedan rocketed to seventy miles an hour.

The SUV tapped her rear bumper again.

Gloria's eyes teared. She was losing it but fought to keep the car on the road.

The SUV slammed into her harder. "Stop it!" she cried.

And then the power punch. Five thousand pounds of steel rammed her compact car.

Gloria couldn't hear her squealing tires over the sound of her own screams as she went into a death spin.

Gloria knew she was going to die a moment before her car came out of the 360 on the opposite side of the road, barreling toward the cliff at seventy miles an hour.

Her Fiat smashed into the rocky berm and went airborne.

Time stood still.

The only sound: the whistling wind and Gloria's beating heart.

The rock-strewn riverbed grew in size, filling her field of vision as she dropped out of the sky and bore witness to her impending death.

The pistachio Fiat that had brought Gloria so much joy in life burst into flames on impact and enveloped her broken body.

CHAPTER 2

FIVE WEEKS LATER

The sky above Marina del Rey was the kind of crystal blue that made the rest of the country put Southern California on their bucket list. Jack Bertolino had never questioned his decision to move across country from Staten Island. He was puttering around his used twenty-eight-foot cabin cruiser, feeling pretty content. He had reached a civilized truce with his contentious ex, and his relationship with his son, a Stanford sophomore with a full baseball scholarship, was on the mend. The gulls riding the thermals and cawing overhead seemed to approve of his good fortune.

Shirtless, in his jeans and black running shoes, he was on his knees sanding teak accent pieces on the aft deck. His back was muscled and gleaming. The scars, along with the remnants of a bullet wound, told his history of working narcotics on the streets of New York City. Jack was a retired NYPD inspector with twenty-five years on the job.

He'd moved west to reinvent himself, but the gods had other plans. He was pulled back into the business when a beautiful confidential informant named Mia showed up in Los Angeles. After a night of mind-blowing sex, Mia turned up dead and Jack stood accused. He ran the killers to ground, and he was now running a successful private investigations firm. After bringing his last case to a successful conclusion, he and his team were taking some hard-earned personal time.

He noticed Deputy District Attorney Leslie Sager standing at the chain-link security gate, watching Jack's labor. Carrying a bottle of wine, she was dressed in her work clothes, white silk blouse, modest gold chain, and a charcoal Donna Karan skirt. Her blonde hair blew off her shoulders like a Greek goddess in the light ocean breeze, and the color of her eyes gave the perfect sky a run for its money.

"Bertolino," she yelled. "Open the gate."

Jack washed the dust off his hands and jeans as he jumped onto the dock and headed for the ramp. A big smile creasing his chiseled face.

His longish black hair had more silver feathering his temples since the last time he and Leslie had spent time together. Jack's caseload was strenuous, but his clearance rate, triple A. She wasn't exactly twiddling her thumbs herself.

They'd been an item after she helped clear him of murder charges. But the violence that followed Jack like a shadow, and some L.A politics where she backed the wrong horse, were their undoing. They decided to take a break and reassess their relationship, but as time passed, it created a schism that was too wide to navigate. That being said, it did nothing to diminish their physical attraction and genuine respect for each other.

"Like a good Italian, you come bearing gifts," he said as he opened the locked gate.

"I'm not Italian."

"Then I taught you well."

"We both have our skill sets."

Jack didn't argue the point. Leslie could always win the verbal game. It was in her DNA and what made her a great litigator.

"You look beautiful."

"You look relaxed."

"Why do I think that's about to change?"

She loved the banter and answered by handing off the bottle of Benziger, Jack's favorite Cabernet. The gesture didn't go unnoticed. "I'm running an errand for the mayor."

"Don't spoil the mood."

"Open the bottle and I'll clock out for the day."

Jack stepped down into the galley of the boat, slipped on a black T-shirt, and grabbed two glasses. As Leslie got comfortable in one of the deck chairs, leaning back, letting the sun warm her face, he realized his blood pressure had spiked a notch. He'd been without female companionship the past few months.

He walked up the teak stairs and handed her a glass of wine. Jack clinked his glass against hers. "All right, let me have it."

"Business before pleasure," she said and studied his face. "Are you up to speed on the Gloria Millhouse case?"

"She's the one that disappeared last month, and they recovered the body a couple of weeks ago in Malibu Canyon?"

"Sad story. Great young lady. Law student. Her father, Keith Millhouse, is a powerhouse of an attorney, politically connected, impeccable reputation, and a personal friend of the mayor. He was aware of our past relationship and called me." And then getting down to the reason for the unexpected visit, "He'd like you to take a look at the case."

Jack sipped his wine, enjoying the finish. "The *Times* said the LAPD was putting the full weight of their department into solving the case. But the reporter intimated the jury was still out as to whether it was a single-car accident or something dirty."

"That's exactly why the mayor wants your help. The cell phone records from the approximate time of her disappearance shows Gloria making a call to her father. He answered, but no one was on the line.

"They think she might have been distracted, lost control, and ran off the road. The drop is so steep, and the vegetation so dense, it took a few weeks to discover the wreck. The car had burnt to the ground, and by the time of discovery there were no distinctive tire tracks above to reconstruct the accident."

"Why does her father think they're on the wrong track?"

"Gloria was working a case for Project for the Innocent and stepped on some political toes. She confided to the professor heading up a cold-case investigation that she thought she was being followed. Her father thinks she unwittingly generated enough heat to motivate someone to break into her car and steal her briefcase containing her notes and interviews the night she went missing.

"The police think there was a good chance the break-in was opportunistic. Keith does not. Gloria was upset over the theft and on the way to his house in Malibu the night she died."

"And now the mayor wants me to step on the LAPD's toes?"

"Light on your feet, Bertolino. Light on your feet. Keith's a good man, and the mayor said to tell you he'd be eternally grateful."

"Doesn't sound like the mayor I know."

"Still, not a bad person to have in your hip pocket."

"You're the political animal in the relationship."

Jack's Freudian slip startled them both into taking big sips of their wine.

"Do you have dinner plans?" he asked.

"Hal's sounds good," she said. Hal's Bar and Grill, a Venice mainstay, was Jack's go-to restaurant if he wasn't in his loft cooking. The pair had shared many romantic meals there—and some of their most contentious.

"Give me ten minutes to clean up."

"I'll reserve a booth," and she pulled out her cell phone.

Jack disappeared into the cabin. His cop-brain kicked in as he washed off. The information Leslie shared didn't sit well. Someone smashed in Gloria's car window to steal her briefcase, and an hour later this young woman does a swan dive off a cliff-side road? The timing left him feeling uneasy.

CHAPTER 3

It was hot, muggy, and the city traffic was unrelenting. Jackhammers pounded, horns blared, and civilians jaywalked like they had all the time in the world. It made driving in downtown Los Angeles a drag. Jack was happy to park and stretch his legs.

Ninety-eight degrees without a hint of a breeze. Not New York humidity, just enough to bitch about. A typical hot winter's day in Los Angeles. He stopped at a donut shop around the corner from the Police Administration Building on 1st. It never hurt to come bearing gifts. Especially when the detectives in charge of the investigation were Lieutenant Gallina and Detective Tompkins.

Gallina and Tompkins were the men responsible for murder charges being filed against Jack, but it was a few years back and there was much water under the bridge.

Tompkins was the more reasonable of the partners, but Gallina had developed a grudging respect. A notion he'd go to the grave with rather than admit.

"Bertolino," Gallina barked when he realized Jack was standing in the doorway. "What the hell are you doing here?"

"The Gloria Millhouse case."

"Why am I not surprised?"

Jack strolled into their office, winked at Tompkins, and set the box of sugared fried dough in front of the lieutenant. "Tompkins," Gallina went on, "did you get a call from Bertolino? No? Me neither. Maybe my secretary failed to notify me of said call. Oh wait… what am I talking… I don't have a secretary."

"Lieutenant … Tompkins, you're my first stop."

"You are so disingenuous, Bertolino. Don't tell me, the case came across the desk of the President, and he had to have Jack Bertolino mucking up real police work?"

"I can see you're busy pounding the pavement, Lieutenant. Have a donut. And it was the mayor."

"Christ, it's time that man ran for governor and moved on."

"How's the family, Tompkins?" Jack asked. It had taken more than a year to discover Tompkins was the father of two beautiful girls. The lieutenant didn't have kids, probably because no one would put up with him long enough to allow procreation.

"Doing great, Jack, thanks for asking. And terrific work down in Long Beach."

"Thank you, a lot of moving parts."

"All right, let's cut the crap and the mutual admiration society." Gallina lifted the lid of the box and snatched a chocolate-covered number. "What, no jelly donuts?"

"Can I get a look at the murder book?"

"You're getting ahead of yourself, Jack. There is no murder book. We're chasing our tails because your benefactor is all over the chief, and the chief's joy drips down until here we sit up to our ankles."

Tompkins grabbed an old-fashioned cake donut out of the box. "I'm a purist," he informed Jack, taking a bite. "We're covering both angles, but there's a strong case to be made for a single-car accident. Cell phone call, high speed, tight turn, distracted driver."

"Father thinks it's tied to the Project for the Innocent," Jack stated without rancor.

"Keith Millhouse is a bleeping defense attorney," Gallina said with plenty of rancor. "He'll put the blame on the cops, the DA's office, the witnesses, anybody who gets in his way."

"How did he sound?" Jack asked.

"He just lost his daughter," Gallina said, turning a hint of sensitivity into a challenge. "What he doesn't want to hear was that his daughter was on the phone, on a dangerous road, with a lot on her mind. Millhouse doesn't want to hear it might have been an accidental death."

"Gloria thought she was being followed earlier in the day," Jack said. "Shared that with her professor who runs the program. Her briefcase with an iPad, and notes on her interviews, was stolen an hour before she died."

"A smash-and-grab, big deal. She left a fancy-pants leather briefcase on the rear compartment of her car, on a side street off Pico. Please." Gallina raised his hands and eyebrows simultaneously in a what-the-fuck gesture.

"Can I take a look at your witness list? Save me some time?"

Gallina glanced at Tompkins, who nodded in the affirmative. "Shit. Okay. But sharing intel goes both ways. I'd ask you to keep us in the loop, but I know better."

Tompkins pulled out his cell phone. "I'll text it to you."

"Thanks." And then, "I'll keep you in the loop."

"Get outta here. We've got police business to attend to." Gallina snatched a glazed donut out of the box.

"What about the car?"

"It's in the impound yard," Tompkins said. "Nothing to see. The rear end crunched on impact. That and the flames melted any tells that might have given conclusive answers."

"Mind if I take a look?"

Tompkins grabbed the landline. "I'll call down."

"Thanks," Jack said, and when Gallina looked up, he was gone.

The LAPD impound yard was hidden behind eight-foot chain-link fencing with green canvas backing to keep out prying eyes. What was left of the Fiat was hoisted three feet off the ground on pneumatic skids. Jack walked slowly around the burnt-out hulk and hoped Gloria had died on impact. He stopped at the rear of the small frame, pulled out his phone, and snapped a few photos.

The rear end was mangled, the interior plastic melted, fabric seats disintegrated, exposing fire-blackened springs. The frame was a twisted mess. There was no way to discern if the Fiat had been pushed off the cliff. No paint scrapes, no paint at all – that could have proven it wasn't an accident – had survived the impact and ensuing inferno.

Zero for him there.

Loyola Law School, which housed Project for the Innocent, was located at 919 Albany Street, in downtown Los Angeles. The campus was designed by architect Frank Gehry and had a modern, minimalist feel.

Jack got directions to the director's office and entered the building. The mayor had cleared the way and he was expected.

The professor's door was open a crack, and Jack could see a wiry man with salt-and-pepper hair, who looked more like a rock 'n' roller than an academic, leaning forward in his chair crying.

When he realized Jack was standing outside his door, he leapt to his feet, wiped the tears, and struggled to put on his fragile wire-rimmed glasses. He cleared his throat and waved Jack in.

"I apologize," was the first thing he said, slightly embarrassed. "Oh, I'm Ted Anderson, and you must be Jack Bertolino." He proffered his hand, and Jack shared a rather moist shake. "I've been expecting you. I, uh, mentally replayed the last conversation I had with Gloria and it got the best of me. This has been a total nightmare. She was one hell of a young lady, and ... I'm sorry." The tears welled again, and Anderson dropped back down in his chair.

"Take your time. I'm in no hurry. Can I get you something to drink?"

"Ah, great, I'm supposed to be helping you and I'm falling apart. No, I'm fine—well, as you can see, not really. I'm going to grab a cup of coffee. Can I get you one?"

"Black will be fine."

"Oh, okay, make yourself at home." The professor took a left outside his office and disappeared down the hallway.

Jack knew it would give the man time to pull himself together so they could get down to work.

"I read her the riot act for taking the meetings that day without me," Anderson said when he returned. "I got pulled into a fire drill." He read the question on Jack's face, and explained. "I had a recanting witness on another case. When the new petition is on the clock, we drop the case we were working on. It gets put on hold.

"I was angry and pulled her off the streets, off the case. I told her to get her files in order, and that's when she admitted she might have been followed. I never should have let her off the phone until I had more specifics, until we got to the bottom of her fears. She said it was an SUV with tinted windows. I lectured her about following her instincts and I didn't heed my own advice. I'm a lawyer, with a background in criminology. I failed miserably. What was the make of the SUV? Did she get a license number? Rookie mistakes."

Jack had no answers for the man. Anything he said would sound trite.

"Her father, have you met him yet?" Anderson said.

"After we're done here."

"He raged at me. Called me incompetent."

"He just lost his daughter."

"You think I don't know that?" he snapped. "I know that. And he was right."

Jack had to keep the distraught man on track. The meeting wasn't about him. "How far along was the investigation?"

"Our Habeas petition was just approved. Gloria would've been pleased. We're waiting on a court date. These cases can drag out for years, but we're prepping for the trial. If a student was a good interrogator, and Gloria was the best in her class, she had the ability to make more than a few witnesses on the list nervous."

"Was she in conflict with anybody in her class? Competitive jealousy?"

"Not that I'm aware of. It's such a daunting task we're up against, it's more a matter of us, the team, against the system."

"Can I get my hands on the transcripts of the original trial, the witness list, and any newspaper articles you've come across?"

"I copied the entire file for you on a flash drive."

Anderson wasn't completely a mess. "What else did you talk about? The last day."

"I chided her for losing focus with Councilman Corcoran. It was an important interview. She took his evasiveness personally and was shown the door."

"Why important?"

"The man knew the victim and the accused. Same neighborhood. Gloria was very hard on herself."

"And your client, the accused? What brought him to your attention."

"His tenacity. His letter-writing skills. His exemplary reputation as an inmate. Gloria is the one who championed him. And then there was the DNA angle. Very few men and women ever get convicted if there isn't DNA involved. None of his DNA was found on or in the victim's body. There was DNA present, discovered with the rape kit, but a match was never found." He went on, not realizing that Jack knew all about DNA. "When you're dealing with extended time frames, all the witnesses, cops, district attorneys, defense lawyers, and physical evidence are as old as the jail time served. It's an uphill battle and we need all the ammunition we can get. Carl Forbes has been in prison for twenty-three years. It was Gloria's dream to set him free. We were here to support her dream."

The professor's emotions were surfacing again. "Where's he serving his time?" Jack said to keep him focused.

"The federal penitentiary in Victorville. I'll call the warden when you're ready to visit. I'm available to you twenty-four/seven, Jack. Any questions, any help, any time."

Jack shook the man's hand and left him to his guilt and sorrow.

CHAPTER 4

Jack had an appointment to meet Keith Millhouse at his home in Malibu. He powered down his Mustang's convertible top, slid on his Ray-Bans, and decided to take the route Gloria drove the night of her death. It was too early in Jack's process to characterize her fatality as an accident or a murder, or to let anyone else's opinion color his investigation. The burnt-out hulk of the Fiat hadn't revealed any secrets.

He remembered that he had to get his young associate, Cruz Feinberg, on board. He tapped Cruz's number on his Bluetooth, and when the call went to voicemail, explained they had a job, and to Google, Gloria Millhouse, and Project for the Innocent. He'd fill in the particulars later in the day.

Jack's car hugged the curves at fifty miles an hour, but he wasn't sure a Fiat, driving at night, would feel as secure. Then he rounded a very tight curve and backed off the pedal.

A bouquet of flowers in a makeshift shrine, as well as tattered yellow police tape flapping in the breeze on the side of the road, marked the spot her car had veered off the cliff.

Jack was forced to drive a few hundred yards past the crash site before he found a safe turnout. He waited for a break in traffic and hoofed it across, making his way back along the ravine's edge. He stopped at the shrine to consider the tragedy and a life cut short. He carefully climbed onto the berm and peered over the edge. There wasn't much to see except thick brush and then burnt undergrowth. Jack had a touch of vertigo and stepped back from the edge.

The ravine was so deep and overgrown, he wasn't surprised it had taken eight days to find the wrecked Fiat with Gloria's body inside. There were no eyewitnesses to the crash unless the SUV that Gloria reported tailing her earlier in the day caused the accident.

As he watched the cars speed by, oblivious to the tragedy below, Jack did a mental reconstruction of possible scenarios. If Gloria had been distracted while driving, it was totally believable she could have lost control of her vehicle and plunged to her death.

Gloria also could have recognized the vehicle, hit the gas, and the SUV rammed her rear bumper, executing a pit maneuver, spinning the subcompact car out of control and off the cliff's edge.

Jack had seen local news coverage of an EMS chopper lifting her body off the rocky riverbed below, but he wasn't sure how they'd extricated the burnt shell of the vehicle. He'd call Detective Tompkins and ask to be copied on the crime-scene photographs.

Keith Millhouse was sitting in a chaise lounge, staring at his unobstructed view of the Pacific Ocean. But the man wasn't lounging. His body was rigid, as if he'd been chiseled from a block of ice. Millhouse cut a rakish figure in his pressed suit slacks and dress shirt casually opened at the collar. His hair was cut tight to his scalp, his body well defined, but on closer inspection, his face was a mask of concern.

Jack sat on a heavy designer patio chair positioned opposite Keith.

"You work a lifetime, to amass...all of this," Keith said. "A great house, a solid career ... and then your daughter is born and everything else pales in comparison. Do you have children, Jack?"

"A son I'd take a bullet for."

Keith nodded in agreement. "We went through a rocky patch after Tracy and I divorced. Gloria blamed me, and hell, I blamed myself. Too many hours at the office, career building. Too many travel days. Guilty as charged."

Jack could relate. It was a scenario right out of his own playbook. "It's one of the reasons I moved west," he said. "My son's up at Stanford, playing baseball. I vowed never to miss another game."

Keith nodded. "We finally reached détente," he went on. "When Gloria found Project for the Innocent, she began to understood how it might happen. A passion for your job, long hours, and all of a sudden you're MIA. She had a big heart, and she forgave me." Jack could see Keith shifting gears before he was carried away with emotion in front of a man he'd just met. "Anyway, thanks for driving out. And thank you for joining the team."

Jack was happy to get down to business. "I'm playing catch-up here. It's going to be rough, so let me apologize ahead of time for the intrusion..."

Keith stopped him with a raised hand. "No apologies necessary."

Jack continued, "I need to know everything and anything you think is important or relevant to the case. And I'd like to get into Gloria's apartment, take a look at the files she left behind."

"She left behind. Sounds so permanent, doesn't it?" Keith didn't expect a response. "She believed Carl Forbes, her client, was an innocent man. And I believed her. It was her case, and she was going to win. Carl was going to be exonerated."

"Where did she run into conflict? Did she share specifics with you?"

"Just about everyone was resistant. Some more than others. Judge Bradley Cole shut her down. He works out of the Airport Courthouse. The man was the ADA when the case went to trial back in 2000. I crossed paths with him back in the day. He was a tough little guy who wanted to get ahead, and he succeeded. With the conviction of Carl Forbes, the accused murderer and rapist, his career took off.

"Gloria reminded him about the case, and wanted to know if she could ask a few questions. He told her the case had been justly adjudicated, revisited four times, appeals overturned. He didn't know who she was and had no desire to continue the conversation. The cocksucker hung up on her. I offered to intercede, and she shut me down. That's what kind of person she was. No free rides for Gloria."

"The detectives working the case said you received a phone call from your daughter around the time of the accident."

"We talked, the first time, when she was in West Hollywood. Her car had been vandalized and she lost a great deal of work when they stole her briefcase. She was devastated. I tried to calm her down, explained we could reconstruct the files. Talked her into coming over and spending the night. She said she had takeout from Twin Dragon, I said I had the wine. It was short and sweet.

"She called again about forty-five minutes later. Her name registered on my phone, but by the time I answered, the call had ended. I redialed, but she didn't pick up."

Jack gave Keith a moment before continuing. "I'm going to copy you on the list of potential witnesses. I'd appreciate if you'd give it a look, and notate any conversations you might have had regarding a particular person, the case, or her thoughts. You know the drill. The smallest detail might seem insignificant, but could bear weight." The lawyer nodded in agreement. "And if I could get the key to her apartment, I'll stop by. I know the police did a thorough search, but I want to go over it again, get a feel for your daughter before anything disappears."

"I've got one inside the house. I don't want to put a crimp in your style, Jack, but anything you can share as you progress, please, anything at all."

Keith didn't wait for an answer. He stood tall, sucked in a breath, and walked into the great house. Jack knew very well that it would feel empty now, forever.

Laurel Canyon was a slice of heaven in the middle of a crowded city. Country living, bisecting Hollywood and the Valley, with an eclectic mix of modern architecture rubbing shoulders with 1940s hunting lodges and nondescript contractor builds clinging precariously to the steep hillsides. The area received international fame in the sixties when it was home to Joni Mitchel, Jim Morrison, and Crosby, Stills, Nash & Young, to name a few. Now it was the exclusive enclave of well-endowed boomers, actors, writers and studio execs.

Gloria's building was a half block from Ventura Boulevard. It was a well-maintained five-story, pink Mediterranean with security locks on the thick glass front doors.

Jack thought he was first to arrive until he saw Cruz Feinberg waiting in the modest lobby. His associate was twenty-four, stood five-foot-nine, with dark skin, intelligent brown eyes, and unruly black hair that was a studied choice. Cruz's mother was Guatemalan, and his father a Brooklyn Jew who founded Bundy Lock and Key. He taught his son everything he knew about installing and, more important, dismantling locks and safes and security systems. Cruz, a tech sponge, expanded his areas of expertise to include computer skills, spyware and all the latest technical gadgetry.

Jack looked at the key in his hand and grinned, shaking his head, as Cruz pushed open the security door. Jack knew better than to ask how he'd gained entrance. He was handed a Starbucks iced Americano, his favorite, and a stack of Gloria's mail Cruz collected from her locked mailbox.

"We're lucky you're on the right side of the law," Jack said dryly.

He stepped past the yellow crime-scene tape hanging loosely off the doorframe. Some deterrent, he thought. He straightened as the locked door to Gloria's apartment swung open, and he heard a sound emanating from the single bedroom. Jack waved Cruz deeper into the hallway, handed him the coffee and mail, then pulled the Glock from his shoulder rig. He entered the apartment, moving silently across the plush carpet toward the sound.

The door was open a crack. Jack stopped for a beat. Kicked the door open and followed the barrel of his gun into the bedroom.

"Shit!" someone screamed from within.

"Hands over your head, down on the floor," Jack ordered, his voice tight.

The intruder immediately complied. "What the hell? Who the hell are you?" he wailed defensively.

Jack assessed the situation and lowered his weapon. The attractive young man was Caucasian, early twenties, toothpick thin, clean cut, and weaponless.

"Cruz! We're clear!"

Jack heard the front door shut. "Get up son. Let's move to the living room and straighten this out."

"You scared the ever-loving shit out of me," he said, standing on shaky legs. "Who are you?"

"I'll ask the questions." He signaled the boy out of the room with his gun. "Who are you, and why are you here?"

"I'm Gloria's boyfriend, or I was." He seemed fragile, ready to crack. "And I'm here to pick up my stuff."

"Let me see some ID," Jack said as he holstered his 9mm.

"Show me yours first." The kid was scared, but he wasn't stupid, Jack thought.

"Fair enough." Jack pulled out his wallet and handed the kid his card. "I'm Jack Bertolino, and this is Cruz Feinberg. I was hired by Gloria's father to look into her death. Nobody mentioned a boyfriend."

"Her father doesn't know me. I never met the man." He handed Jack his driver's license.

"How did you get in, Jeremy?"

"We exchanged keys."

"You didn't see the crime-scene tape?"

Jeremy grunted a yeah and then, leading with attitude, "Is it all right if I use the john?"

Jack walked over to the bathroom and cleared it. It was well appointed and spotless, with a modern sink, shower, and freestanding tub. There was one small window and no way the boy would be jumping from the fourth floor.

"God," the kid said as he passed Jack and closed the door behind him.

"Hell of a way to start the day," Jack said to Cruz, who was already scoping out the apartment. Files, photographs, and yellow pads with hastily penned notes covered the kitchen table and the modest couch.

Jack typed Jeremy's full name and address into his phone. "We'll need a copy of all her files, and then drop the originals off to the professor. The intellectual property belongs to Project for the Innocent.

Then I want you to cross-reference the professor's lists with the remaining hard copy. It'll be interesting to find out who was important enough for Gloria to carry their files in her briefcase."

"This was one serious woman," Cruz said, impressed.

Both men looked up at the sound of a toilet flushing. Jeremy walked into the living room looking green at the gills.

"Can I grab my stuff and leave?"

"No, you've got some explaining to do."

"I think I'm going to puke."

"You know where the bathroom is."

"What?"

Jack handed Jeremy his license back. "When was the last time you spoke with Gloria?"

"The night she died. She called on her way to Malibu. Told me about the break-in, and how upset she was, and how she blew it with Councilman Corcoran. She was having a bad day and we made plans to see each other over the weekend."

"When did you hear about her death?"

"That was a few weeks later. The news reported her missing the next day."

"Why didn't you come forward? The police will want a sit-down."

"I'm not sure. I didn't know anything I thought would be helpful." Then his face fell. "I screwed up."

"Did you think to help with the search?" Jack said, trying to keep the frustration out of his voice.

"By the time it made the news… yes, I thought about it, no, I didn't. I did nothing. I feel terrible."

"Did anybody else know you two were an item?"

"Sure."

"Who?"

"Friends."

"Why the secrecy?"

Jeremy gave that some thought. "I was a little shy about the interracial thing. I wasn't sure how her father would react. Gloria said I was being ridiculous and was going to set up a dinner. I said fine. She never got the chance."

"Did Gloria mention being followed?"

"Yeah, but she said it happened earlier in the day on her way to an interview."

"Where were you when you made the call?"

"Sherman Oaks, Coffee Bean and Tea Leaf. I was working on a term paper."

"Can anybody corroborate that?"

Jeremy was getting antsy again but fighting for cool. "Um, yeah, Mark was working that night. The barista. He knows me."

"Did Gloria mention any other friction regarding the Carl Forbes's case?"

"Not really. She was on a mission, though, building a hell of a case."

"What direction was she leaning?"

"Don't know. She blamed the cops, the DA's office, the eyewitness, the whole lot of them. She didn't want to talk too much about it until she had concrete proof, but I got the feeling she was getting close."

"Was she in conflict with anybody else? Had concerns about? Outside the case. Friends, family?"

"Not that I'm aware of."

"How was your relationship with Gloria?"

"Good. Real good. We were both busy but had fun when we hooked up. Look, can I go now?"

"Write down your phone number and address. And I'll need a list of the friends you shared in common."

Jeremy scribbled his information onto one of Gloria's blank yellow pads Cruz handed him.

"I don't know all their phone numbers."

Jack wasn't taking lazy for an answer. "Is your phone with you?"

Jeremy sighed, pulled out his cell, and copied the information off the screen.

Jack nodded to Cruz, who nodded back and tapped a few keys on his laptop, making short work of hacking into the kid's phone.

Jack walked into the bedroom and used his cell to photograph the handwritten letters from Carl, his headshot, and his mug shots. He tore through the bedroom, finding nothing else related to the case.

Prominently placed on her makeup table was a framed photograph of Keith Millhouse and his ex-wife, Tracy. Happier times. Jack flashed on his own contentious divorce and the negative effect it had on his son. He quickly put that to bed and got back to the business at hand.

He called Gallina and Tompkins, filled them in on Jeremy, his relationship to Gloria, and his phone call the night she disappeared. Tompkins was in Studio City, and agreed to head over.

"I'm done," Jeremy shouted from the other room.

"There's a detective running the case, good guy, wants to have a few words," Jack said, getting the nod from Cruz, who had finished downloading Jeremy's cell phone hard drive.

"What?" Jeremy started to panic again.

"Your call, but it'll be a lot nicer than having a police car pick you up at home." And then, "Jeremy, what kind of a car do you drive?"

"Why?"

"To cross it off my list."

"Do I need a lawyer?"

"Car?" he pushed.

"Camry. Do I need a lawyer?"

"Only if you're guilty."

"That's what they told Carl."

Jack let that slide. He couldn't argue the point. "Show me what you came to retrieve, and I'll make sure nothing happens to your property," Jack said, knowing if Gallina thought the boyfriend was a person of interest, he'd never see his belongings again.

"Why can't I take it with me?"

"It's potential evidence until it's cleared by the police."

Jeremy ran into the bathroom and slammed the door.

CHAPTER 5

"Jack, you're killin' me here." Narcotics Detective Nick Aprea knocked back a shot of Herradura silver, chased it with a lick of salt and a savage bite of lime like he was ripping the head off a lizard. Nick was tall, hard, with a faded blue marine tattoo on his meaty forearm. Intense dark eyes made lesser men blink first. "Why do you want to get caught up in a no-win dog-and-pony show? Who do you owe a favor?"

"No debt. My cards clean. I owe no man." Jack said, air toasting and then taking a swallow of red wine, not giving an inch but enjoying the game.

"Pullease," Nick said, torturing the word. "Who the fuck do you think you're talking to? You're going into a no-win situation. You're gonna be ruffling feathers of former comrades, asking embarrassing questions of power brokers, and if the young woman, God forbid, lost control of her vehicle and wasn't pushed over the side, it'll all be for naught."

"For naught?"

"Whatever."

"Speaking of comrades," Jack said. "You ever cross paths with Commander Terry Brannigan? He was part of the arrest team."

Nick's face creased into a grin. "I can save you some shoe leather there, pard. Brannigan, he's one of the good guys. Ex-Marine, we did a joint drug task force deal on a local gang tied to the cartels. Early morning raid, I was on the assault team. A banger stepped around the side of the house and had me in his sights. Brannigan took him down before he could shoot me in the back.

"He's a commander now, runs the Metro Division. Not your stuffed-shirt manager. Likes to get his hands dirty, spend time with his men in the field. I see him on the tube once in a while. Hostage situations and whatnot. He's also on the short list of men the Police Commission is interviewing for possibly replacing the outgoing chief."

"Good to know."

"So, if it's not a favor owed," Nick went on, "and you owe no man, ah… don't tell me." A wolf grin split Nick's face. "It's political in nature. And if it's political, there's only one person who runs in those same circles, and that same person, who you've been known to spend more than a few intimate moments with, is DDA Leslie Sager."

Jack sat stone-faced.

"Tell me I'm wrong. No, tell me I'm right, 'cause then drinks are on you…"

"You should become a detective, Aprea. You look worse for the wear, but your sleuthing skills are firing on all cylinders."

Nick had taken a bone-crushing bullet to the shoulder on a case he was working with Jack, running a ruthless gang of brothers to ground. After six months on the mend and painful rehab, he was off desk duty and back on the streets.

"Bet your ass, pard …" And then giving Jack's situation some thought, "Eh, it's time to test the waters, see if you've still got what it takes," Nick said, referring to Jack's sexual prowess.

"Don't get ahead of yourself." It had been Jack's choice to end his last relationship, but the experience hit home. He took an emotional hiatus. Maybe it was time to get back in the game, he thought, and not for the first time.

"When are you going to see her?"

Jack grinned as a contrail of blonde hair moved past the front picture windows, and Leslie Sager, looking fabulous, entered the restaurant and made her way through the dining room at Hal's Bar & Grill.

Nick read Jack's expression, knowing without turning around who had just entered the room.

Both men stood, grinning like brothers. Jack stepped out of the booth and let Leslie slide in.

"I hope I'm not the punch line," she said knowingly. "How are you, Nick? You look terrific."

"You look like a million bucks."

"He's prescient," Jack said to Leslie. "You were supposed to be a surprise."

Arsinio, Jack's favorite waiter, arrived tableside with two glasses of Benziger Cabernet, another icy shot with a small tray of cut limes, and satisfied his table was well taken care of, disappeared.

"Are you joining us for dinner?" Leslie asked.

"No, just some liquid appetizers," Nick said. "I've been burning it at both ends on the MS-13 task force. And my beautiful wife got used to having my delightful mug around the house. I'm trying to keep Jack on the straight and narrow here. Don't want him burning too many bridges on a no-win case."

Leslie's smile dimmed some. "Have you seen a picture of Gloria Millhouse?"

"Haven't had the pleasure."

Jack pulled a photograph out of his manila envelope and slid it in front of Nick.

"Yeah. She's beautiful," Nick said.

"So knowing your girl, Sammy, is what, five now? You have some idea how her father might feel."

Jack could see that Nick knew it was time to cut his losses. There was no winning this conversation. He polished off the last shot. "He must feel better having Jack on the case. She was operating in a snake pit that might have something, or nothing, to do with the tragedy. That's all I was saying."

"You're a good friend, Nick," Leslie said, letting him off the hook. "Send my best to Alicia."

"Stay in touch," he said to Jack, who waved away the wallet pull.

"On me, partner."

"You kids have fun, you hear." On the way out of the booth, he palmed Arsinio a twenty.

"At least I didn't clear the entire table," Leslie said.

"He means well, and he got your point. I've never been in the game to make friends, and so I'll take the good with the bad. You can tell the mayor I'm all in. It's just a gut feeling at this point, but what I've learned about Gloria today … I'm not picking up the kind of woman who lost control of much in her life."

"You, Mr. Bertolino, are a keeper."

They clicked glasses, took a sip, and picked up their menus. Jack didn't respond to the compliment. But the night was young.

CHAPTER 6

Nick was sitting at his desk at the Pacific Division. His ham fist reached for the phone. His eyes came to rest on the photo of his daughter and wife at SeaWorld. They were standing in front of the central tank, with white sharks circling behind them. It reminded Nick to stay vigilant.

He tapped in a number, and it was picked up on the second ring.

"Nick Aprea, it's been too long."

Brannigan was seated at his desk in LAPD headquarters. With silver close-cropped hair, steel gray eyes, and angular face, he looked every bit the commander he was. He palmed the receiver, and his face creasing into a tight grin told the young cop seated in front of him to give him some privacy. The young cop jumped up and left the room. "How the hell are you?"

"Doing good. Shoulders healed, and I'm back in the thick of it. I just wanted to give you a heads-up. Friend of mine, Jack Bertolino, is working the Gloria Millhouse case."

"I'm up to speed on that."

"The mayor and the girl's father brought him on. I gave you a triple-A rating, but don't be surprised if he comes around and asks a few questions. Just give him the facts, ma'am, and he'll be on his way."

"Oh, Christ. What a pain in the ass. You can't run interference?"

Nick chuckled. "It's not in Jack's DNA to leave any stone unturned. He's as stubborn as we are, Terry. And being as you were one of the arresting officers, you'll see him."

"The Millhouse girl came around last week with her professor."

"What was your take on Gloria?"

"She had a mouth on her. Asked the right questions. Wasn't going away anytime soon. I offered to help if they found anything we might have missed. Told them to reach out if they discovered anything new, but it was a solid case, a clean arrest, and a unanimous guilty verdict."

"Like I said, Terry, just the facts. Nothing to worry about."

"All right. And listen, we need to talk about your future. If all goes according to plan and I'm running things around here in the near future, you'll be one of the first calls I make. Battle tested, battle hardened, you're the kind of no-bullshit soldier I want standing at my side."

"Sounds like a plan," Nick said. "Gotta run."

"Roger that." Brannigan hung up. His face hardened with the news. He was aware of Bertolino's history, and from his point of view, the man was a bad operator. Nothing but trouble.

Cruz was working at the dining table in Jack's loft when Jack keyed the front door and entered. Reams of paper, an open laptop, iPhone, and inked-on yellow pads were strewn around an empty coffee cup.

"There's a pot of coffee," Cruz said by way of hello. "Hey, what's up?"

"What do you mean?"

"I don't know, you look different."

Jack's eyes narrowed. He knew his bed hadn't been slept in, and Cruz knew his bed hadn't been slept in. And he was wearing the same clothes he had on yesterday. But Jack wasn't a man who talked out of school.

"Spent the night on the boat," he said and walked to the back of the loft to change.

"Yeah, right," not buying it, but not about to push the point. Cruz continued cross-referencing the lists from the prof, the reams of pages from Gloria's apartment, and the LAPD's list of witnesses from the trial. "It'll take me a few days to collate, but I should have a preliminary list for you by the end of the day. Give us some idea what was stolen with her briefcase, and her iPad. I'll start on the people Gloria interviewed, what her thoughts were, and walk you through her last few days on earth."

"Good," Jack shouted from the back of the loft.

The modern loft space was fifteen hundred square feet of concrete, open floor plan, and the entire back wall consisted of sliding glass panels that opened onto a balcony that overlooked a FedEx lot. Two bedrooms, two baths. High-tech design, stainless steel appliances, and center island. The loft served as their office when they were on a job. The second bedroom was Jack's office, and Cruz, a creature of habit, called the sand-blasted glass and steel dining room table his workspace.

"I connected with the people on Jeremy's list. They all checked out. Knew about his relationship with Gloria. Thought he was self-centered but an okay guy. Everyone loved Gloria. Said she outclassed him.

"Oh, and I paid a visit to Mark, the barista at the coffee shop. Guy was crazy wired, drinking too much of his product. But he vouched for Jeremy the day she died."

"Okay. We can cross him off our list. I'm taking a road trip to the federal pen up in Victorville. Get a feel for our inmate."

Jack, wearing black slacks, black loafers, and a blue button-down shirt, headed for the kitchen sink and grabbed two Excedrin and a Vicodin out of the cupboard. He knew the two-hour drive would wreak havoc with his back, and he chose to stay in front of the pain. He grabbed a bottle of water out of the fridge, slugged down the pills, and slung a black leather jacket over his arm. "You can reach me by phone if anything comes up."

"Cool."

"And don't work too late. I'll probably catch afternoon traffic, and I can fill you in on my way back to town." Jack walked out the door looking forward to hitting the road with the top down.

The United States Penitentiary, Victorville, was a high-security prison designed to house 960 male inmates but was pushing 1,400 violent offenders. Six V-shaped buildings surrounded the central yard with a gun tower in the middle. Six more towers lined the perimeter of the facility along with a lethal electric double fence.

"Survival, that's the name of the game," Carl Forbes said to Jack. He was seated at a metal table in a windowless jailhouse interview room dedicated to convicts and their lawyers. "The long and the short. In my case, the long," Carl said without humor, just truth telling. He was a thin man, with skin the color of caramel, lightly freckled. Salt-and-pepper hair, jailhouse short, cut close enough to see the sheen of his scalp. His eyes were copper, probing, world-weary. His hands, palms held upward in his lap, lent a feeling of ease that belied the cacophony of shrill sounds that echoed on a constant loop in the high-security prison. This was a man who had turned living in the moment into an art form, stringing enough of those moments together until a minute turned into an hour, and one day turned into the next. This was day eight thousand, three hundred, and ninety-five.

Carl stared at Jack, searching his eyes, trying to suss out whether this ex-cop was there to fuck him around or was the real deal.

Jack let him make his assessment.

"In here, I'm invisible. A ghost. The unseen. You got no name, no control, no judgment, no point of view, no one gives a damn. No need for plans, not today, not tomorrow. It's bad enough if you did the crime, but if you're innocent... well, purgatory's too kind a word. Because in here it's hell on earth. But then, you're a cop," he said with a visceral flare of anger on *cop* that disappeared as quickly as it appeared. "You heard it all before. We're all innocent."

Jack couldn't deny it. He'd put many bad guys behind bars and spent many hours in federal pens deposing witnesses on a case he was running, making deals, trading time off for information. He always felt claustrophobic and couldn't wait to hear that steel door clang shut behind him as he walked out into the sunlight.

Jack didn't weigh in. He let the man continue.

"I was in one week before word was sent down from cell block C. Two men were fighting over me. The winner would own me. I was seventeen when I was arrested, but eighteen before the trial was over. I weighed in at ninety-eight pounds, and the girls in my high school found me attractive. Thought I looked good. You could've knocked me over with a feather. With all this ... I never slept with a woman. Dreamt about it. Still do, twenty-three years later. That ain't right."

Carl rolled up his sleeves. Angry scars ran the length of both forearms. Pink squiggly raised lines from his wrists to the crook of his arm. "I used a soda can pop-top. Wasn't gonna be nobody's bitch. Only mistake I made was timing. The guards did a cell check before I bled out.

"The doctors who saved my life didn't know who the hell I was, but they worked for five hours and through four transfusions to save my sorry soul. Had to steal veins from my legs to keep blood flowing to my hands or I'd be brushing my teeth, and worse, with hooks. When I woke and realized what those good men and women did to save me, I figured God musta had a plan and who was I to punk out on him?"

Carl let that revelation take hold. "So, what do you know about me that's true?"

Jack knew better than to make up a story if he wanted chance one of getting the inmate's help. "I know Gloria Millhouse believed in your innocence. And she was working hard on your behalf. I don't know how far she got, so I don't have an opinion one way or the other. Don't have enough information. But I'll do everything in my power to get to the bottom of Gloria's death. If she was murdered and it was tied to your case, and if it helps exonerate you, I'll share that information with the proper authorities. The people at Loyola who have your back."

Carl seemed content with that, so Jack set down the rules. "You don't lie to me, I won't lie to you. What I need now is to reconstruct all of your conversations with Gloria. All the notes and files lost in the West LA robbery. I want to know what your story is, how you ended up here, what Gloria was pursuing to overturn your sentence."

He watched Carl roll that around. He didn't give quick answers to hard questions. He probably didn't want to get hurt again, open old wounds, live with false hope. Carl nodded as if he was answering an internal question. But then, "So here's the thing. I'm inclined to say yes."

Jack knew there was more coming.

"You see, someone's still out there. Breathing my air. And I've got an awful short list of people who still believe in me. Now, Gloria ..." Carl took a deep breath and pushed down the emotion that was threatening to take hold. "Someone's out there breathing her air. You look like a man who can take care of business. Let's give it a go."

Carl extended his hand. Jack accepted.

Jack's dark hair was buffeted in the warm afternoon breeze as he powered down I-15. Traffic was light, and it felt good to drive with the top down. The glare of the sun was a welcome friend, and it was a relief to be out of the oppressive prison. He had a lot of work to do before rendering an opinion as to Carl's guilt or innocence, but his first impressions were positive.

Many men broke mentally from long-term incarceration. Carl seemed to have his head screwed on straight. Not an easy feat, he thought. And Jack wasn't a bleeding heart when it came to putting away bad guys. He liked to believe that everyone he arrested was good for the crime, but he wasn't naïve enough to think mistakes couldn't be made.

The professor told him two hundred men had been exonerated in his program. Men who had spent a lifetime behind bars for a crime they hadn't committed. And the countless number of death row inmates who had already been put to death. Something to think about.

Jack cleared his mind as he flew across the high desert. The area was filled with scattered boulders, tan sand and little else. By the time he hit the I-10, small towns and building developments mushroomed between hills along the five-lane highway before he dropped into the valley and dense suburbia. Then the scenic drive over the Santa Monica Mountains, ending up at the Pacific Ocean. All in eighty-five miles.

As he merged with the 405, he slammed on the brakes. It was toe and heel for the next hour. The downside of urban sprawl.

Jack knew that Terry Brannigan, the only arresting officer still alive, should be next on his list. But inmate Carl Forbes had told him he'd been tortured and coerced into giving a false statement at the hands of Brannigan and his partner Kevin Cook. It was that statement, the young man's own damning words, that caused the jury to find him guilty of murder.

Jack decided to do an end run and talk to Kevin's ex-wife. She might be able to provide a more honest opinion of what her husband's life was like back in 2000.

He called Cruz, filled him in on his conversation with Carl, and got the address to Hanna's house in Del Rey.

Jack pulled his sterling-silver Mustang to the curb in a modest neighborhood. Many of the houses were built on half lots, and comingled with the occasional McMansion that loomed over the smaller homes and changed the feel of the street.

He checked his GPS against the address of the house. The dwelling looked the worse for the wear, and the picture window was boarded up with a clean sheet of plywood. A disturbing recent addition.

He slid out of his car and stretched his back. It was going into spasms from the punishing traffic. He didn't have a spare Vicodin and would have to gut it out until he got back to the loft.

"She's not home," a young mother carrying a baby on her hip said to Jack.

"Do you know when she's returning?"

The woman shook her head and hiked up the boy, who was getting restless. "We had a drive-by shooting two nights ago. Hanna was sitting in her living room and someone blew out her picture window. She left with a packed bag as soon as the police took off. I didn't have a chance to say goodbye."

"Did they catch the shooter?"

"Right," she said derisively. "I saw her face, and the woman looked freaked."

"Was anybody injured?"

"Not physically, but damn if Hanna didn't look like a hot mess. Are you a cop?" she said, trying to match the convertible with Jack's face.

"Retired," he said. "Jack Bertolino. I'm looking into the suspicious death of a young woman. Hanna was one of the last people to see her alive."

"Jean Bradshaw. Pleased to be talking to an adult. What was the woman's story? I mean connection with Hanna?"

"She was questioning her about a man who might have been falsely convicted of a crime."

"Yeah. Her husband was a cop. No love lost there. Hmmm."

Jack raised his eyes. "What?"

"Someone comes around asking questions. About an old case." The woman was riffing now. "Maybe a bad cop. Hanna gets her window shot out. And now she's on the run."

"What're you thinking?" Jack asked.

"If that's not a message sent, then I'm gonna stop watching *Law and Order.*"

"Anybody see the car?"

"No. I ran out when I heard the window shatter and was joined by a few of the neighbors. No one saw a thing."

"Any idea where she might be headed? Family, friends?"

"No, but I'll ask around. It's a tight-knit group around here. Except for the assholes," she said throwing an angry glance toward the McMansion blocking their neighbor's sun. "Pardon my French."

"No worries," Jack said, grinning. He liked this woman.

"If I hear anything, I could give you a call."

"That works for me." Jack handed her one of his cards. "Anything you come up with would be a help."

"Give me something to do besides chase after this tornado," she said, tousling her boy's hair.

"I'm going to look over the property. Don't call the cops on me."

Jean grinned, the baby squirmed, and Jack walked across the street.

He looked into a side window next to the plywood. Glass was

strewn over the rug. A framed poster of Monet's *Gardens of Giverny* was listing to the side. The shattered glass was sprayed across the off-white couch.

There was nothing of interest around the house. The window on the side of the garage showed it was filled with clutter, but minus a car.

As he walked back down the driveway, he checked the mailbox. There were a few bills and an oversized red envelope that looked like a personal card of some kind. He pulled out his cell and took a photo of the return address. Then he stepped onto the porch and slid the mail under the doorjamb.

Jean was sitting on the lawn, rolling a soccer ball to her son as Jack got into his car. "Do you know what kind of car Hanna drove?" he asked.

"A beat-up old Plymouth. Kind of gold colored. Faded on the roof."

"A license number?"

"Hey, I'm good, but not that good."

Jack waved and drove down the street thinking she was damn fine.

CHAPTER 7

Jack was back in his car at first light. He tried connecting with Commander Brannigan at LAPD headquarters and was told he was working one of his SWAT teams at the G. Dawson Regional Training Center.

The compound was a sprawling eight-hundred-acre affair in the forested foothills of the San Bernardino Mountains. Jack checked into the main building, where a phone call from the mayor's office had cleared the way, and was given directions to the fifty-yard small arms range where Brannigan and his team were executing shooting drills.

Ten men, dressed in full tactical uniforms, helmets, boots, and ballistic vests were going down the line, taking turns doing a grueling series of pushups, then jumping to their feet, drawing their semi-automatic pistols, and firing at close-range targets. And that was in eighty-degree heat, wearing an extra fifty pounds of equipment.

One man not in assault gear, with a brisling silver flat top and a powerful military bearing, was clearly running the show. A team member waiting his turn spotted Jack standing next to a corrugated metal supply shed and signaled the squad leader.

Terry Brannigan turned, pulled out his earplugs, and strode toward Jack. "This is a closed area. Civilians aren't allowed," he said with brusque condescension. "We're using live ammo. Not looking to get anybody hurt."

"Jack Bertolino," he said, ignoring the snub. Brannigan knew damn well who he was.

"You're not a cop anymore. You want to talk, we'll do it downtown."

"Tell that to your boss."

Brannigan's face creased into a tight grin. "It's all politics with you guys, huh? Make it short."

Jack had had just about enough of the commander's attitude. "I heard something interesting yesterday. Have you been around to visit your partner's ex-wife lately?"

"Why in God's name would I visit that cold bitch? She kicked Kevin when he was down. He had the big C, and she let him die alone."

The memory seemed to calm the commander some.

"You weren't around?" Jack asked.

"As much as I could. I was on the job. You know how that goes. What did she have to say for herself?"

"She's in the wind. Somebody tried to take her out."

Brannigan cocked his head but didn't blink. "How?"

"Drive-by."

"Hmmm. Sorry to hear it. Not like Kevin wasn't a handful, but why would someone take a shot at old Hanna?"

"I was hoping you had some idea."

"What the fuck does that mean? You get hit in the head one too many times?"

"Gloria Millhouse. You had a conversation with her."

"We talked. Her and that professor. So what?"

"She also met with Hanna. The same day she died."

"I heard about that. Car accident, right? Tough luck. Seemed like a nice kid. So?"

"Same reason she reached out to you."

"That makes sense. She asked questions about a cold case. Makes sense she'd follow up with Hanna. I told her if there was anything new with the case, ring me up, and I'd do what I could to help. Where are you headed with this, Bertolino? The case is old news. It was a righteous bust. Clean arrest, kid confessed, jury convicted, end of story."

Jack changed tack. "You think someone was trying to send a message to Hanna?"

"How the hell would I know? She lives in a shitty neighborhood. Gangs, a few blocks over. They're like cockroaches."

"You're a cop. You believe in coincidences?"

"I'm starting to lose my patience here." The vein on Brannigan's temple throbbed, his voice tightened. "If it weren't for Aprea, I wouldn't give you the time of day, and you know what? We're done here."

He turned to walk away but then spun back, stepped in close, violating Jack's personal space, inches from his face. "And nice job getting my friend busted up. You were supposed to have his back. He's supporting your fucking caseload, and my friend takes a bullet. You get the glory, but that's it right. You're nothing but a half-assed, washed-out glory hound who—"

Brannigan's proximity worked against him. Jack's hands struck like cobras. He two-fisted Brannigan's jacket, muscled him up, and slammed him against the shed. His head whipped back, and the sound echoed off the metal siding.

Ten automatics ratcheting bullets stopped the action. Jack eased his grip on a red-faced Brannigan, who smacked his hands away.

"We got a problem, boss?" a twenty-something hotshot said as smooth as a python.

"No, Bertolino was just leaving." His eyes burned into Jack's.

"He's got a funny way of saying goodbye." The hotshot drilled a searing punch to Jack's kidney.

Jack's knees started to buckle, but he spun and locked his arm around the hotshot's neck, choking him out, while using him as a crutch. The man struggled, his face turning beet-red, but Jack tightened his grip. The other men knew better than to make a move without a signal from their leader.

"Let him go," Brannigan hissed.

Jack pushed the warrior away and the wise guy dropped hard. "You just drew a line in the sand and stepped over it, Brannigan."

Brannigan spat on the ground next to Jack.

Jack stood his ground, his eyes raking the assembled team. He turned on his heel.

"Where you going, wise guy?" Brannigan said, tight. "You just assaulted an LAPD police officer. Arrest him."

Five men moved as one, swarming Jack, who didn't struggle as cuffs were tightened on his thick wrists.

The echo of rounds being fired accompanied Jack's perp walk as he was shoved through the knot of men and pushed down the dirt path toward an awaiting unmarked government-issue Ford.

One of the commander's men palmed his head down and pushed him roughly into the rear of his plain-wrap sedan, slamming the door, locking him in.

Jack's back was a sheet of burning pain. But his breathing and heart rate were trending back toward normal.

This wasn't the last time he'd be confronting Brannigan. He'd worked with men like him in the past. The commander showed his true colors today. He might have snowed the professor with his offer of help, but Gloria had it right. Brannigan was now firmly on Jack's shit list.

Nick had made it home early for a change. As he poured charcoals onto the Weber grill, his daughter, Sammy, wearing a yellow summer dress, turned in circles until she got dizzy, giggled and fell to the grass laughing and watched the clouds spin. Nick grinned at her little girl's infectious laughter.

The family's California bungalow was modest, set in the hills of Northridge, with a treetop view of the valley. When Alicia banged out the screen door with a cocktail for her husband, Nick felt like the wealthiest man on the planet.

Alicia was a first-generation Filipino beauty, with chestnut skin that drove Nick to distraction. Twice divorced, Nick hadn't thought the life he was now living would ever be in the cards. The third time was definitely the charm, he thought, and he vowed never to take her perfect love and the love they shared for their daughter for granted.

Nick set down his drink, uncapped the lighter fluid, and gave it a healthy spray. He struck one of his wooden matches and tossed it onto the coals that lit with a whoosh. The smell transported him back to nights and bonfires and burgers on the grill at Dockweiler Beach, where teenage hormones roared and dreams were still possible. From Nick's perspective, his had finally come true.

He was pulled out of his reverie when he heard the sound of a car pulling up the driveway. When the car door slammed, he shouted, "We're in the back," not knowing who the mystery guest was.

The redwood fence's rusted hinges squealed as it swung open, and Commander Brannigan walked across the lawn, with perfect posture, a light grin, and a bottle of Herradura silver in his hand.

"He comes bearing gifts," Nick said, proffering his hand, and accepting the tequila with the other.

"Hello, Alicia, you're looking lovely as ever," Brannigan said, as charming as he could muster. "And who's this big girl?"

"Sammy, say hello to Mr. Brannigan," Nick said.

Sammy, not usually shy, sidled up to Nick and snugged an arm tight around his leg, her smile gone. Alicia jumped in, "What a nice surprise, Terry. May I pour you a drink?"

"The day I had, I could sure use one."

"You still drinking Macallan?" Nick asked.

"You got it."

"Honey, would you mind pouring a scotch, one cube for the commander?"

"Terry," he corrected with a smile. "We're not on the clock, and we've been through too much to stand on ceremony."

"Will you be joining us for dinner?" Alicia asked as she headed across the lawn.

"Just a cocktail tonight, and a few words with the old man."

Sammy looked over her shoulder and followed her mother into the house.

Nick and Brannigan made themselves comfortable on two blue

Adirondack chairs, drinks in hand, listening to the ambient sound of summer.

"You remembered my brand."

"I take care of my friends," Nick said.

"Good to hear."

Nick wasn't sure what Brannigan meant but knew it was the reason for his visit.

"You know, we're the same, you and me," the commander said.

"How so?"

"Cream rises to the top. And I'm gonna bring you along."

"So you said."

"Do me a favor and keep your buddy out of my face."

"Jack's okay."

Brannigan's demeanor changed. "I'm just saying."

"So, what happened? It's been a long time since you've driven up the hill. Bertolino make an appearance?"

"More than an appearance. Your guy's sitting in a holding tank as we speak."

Nick smile disappeared, his eyes narrowed. "Keep talking."

"He attacked me in front of my men, and when Joe Moran tried to help, he choked him out."

"He took two of you down?"

"He's lucky he's not dead. My men were training with live rounds."

"What was the play?"

"He started getting in my face, tossing around not too subtle accusations."

"Yeah?"

"And I may have called him a 'fucking glory hound.'"

"There you go."

"There you go what?" The collegial attitude evaporated quicker than the two fingers of scotch.

"You know you can't prosecute him," Nick said.

"The hell you say."

"Here's what I'm hearing," Nick went on. "Jack Bertolino took on two of LAPD's finest and got the upper hand. Now, the more senior of the officers is looking to be the next chief of police. Make a good headline. And I'm sure Moran doesn't want his reputation marred by that kind of publicity."

"You piss me off, Aprea. I thought you were my friend."

"That's why I'm giving you advice you didn't ask for and nobody else would have the balls to tell you. You want a refill?"

"Hell, yeah. Neat this time. And make it a double."

Nick pushed off the chair, hiding the knifing pain in his shoulder as he walked toward the house. He gave a quick check on the charcoals, saw they were still ten minutes away and shut the lid.

Brannigan stopped him at the screen door, "Nick."

Nick turned on his heel.

"Thank you."

Nick nodded and let the screen door slam behind him.

Jack pushed off the stainless steel bench in his holding cell at the Metropolitan Detention Center. He stepped close to the bars and when he was sure no guards were in the area, pulled two Excedrin out of the watch pocket in his jeans and dry-chewed them. Then he popped his only Vicodin to stave off the pain, hoping no serious damage had been done to his back.

He heard footfalls on the linoleum floor and recognized the rhythm of the stride before Leslie stepped into view.

"Hey, cowboy," she said as she tossed her blonde hair back.

"Ma'am."

"How do you like the accommodations?"

"Had better."

Leslie nodded in agreement. "I can't spring you, Jack. Conflict of interest and all, you know, because of our past. I've had to recuse myself."

"Sorry to hear that."

"Hmmm. Do you think they'll allow conjugal visits in this hotel?"

She always kept her sense of humor. "I'll call my lawyer and get back to you."

"Good. So I can't get you out of here … but the mayor made a few calls and interceded on your behalf. He spoke with Commander Terry Brannigan – who is in his pocket – who spoke with Joe Moran, the detective you choked out. As it turns out, Moran, decided not to press charges. Truth be told, the mayor thinks both men were embarrassed you got the upper hand in front of the team, and the commander wouldn't want the full story to come out during an arraignment hearing. It wouldn't help his chances of replacing the police chief when the confirmation vote is put to the city council."

"My lucky day."

"You've made some powerful enemies, Jack. A week on the job, and you're the one sitting in a jail cell. You are aware that's not the way it's supposed to work?"

"So I've been told."

"What am I going to do with you, Bertolino?"

Jack sauntered up to the bars. "I've got a few ideas."

"Huh. While I've got your undivided attention, what are your thoughts on the concept of 'friends with benefits'?"

"Hmmm. It's definitely something I want to explore."

"Good answer. You'll be out within the hour. We can continue the conversation then."

Leslie turned on her heel, enjoying the feel of Jack's eyes on her body as she walked down the hallway.

Jack was lying face down on Leslie's down-filled mattress. Her bedroom, on the twenty-third-floor of the Wilshire Corridor condo tower, was well appointed. Modern furniture, a white plush rug, and walls painted muted shades of gray. A red Barcelona chair was the accent piece and faced the modest flat-screen television. Light jazz emanated from hidden speakers.

Two pizza boxes from Mozza lay open and empty on a side table next to a half empty bottle of red. Jack's empty glass sat on a modern Italian end table.

From the balcony, Leslie could see Wilshire Boulevard ribbon its way west all the way to the moonlit slash of silver that reflected off the Pacific Ocean. She never got tired of the view. She parted the diaphanous white curtains, took a last sip of wine, and joined Jack on the bed.

His shirt was off, jeans on, barefoot, as Leslie pulled back the ice pack and winced in unison with Jack as she exposed the purple and yellow bruise the size of a softball on his lower back.

"You look like you were gored by a bull."

"Close, but he got the worst of it."

"You're like a teenager, Bertolino. Oozing bravado. But your body's paying the price. What am I going to do with you?"

"You could start with my neck, please."

Leslie, wearing nothing but her favorite bathrobe from Ventana, kissed Jack lightly on the back of his neck, grabbed some lotion from her end table and went to work trying to loosen some of Jack's knots. She straddled his bare back, her knees lightly pressing into the sides of his ribs. Jack fought the urge to growl in pain, but couldn't stop his body from arousal.

He spun onto his back, and Leslie rose to her knees and leaned down to kiss him on the lips. Her bathrobe fell open and she raked his chest with her breasts.

Jack's pain started to subside as he unbuckled his belt and slid his jeans off the side of the bed. His hands moved to Leslie's waist, slowly guiding her onto his erection.

Leslie held Jack tight, pushed up, and pulled her bathrobe off, tossing it onto the rug. Their eyes locked as she slowly slid down, offering her perfect breasts, her nipples rock hard from the light ocean breeze that moved the curtains from the open door of her balcony.

They groaned in unison and their breathing became slow and sensuous. Her lips, inches from Jack's, her breath warm, her light scent intoxicating.

Leslie's deep blue eyes were hypnotic, her blonde hair draped over the sides of his face. The pain in his back miraculously disappeared. Their eyes locked as his tongue met hers and the electricity that flowed from their lips overwhelmed them both.

Leslie came up for air. "Does it hurt?" she asked, her voice thick.

Jack moved his hips slightly, slowly, and then pulled her deeper, the only answer he gave. Then he disengaged and rolled Leslie onto her side, with one arm around the back of her neck, and the other snugged between her legs he drew her close.

He lifted her slightly and gently lowered her onto her back. Jack slid between her legs, losing himself in her heat.

The lovers shared slow, orgasmic sex that left them both breathless as they rediscovered their perfect chemistry.

Nick and Alicia stood at Sammy's doorway. The angel night-light was plugged in, emitting a reassuring glow in her room. She was asleep on her back, still wearing her princess tiara. Nick kissed Alicia on her neck, and walked into the room. Carefully lifting the tiara off his daughter's perfect head, he placed it on her bedside table.

He stepped out of the room, took his wife by the hand, and walked her into the living room, where they settled in on the overstuffed couch.

"So, what did he want? You do know he scared Sammy?"

"I noticed. It's just a gift he has. Scaring little girls and grown men."

"He wanted something. I could tell."

"Yeah, he did. He's offering me a job, not sure doing what, in his administration if he gets appointed police chief. He said that I was a lot like him."

"No you're not. You are a kind, generous man. A man who takes care of his family, and his friends. You are not a thing like him, Nicky. You don't scare your five-year-old child even when you're loud."

Nick took his wife's delicate face in his big mitts and pulled it close to his cheek. He could no longer talk, so full was his love for Alicia.

Jack stepped out of the bathroom, wrapped in a towel, and slid gingerly under the sheets. Leslie was watching MSNBC and muted it.

She took a pensive sip of wine and Jack, picking up on her energy, asked, *what*?

"Did I hurt you?" she said.

"Hardly. You worked out some of the kinks." From her distant tone he wasn't sure the direction the conversation was taking.

"Am I too old for you?"

Jack sat back up, grimacing with the effort. "What are you talking about?" But Jack knew the answer before it was stated. He realized he should have immediately said no.

"Angelica Cardona."

And there it was. He took a hit of wine and looked squarely into Leslie's attorney eyes. He leaned in and placed a light kiss on her lips. "No. And there's absolutely no reason to go there. You're younger than me."

Leslie rolled her eyes.

What she didn't know, and what Jack wasn't ready to share, was that Vincent Cardona, Angelica's father, was an inmate at the same prison as Carl Forbes. It was only a matter of time before Vincent would call in a favor.

CHAPTER 8

Nick Aprea's face was redder than the dried hot sauce on the scarred wooden picnic table where he sat devouring his lunch. The ancient taco stand was located a stone's throw from Whole Foods on Lincoln Boulevard, and the noise and soot rising from the dense traffic suited his foul mood. Nick didn't raise his head when Jack walked up. Instead he doused his carnitas tacos with enough of the fiery sauce to take a lesser man down.

"You first came to town, Gallina had a pretty good case against you," Nick said. "It was a setup, but could've gone either way. Who on the force took you at your word? No questions asked?" Nick said, wiping his mouth with the back of his ham fist.

"You."

"Right. So that banger, one of the 18th Street Angels, he's still walking with a limp, I hear. How did that one go down?"

Silence from Jack. He knew where Nick was headed.

"Right. I could've turned you in. What do you always say? Whatever serves the greater good? Right? Like Mateo. That's right, except he was never innocent. He was a major drug dealer, right, pard?"

"Look, something stinks here, Nick. I don't have the answer, but I'll get to the bottom of it. You can't take the ride with me, it'll be my loss."

Nick balled up his paper plate and jammed it into the overfilled can. He pushed off from the table and swatted the remnants of lunch off his wrinkled blue shirt. "You had to get in his face in front of his men? What part of don't waste your time didn't you understand?"

"The question had to be asked."

"Bullshit. You didn't believe me. Shoulder to shoulder, you and me, under fire, you prick," Nick took a menacing step toward Jack. He balled both fists and pounded Jack in the chest, knocking him back a step. "C'mon," he said, flicking the air with his thick fingers, challenging.

Jack stood tall. "One good shot to your shoulder, you're on your knees, crawling like a bitch."

"Low blow, brother," but it gave Nick pause. "Man's the only other cop saved my bacon when it needed saving, and you're lookin' to end his career."

"I'm just looking for the truth. If he was heavy-handed, forced the issue, got a confession that stretched the truth, then yeah. If it's a career ender, it's on him. Not the man who was a fucking kid at the time of his arrest, and might've served twenty-three years on trumped-up charges." Jack knew he was getting through. "I love you, brother, and I know you live by the truth. If you've changed, be sure to let me know."

Jack turned his back on Nick and walked to his car.

Nick viciously back-kicked the can of trash, overturning it, sending dirty plates, cans, half-filled coffee cups, and soiled napkins scattering on the oily dirt.

As Jack pulled away from the curb, he could see his old friend in the rearview mirror, righting the can and scooping up the nasty garbage with his bare hands. Nick Aprea was never one to let someone else clean up his mess.

Councilman Mark Corcoran's City Hall office was one of three he had at his disposal. He was the council member of the 11th district for the City of Los Angeles. And his district covered Brentwood, Marina del

Rey, Mar Vista, Marina Peninsula, Playa del Rey, Pacific palisades, and Playa Vista. All upscale zip codes, perfect for fundraising.

Corcoran's head rose from a desk full of paperwork as raised voices spilled in from the outer office. "You can't go in there without an—"

Jack stepped into the room, his hand outstretched. "Jack Bertolino, pleased to meet you."

Corcoran had obviously gotten a heads-up from the mayor's office. Information he hadn't shared with his secretary. She was waved out of the room before she could explain the intrusion.

"Natalie is overly protective, but without parameters I'd never get anything accomplished. And as you can see, I'm drowning in paperwork. Now isn't a good time."

"Should've thought of that before you gave Gloria Millhouse the bum's rush. She said you all but threw her out of your office."

"She exaggerated." Corcoran tried for the breezy approach. "You know, we work our asses off to get elected, and then the real work starts, fundraising for the next election. Time is money."

"You're breaking my heart. And all along I thought you were doing the people's work."

Corcoran ignored the dig and explained. "The last thing I needed politically was to be tied to a twenty-three-year-old murder case."

"And I thought the last thing you needed was to piss off the mayor. Bad enemy to have in your line of work. And so, you can either share what you know about the case and what you spoke to Gloria about, or I can get Lieutenant Gallina over here and make sure there's a news crew on hand. Councilman Mark Corcoran was one of the last persons to see Gloria Millhouse alive. The young woman, representing Project for the Innocent, was questioning the Councilman about a murder… well, you see how this'll play out."

Corcoran got the message. "You want coffee?" he asked.

"Black," Jack said.

"Natalie, would you bring us two cups of coffee, black." Then he turned to Jack, "Okay, let's do this."

Jack laid a file on Corcoran's desk. "I want you to look over the names on the witness list. Especially your pals. I want your take on them. Things they talked about after a few beers. Anybody who was really sexually charged and let his hormones do the talking. We all knew guys like that. Always mouthing off. Always took things a bit too far. You can add anybody you ran with who didn't make the list. I want any thoughts you might have had during or after the trial that put Carl Forbes away for a lifetime."

Natalie entered and set down two mugs of steaming coffee. She was miffed and didn't hide it. Corcoran let out an audible sigh and took a sip after she turned stiffly and left the room.

"Look," he said. "It was a terrible tragedy, Gloria's death. I followed the report on the news – and let me tell you, I suffered some guilt. But if it was an accident, why are we spinning wheels?"

Jack had never been fond of politicians. He'd had his fill when he was running the Drug Enforcement Task Force for the NYPD. It took all of his control not to slap the hypocritical concern off the councilman's face for saying he'd suffered guilt when he heard about Gloria's death.

Instead, he answered the question. "Because the jury's still out. The evidence is inconclusive. If it wasn't an accident … someone killed her. Someone who had something to hide. Possibly someone from your past. And there's a good chance it's tied to the sexual assault and murder of Shelley Goldstein. A woman you had a mad crush on in high school and who wouldn't give you the time of day. Ego like yours … must've been hard to take."

"I've suffered worse rejection in my life. It never slowed me down."

"And you suffered when you heard about Gloria's death?"

"You have a problem with that?" the councilman said, unable to hide his irritation.

"I didn't think guilt was in a politician's lexicon."

"Thanks for stopping by, Jack."

Jack tossed one of his cards onto the councilman's desk. "Send me that list. I'll be seeing you."

As Jack started out the councilman said, "Call first."

Jack smiled at the secretary on his way out the door. Natalie returned the favor.

Jack was in stop-and-go traffic on the I-10, heading for the marina. He decided it was time to bring his old friend Tommy Aronsohn into the mix. He tapped the car's Bluetooth, hoping to catch him in the office with the three-hour time difference.

"Jack!" Tommy shouted into the phone.

Tommy was forty-six, medium height, broad shouldered, ruddy skin. He had a light East Coast accent and a heavy New York attitude. His easy smile could turn dark on a lie if it was leveled in a courtroom. "You wanna know what kind of a week I'm having?"

"Talk to me."

"The kind where I'm waiting on a call from you, my friend. To pull me out of my malaise. This corporate bullshit. Cleaning up after rich men I wouldn't break bread with."

"But you cash their checks," Jack said, feeling better himself for the first time all day.

"I'm a lawyer, for chrissake." Both men laughed.

Jack and Tommy had major history. They'd worked a case together when Jack was a rookie undercover narcotics detective and Tommy a baby DA. They made their bones taking down a vicious gang of Jamaican drug dealers, moved up through the ranks, and remained steadfast friends. Tommy, Manhattan's District Attorney, and Jack, Inspector in the NYPD. Tommy was the reason Jack went into the PI business and directed lucrative clients his way, as promised.

"Tell me you need me to book a flight. I think Elizabeth's bored. She'd like me out of the house for a few weeks, and I'd like to comply."

"You're on."

"What do you need, Jack? Are you ready to go back to work?"

"I got pulled onto a case. A personal situation. I'll need your expertise if I'm going to make any headway. It's a mystery at this point, but it feels like a murder."

Tommy, no longer a civil servant, ran an upscale law practice with an office on Park Avenue that afforded him an opulent home on Long Island. But he was still connected and owed favors he was happy to call in for Jack.

Jack laid out what he knew about the victim, the case, and then dropped the bomb. "I'll need court records of the murder case that was litigated back in 2000. And excessive-force complaints against the arresting detectives, Terry Brannigan, and his partner Kevin Cook, who died a few years ago.

"If Gloria was murdered because of the dirt she was digging, there are only so many people who would benefit from her being silenced. The cops, the prosecution, the judge, the eyewitness, the killer."

"A hornet's nest, Jack. Good for you. Can't Leslie help?"

"She pulled me onto the case. Delivered the request in person. A favor for the mayor. I don't want to tap that well, don't want to mix personal with politics."

"But you are mixing?" Tommy asked like a goofy freshman.

"The master of double entendre," Jack shot back.

"You know I live vicariously off your sexual exploits."

"So, are you in or what?"

"E-mail me names, dates, and thoughts. I'll clear my desk and book a flight."

Tommy never disappointed, Jack thought, as he clicked off the Bluetooth and headed for home.

CHAPTER 9

The next morning Jack and Cruz drove through a middle-class neighborhood in Mar Vista, following a hand-drawn map Gloria had penned. It concentrated on a four-block radius, but other sites of interest were drawn along the yellow pad's borders. She'd marked X's over particular houses where Councilman Corcoran and his friends lived back in 2000. Their names carefully printed above the rough sketches. The house X'd in red was where Shelley Goldstein, the murder victim, had lived.

Jack wanted to get a feel for the neighborhood and see where the accused, Carl Forbes, lived in proximity to the rest of the crew. As it turned out, Carl's house was five blocks east of the core group of friends—and on the other side off Washington Boulevard. It would have dictated a different route walking to their high school. Jack knew kids were pack animals at that age, and cross-pollination was not an everyday occurrence.

Jack pulled the Mustang to the curb next to a litter-strewn field and a large, round concrete storm drain, with an opening tall enough to enter on a crouch. The city-owned property was located a quarter mile to the west of Shelley's home, where runoff from rainwater, discarded oil, plastic bottles, cans, Styrofoam containers, and human waste spilled into the L.A River and then dumped into the Pacific Ocean below Marina del Rey. It was where Shelley's body had been found, raped and stabbed multiple times.

"Because of the lack of blood at the scene, the detectives concluded the murder hadn't occurred in the storm drain that was dry at the time of her death and filled with sand and garbage. They were confident the body had been transported and dropped there."

"Where was she killed?" Cruz asked.

"Cops never discovered the location. She could have been forced into a vehicle, but if that's the case, Carl didn't have a car. And it's one hell of a hump to carry a body if she was attacked closer to home."

Cruz leafed through Gloria's notes on the teenagers on the original suspect list. They had all been questioned and released. One of the boys died in 2000, the other lived in Reno. Gloria had run down his phone number, but the guy wasn't cooperative.

Jack decided to introduce himself to Carl's mother, who was a ferocious advocate for her son and still lived at the old address.

"I'm sorry for the way I acted, getting all up in your business when you knocked on my door. But you have to understand, there is no love lost between me and the police."

"I understand," Jack said as Cruz took another mouthful of cherry cobbler Eunice Forbes had placed in front of him on the dining room table, letting an unconscious sigh of pleasure escape.

"And you look like the police," Eunice said, eyebrows raised.

"Guilty as charged," Jack said.

Cruz snorted and said, "This is delicious, Mrs. Forbes. I mean, unbelievably good."

"There's more where that came from," she said approvingly. "Don't you feed the young man?" she scolded.

Jack took a sip of coffee from a flowered cup, too delicate for his large hands. "Oh, he eats, all right."

Eunice was a scrappy woman in her eighties who couldn't have weighed more than ninety pounds. Her silver hair was tightly braided and her brown eyes probed. She exuded a faith-based strength.

"I can't make promises," Jack went on, carefully placing the flowered china cup back on its saucer, which had cracked and been repaired. "But I want you to understand that if there's a connection between Gloria's death and the murder twenty-three years ago—and I'm leaning in that direction—it might shed light on Carl's case. Gloria was poking a hornet's nest, and somebody stung her. If I discover the link, it could help your son."

Eunice gave that some thought and freshened Jack's coffee. "That girl was a bright star. I cried when I heard the news. Carl was depressed for weeks. I was worried about my boy, as you can imagine. I've never lost faith in his innocence; my boy was as pure as the driven snow. But I have lost faith in the process now and again. Gloria, well, she was my boy's angel, and it was quite a blow. Anything you can do to help, well ..." Eunice's face reddened. She swiped away a welling tear, stepped into the kitchen and leaned against the sink, her back ramrod straight.

Jack and Cruz didn't want to intrude on the woman's personal pain. The only sound emanating from the dining room was Cruz's fork scraping the plate, scooping up the last bit of crust etched in cherry filling.

Eunice came out, eyes blazing. "Anything I can do to help, I'm here, I'm ready and able, Mr. Bertolino. You can take that to the bank."

And Jack knew he could. "Did you testify at Carl's trial?"

"They never put me on the stand. Carl was home with me the night of the murder. We were watching television. I told the police the night I found him, forty-eight hours after his arrest. I filed a report. By that time he had already confessed."

"And his lawyer never brought it up in court?" Jack asked.

"He said no one would believe the mother of the accused."

Jack thought that was a mistake and it made him angry. She would have made a fine advocate for her son.

"What did you think of his lawyer?"

Her eyes scolded. "My boy's been in prison for twenty-three years. There's no love lost."

"Point taken."

"The police grabbed my boy walking home from school and tortured him. My husband and I didn't know where he was for two full days and nights. And when we tracked him down, Carl didn't know what he was saying, or what he'd signed. They broke him. He just wanted to come home, and they lied to him. They lied. We didn't believe the case was ever going to trial let alone be enough to convict our child."

"What about the eyewitness?"

"That woman was not to be trusted. Cheryl Lee Williams was a single mother that knew the inside of a barroom, if you know what I mean. She moved away the moment she finished testifying. Told the reporters she feared for her life. I'm still not sure where she got her travel money."

Jack glanced at Cruz, who picked up the silent signal. They'd look into the woman's finances.

"She knew my Carl. He used to mow her lawn. She pointed him out to the policemen when they were doing a drive-through of the neighborhood, but she didn't accuse him then. Just called him by name. It's in the court records that she didn't accuse him until the police stood him in a lineup. Something was out of kilter. She changed her mind, or someone changed it for her. And you know what I think?" she said as a statement of fact.

Jack did, but let her continue.

"The police, they did it. Manipulated her. Changed her mind, just like they made Carl believe if he signed the confession he could sleep in his own bed."

"What did you think of the DA?"

She was fired up, blazing at the sour memories. "He was an unlikeable man. He told my son if he didn't plead guilty he'd be looking at the death penalty. They're the killers. They're all trying to kill my boy."

"Did your son know the victim? Shelley Goldstein?"

She shook her head firmly. "They were in the same class, but that's as far as it went. Her family had the biggest house in the neighborhood, and well, I won't accuse them of prejudice, but there wasn't an open door. He wasn't invited to any parties."

"I'd like you to look at these pictures and tell me if you knew any of the young men."

Eunice carefully placed the short stack of photos on the dining room table like laying down a canasta hand. "Oh, I know them all. This one here's in politics now. He was the alpha of the group. Cocky. Tony, he works at the brewery. This one moved out of the neighborhood and I don't know whether he's alive or dead. They were all kids, never close to my boy, but not bullies. Not bad kids. They'd come around on Halloween but didn't get in much trouble as far as we were concerned. I think there was one other boy that hung with their crowd. But if I'm not mistaken, their family moved before the trial began. I'm blanking on names.

"Someone knows something," she said, back on track. "Someone killed that sweet child. Someone who's still walking around free while my boy pays the price."

Jack nodded to Cruz, who thanked Eunice again for the cobbler. Jack handed her his card. "I want you to get into a comfortable chair and spend some time thinking, Eunice. Go over the arrest, the trial. The reporting. Your feelings. As memories come up, I want you to share them with me. Call me, even if they don't seem important. Call me."

"Thank you. You'll be in my prayers, son."

"It couldn't hurt, Eunice."

The screen door hushed closed. Jack glanced back and could just make out the slight woman silhouetted behind the screen. He had a flash memory of the confessional at Queen of the Most Holy Rosary, along with the priest who sat behind the screen when he was a boy. He was no longer a practicing Catholic, but he never turned down the offer of a prayer.

"I don't know if I could do it," Cruz said as they got into the Mustang.

"What?"

"Spend so many years inside. Locked up in a cell. Especially if I was innocent."

"Do you think Carl's innocent?" Jack asked as he powered down the convertible top.

"I'm not sure. I need more information."

"Good answer."

"I always had trouble understanding the concept of a false confession. I mean, why would anyone give it up if they were innocent? But now, reading some of these case files, I mean, throw in sleep deprivation, physical violence, youth, the effing horror of the crime, hunger, loneliness, and well, it starts to become a possibility. What's your take on it?"

"We had a lot of tricks in our bag that we used to get a confession. But we never resorted to physical or emotional torture. Not that it didn't happen, but not on my watch."

"So, you think Carl's confession could have been coerced?"

"I'll let you know when I have more information."

That seemed to satisfy his young charge for the moment. Jack pulled away from the curb. He was on the hunt and wouldn't stop until he had the answer.

CHAPTER 10

Carl Forbes was sprawled on the bunk in his eight-by-ten cell. Lunch had just wrapped up and he had two hours of free time before reporting to his job in the library. He was working on a writ of habeas corpus for inmate 11278. The man had been incarcerated for eighteen years for killing an entire family of six that lived in Walnut Grove, California.

With his own success garnering the support of Project for the Innocent after pestering them for three years, he spent much of his free time helping other inmates wade through the sea of paperwork needed to get a new trial and hopefully overturn their convictions. His vetting process was very much the same as the professionals, and he'd only spend his time on inmates whose cases spoke to him. Wrongs he thought he could right.

Carl didn't feel the inmate silently enter his cell, but as he heard the familiar sound of a Bic lighter ratcheting, he instinctively rolled onto the concrete floor of his cell.

Larry-the-Rat Durkin held a can of hairspray in one hand and a lit green Bic lighter in the other. The spray fanned out in slow motion. As it hit the flame, the combination became a lethal, roiling jailhouse flame thrower. Carl's mattress, plus the reams of paperwork, were immediately inundated in flames.

As Larry moved in for the kill, he was slammed in the back of the head by inmate 11278's beefy fist. The Rat's head snapped forward, dropping his arms. The fire hit his pant leg and the flames jumped up his government-issue grays toward his neck.

Larry-the-Rat madly pushed past his tormentor, running down the cell block screaming in anguish until the flames overwhelmed him and took him down. A guard ran up, grabbed a blanket from an open cell and smothered the fire. The Rat's primal howls elicited no sympathy from anyone on cell block B.

Inmate 11278 finished beating the flames in Carl's cell with his pillow until they were extinguished. He reached down and pulled a shaken Carl to his feet.

"Was that my papers?" he asked, pained. Knowing the truth.

"Yes, Daryl. I'm sorry. I'll start again when we get my place cleaned up."

"I shoulda killed him."

"Yeah? Woulda defeated the purpose. No?"

"I guess."

"Thank you, Daryl. I was gonna be a crispy critter, you hadn't showed."

Four prison guards ran to the cell and ordered both men onto the ground. They assumed the position and accepted the cuffs. They had a long day ahead of them until the crime was sorted out.

Carl wasn't really worried. The Rat's prints were all over the spray can, and it was clear *he* was the intended target. It was just another episode in the nightmare that was life on the inside.

Jack and Cruz were pulling to a curb in Glendale when he fielded a call from the professor at Loyola. Anderson filled him in on the attack at the penitentiary. Jack decided to take another trip to Victorville. First, he got Leslie on the phone.

"I'll need some help getting the video and a list of anybody who visited inmate Larry Durkin the past two months. It might have been a jailhouse beef, but it was too close for comfort."

"Done," she said. "I'll get the mayor's office on it. How's your back?"

"You're a miracle worker."

"Hah!" Leslie barked, eliciting a laugh from Jack.

"Cruz worked his magic and we traced the ex-wife of one of the arresting officers I was talking about. Did a reverse search off the address on an envelope, got a phone number, and we know somebody's home because Cruz called the house. Man's a fine actor. Have to run before she takes off again."

"I'll get back to you," Leslie said. "Thank God Carl's all right. It's a snake pit up there."

Jack clicked off and they sat scoping out the house at the end of the block. A gold Plymouth was parked in the driveway, which matched her neighbor Jean's description. Rust spots on the chrome and wheel wells. The roof was faded and cracked from the ever-present salt air and unrelenting sun. Another car sat in the garage.

"Ready?" Jack asked.

"Am I the good cop or the bad cop?" Cruz said as he slid out of the passenger seat, ran his hands through his spiky black hair and hand-ironed his work shirt.

"Let's not lose our minds here. A…you're not a cop. And B…you're not a cop. Just be smart and let me do the talking."

"You are so easy."

Jack's eyes narrowed as he stared down Cruz. Satisfied he'd been had, his eyes crinkled into a smile. The smile faded as the front door of the house in question swung open and Hanna ran down the path, jumped into her car, and fired up the engine.

Jack hit the gas and the passenger door slammed shut. He pulled to the side, blocking Hanna's egress from the driveway. She stopped inches from Jack's passenger door.

"Leave me alone!" She leapt from her vehicle. "Move your car!" Hanna shouted red-faced, eyes wild with fear. "Sue!" she screamed.

Jack jumped from the Mustang and pulled out his wallet, showing his license in an attempt to diffuse the energy. "I'm Jack Bertolino. I'm looking into the death of Gloria Millhouse."

Hanna's friend Sue appeared on the porch, cell phone to her head.

"I dialed 911. Get the hell out of here."

Jack continued, "You spoke with her the day she died." His eyes shifted from Hanna to her friend, trying to bring her into his sphere. "I work for her father. Keith Millhouse. Five minutes of your time and we'll be out of your hair."

Hanna's friend nodded to Hanna, lowered the cell phone and clicked off. "Damn 911 put me on hold."

"Thank you," Jack said to both women as Cruz, looking choirboy honest, stepped up next to Jack.

"You might as well come into the house," Sue said. "I don't need my neighbors knowing all my business." She waved gaily across the street, and the curtain in her neighbor's picture window was pulled shut.

"I told her they were all in the bag and Brannigan was holding court," Hanna said. "Bragged he could beat a confession out of a dead man! I saw her taking notes in her little car before she drove away, okay? And now she's dead. And now the scumbag's scaring the bejeezus outta me. I'm too old for this shit. Where am I going to go? You tell me. Are you going to protect me?"

Before Jack could answer, "Don't make me laugh. And if you found me here, he can find me too. I will not put Sue in danger. But that leaves me twisting in the wind."

"I can find you a safe house until the case is settled. I have friends in the LAPD."

"Big whoops. Were you really a cop? Because if you think they're gonna go after their own—if you think anything I have to say would make a difference and overturn a verdict from God knows how many years ago—you were one shitty cop."

Jack let her vent.

"Let me make myself absolutely clear. I will not go on record giving testimony against Terry Brannigan. I will not appear in a court of law if he's the defendant. My husband was no saint, but I'll go to the grave believing the guilt he felt, and his drinking, gave him the cancer that killed him."

"But not Brannigan?" Jack asked.

"Hell no. He rode the wave right to the top, and my guess, he sleeps like a stinking baby."

"I have friends in the FBI I can reach out to," Jack said. "Find you a place until things settle down. I'm doing a full-court press. I think Gloria pissed someone off enough to run her off the road. Plus, there's a man who's already served twenty-three years for a crime he didn't commit. And I think the killer took out Gloria, and he won't stop there. If I can prove Brannigan's complicity in the crime, would you reconsider telling your story?"

"Are you deaf, man? Not on your life."

"How about Gloria's life?" he said, taking off the gloves. "If what she said was true, your husband was part of the setup. Brannigan didn't work alone."

"Leave me be… Now, I don't want your help, and I want you out of here."

Jack signaled to Cruz, who thanked the homeowner and headed for the door.

Jack left two cards on the table. "If you get scared again, you can call me, twenty-four/seven. I'll come running. If you need to communicate with me and don't want a direct link, leave a message with Sue. She can make contact. If Brannigan's guilty, I'm gonna run him to ground." Jack walked out the door and closed it quietly behind him.

Jack slid into the car and turned over the engine. As he pulled away from the curb, Hanna's high-pitched voice emanated from Cruz's cell phone. "Bragged he could beat a confession out of a dead man."

Cruz nodded, pleased with himself, and clicked off the recording as Jack snapped on the radio.

Bruce Springsteen sang "Born to Run" while band member Clarence Clemons wailed on his tenor sax, grooving down-and-dirty. It fit Jack's mood. It felt righteous. He now believed Gloria's death wasn't a single-car accident. Someone was clearly trying to stop Carl's case from moving forward. Putting the fear of God into witnesses, even willing to kill Carl to make exoneration a moot issue. Jack didn't have the answer, but he was angry, and he'd let that fuel the fire in his gut. Jack turned up the volume and stomped on the gas pedal.

CHAPTER 11

Sitting at the desk in his loft, Jack placed a call to Lieutenant Gallina and Detective Tompkins, but the partners were out in the field. Jack scrolled down his cell's address book. He grabbed his landline, dialed the number and put the call on speaker.

Cruz was at his workstation on the dining table, sifting through reams of paper he'd copied from Gloria's Laurel Canyon apartment.

Gallina picked up on the seventh ring.

"I get you at a bad time?" Jack asked, wondering what caused the delay.

"So, I'm standing outside of Hanna Cook's house, trying to run down the victim of a reported drive-by. That would be Hanna. And her neighbor tells me that you've already been here. What happened to sharing intel, Jack? We gave you our files, and you've given us bupkis."

"You think there might be a reason I dialed your number?"

"You need something. You always need something."

"I just talked to Hanna. I've got her on tape opening up about her thoughts on Terry Brannigan. She won't talk on record, 'cause she's scared out of her gourd."

"Jesus, Jack. Commander Brannigan?"

"Do you happen to know where he was around the time the drive-by occurred?"

"You're losing your touch, Bertolino. Barking up the wrong tree."

"Not the first time I heard that."

"Don't you watch the news? Your boy was running one of his squads at an armed standoff in Culver City. Whacked-out boyfriend of a teenage mother grabbed their eighteen-month-old child and was using him as a shield. The commander picked up a rifle and took him out with a single bullet. One of his men grabbed the baby before the dead man hit the ground. Don't you feel like shit now, Jack? A fellow officer, for Chrissake, he's a damn hero."

Jack let it go while Cruz surfed the web for the news story.

"Someone tried killing Carl Forbes in his cell today," Jack said. "Tried to light him up with a jailhouse torch."

"Shit. Well, who knows? A grudge hit?"

"I'm looking into it. Checking out the visitors list on the hitter. I'll run that down and get an interview with the man. He's got burns on twenty percent of his body and might be inclined to talk. I'll get back to you."

"Where's Hanna?" Gallina asked before answering.

"At a friend's house. But my guess, she's in the wind by now. I'll send over a copy of the tape."

"Text me the friend's address. I'll keep it on the QT."

"Later." Jack clicked off while Cruz pulled up Channel 4's news report of the standoff on his computer. The story had been recorded live during the time frame the drive-by had occurred. Jack watched until the end, wondering if he could identify the wise guy who had cold-cocked him with the blistering stinger to his back. No sign of him until the shot was fired. Then he saw Detective Joe Moran as he sprinted around the side of the house and caught the baby, a split second before the gunshot man's knees buckled.

The baby's mother ran out of the house, hysterical, and grabbed her child. The cameraman pushed in tight on the gut-wrenching emotion and made the young detective look like a hero. Jack couldn't argue the point. He'd have to start laying out the case again, from the beginning.

"We've got to re-rack. Take a fresh look," Jack said to Cruz. "It's not that Brannigan isn't a bad actor, but we can't let him control our investigation. He appears to be clean on Gloria and Hanna. But just because he didn't pull the trigger doesn't mean he didn't order the play. And it sure doesn't mean he didn't coerce a confession out of Carl. So what does he have to gain?"

"Is statute of limitations in play?" Cruz asked.

"I think so, but check it out. Let's go over the list and try a different tack. I'm thinking the eyewitness, the DA, and the judge. Let's start with the witness."

Cruz rifled through a short stack of computer printouts and pulled out a particular sheet. "Cheryl Lee Williams left town before the jury came in with a guilty verdict."

"Carl's mother wasn't sure where she got her traveling money. I want the answer to that. If cash changed hands, we're looking at the DA's office or LAPD."

"You're not going to get the time of day from Brannigan," Cruz said.

"But we should be able to discover if the DA cut her a check to stay in town and testify. I'll call Tommy and see what he can dig up." Jack thought through what his next steps would have to be. "And I'll talk to Carl again. Get his read on Cheryl Lee. His mother said he knew the woman. Check the list we got from the professor, see if there's a contact number and address for our eyewitness."

Jack had the top down, his shades on, and Gato Barbieri's plaintive sax drifting out of the twelve-speaker audio system playing "Europa." He was in a sax kind of mood.

This was Jack's third Mustang in as many years. The first one got shot up. The second, burned down to the tires. He was betting the third was going to be the charm.

Jack had a bad feeling as he crossed the Colorado River, forming the border between California and Arizona. Cheryl Lee Williams lived in a fifty-plus trailer community in Wickenburg, Arizona. Horse and gold country. From L.A. it was a straight shot on the I-10. A little over five hours and Jack's GPS had him reaching his destination before sunset.

Cruz hadn't had any luck getting Cheryl Lee on the phone. All he received was a message stating her voicemail system was full and no message could be left at this time.

Jack's cop radar was going off. He felt it in his bones. Someone was responsible for the death of Gloria Millhouse. And that same party was trying to scare off, or take out, any witness who could exonerate Carl.

The burnt orange sun hung low against the cloudless powder-blue sky and cast a golden wash over the high desert plateaus and mountains along the interstate. Large olive-green saguaro cactus were scattered along the roadside and vast plains, standing guard like ancient Indian totems.

Jack turned off the road a mile before reaching downtown Wickenburg. The senior community was a nice affair. A well-maintained campus filled with double-wides, three pools, a game room, and more than a few modern prefabricated homes. Two hundred and fifty lots in all.

The woman at the gate smiled at Jack as he rolled to a stop at the gatehouse, and gave him directions to Cheryl Lee's home. "I haven't seen her today, but I just came on shift. I reckon she'll be out on her porch about now. Cocktail time," she said knowingly, without judgment.

Jack thanked the woman and chided himself for worrying. He observed the 5MPH speed limit and pulled to a stop a few units from his destination. The first thing he noticed when he stepped from the car and stretched his back was the absolute silence. Other than the odd bark of a distant dog, or the sound of local birds flitting through the scrub-filled dry-riverbed that surrounded the complex, it was quiet. Too quiet for Jack's liking.

He walked down the middle of the road because there was no other traffic. Other than a few vehicles tucked into carports, the place looked desolate. It was prime season for the snowbirds who owned a large portion of the dwellings. Maybe they were waiting for the sun to go down before leaving their air-conditioned homes. Retirees would spend spring and summers in places like Portland, Seattle, and Vancouver, and then fall and winter in Wickenburg.

The homes all had well-groomed, drought-tolerant, micro-sized front yards filled with succulents and cactus of every variety. Whirligigs, wind chimes, and lots of white ornamental rocks reflected the blazing desert sun.

Jack walked slowly up the path to Cheryl Lee's tan double-wide home. The siding appeared new, the wooden trim recently painted a glossy white. A light blue late-model Volkswagen Beetle sat in the carport, and a window box filled with colorful annuals hung under the kitchen window.

The open side porch was covered in clean Astroturf with two high-end wicker chairs with bright tropical motif pillows and an outdoor coffee table. He headed in that direction. There was an ashtray on the table with a few cigarette butts that had been smoked down to the filter.

Jack could see through the glass-paned door into the empty living room and rang the bell, hoping he wouldn't startle the woman. He rang again and got no response. The house appeared empty. Maybe Jack's timing was off. He started down the steps and walked back along the road toward the carport he'd passed on his way in. Maybe Cheryl Lee was visiting friends, Jack thought.

He decided to drive into town, grab some Mexican food and a motel room for the night, and try again in an hour or so. But something felt wrong. Jack walked to the middle of the street and turned back toward the house. He now took notice of an open door to what looked like a potting shed or storage unit on the far side of the carport, painted the same tan color as the home.

As Jack stepped closer, his blood pressure ratcheted a notch.

Cheryl Lee sat in a simple wooden chair, slumped over a potting table. Her lifeless hands hung down at her sides. Her face was turned toward the door, her right cheek flat against the table: dead eyes staring, covered in an opaque film. Her short brown hair nestled in a pile of potting soil. Purple pansies shriveled by the heat surrounded her head like a crown.

As Jack stepped closer, he could see a single bullet hole on the side of her temple. The blood had already coagulated to a dark purple.

Cheryl Lee's face showed no expression at all. As if she were lost in thought—and then she was dead. No fear, no shock. She'd been shot from long range, medium-entry hole, and a bloody crater where the back of her skull used to be.

The killer could have been hiding in the riverbed until he got the perfect shot. Jack would share all of his thoughts with the local police as soon as he made a call to Lieutenant Gallina and another to Leslie. He'd let the LAPD and the Los Angeles District Attorney's office explain why Jack was on scene and corroborate his story about the case he was working.

But as long as the neighborhood was quiet, he'd do a quick search of her house. He trotted to his car, grabbed latex gloves from the evidence bag he always kept in the trunk, and pulled a thumb drive out of a pack. He let himself in through the unlocked kitchen door.

Jack cleared the house and went right for the desk in the hallway between one of two bedrooms and the living room. It appeared to be her home office, proven when he pulled the center drawer open. Jack snapped photos of her checkbook deposits and her monthly stack of bills, banking statements, telephone, mortgage: the works. She was old school and left a clear paper trail. He found her address book and copied it digitally. There were a few numbers on a scratch pad, and Jack snapped photos of those.

The prize was a laptop that powered up and opened without a password. Jack put in the thumb drive and downloaded the computer's hard drive. He'd let Cruz plow through that information.

He picked up the landline and copied the incoming calls that filled her voice mail account.

In his search he passed a frame with two photographs. One showed a young girl, and the second, the same girl, now a woman. Carl's mother had mentioned that Cheryl Lee was a single mom. He'd let the local cops make the death notification.

He put everything back where he found it and started in the bathroom. Nothing of interest. Generic drugs, the usual.

An ashtray in the bedroom held a single cigarette butt. In her chest of drawers was a jewelry box covered with her intimate lingerie. A few nice pieces. At least a carat of diamond in an engagement ring, plus two thousand dollars in hundreds. Clearly, the shooter hadn't robbed the place. Jack, again, placed everything back where he found it.

The living room had a large-flat screen TV, and the furniture was tasteful, modern. She was an upscale version of trailer-park living.

He looked in the freezer, no drugs or money, just a bottle of Stoli. A fully stocked fridge, two cartons of cigarettes in a cabinet alongside crackers, chips and canned goods. The woman led a seemingly normal life. Jack wondered what secrets died with her. How did she pay her bills? Did she give false testimony, damning Carl for a new start at life? He hoped not, but wasn't optimistic. The paper trail might reveal the answer.

Jack pocketed the flash drive, e-mailed Cruz the photos he'd taken, and made his calls to L.A. By the time he'd secured the latex gloves, thumb drive, and his 9mm and shoulder rig in the trunk of his car, he heard police sirens shatter the desert calm.

Jack sat on one of the porch chairs and steeled himself for the interrogation to come. It was going to be a long night.

CHAPTER 12

The gray SUV was parked on top of a red sand mesa with a panoramic view of the desert floor. Its rear door was hinged open with a straight shot of the I-10 freeway, the only direct route to Los Angeles from Wickenburg, Arizona. With the back seats removed it made a comfortable sniper's nest.

The distance from the SUV to the ribbon of blacktop was nearly a half-mile, but with his M24 sniper system set on a tripod, his state-of-the-art telescopic sight, and his sniper skills honed for long-distance shooting, the gunman wasn't sweating the small stuff. The Remington's effective range was over a thousand meters. The distance to the target, well within his wheelhouse. He took a relaxed swig from his canteen. It was only 7:30, but the sun was rising along with the temperature.

Jack Bertolino's car was still parked in the lot of his motel when the man did reconnaissance at five o'clock. It gave him time to motor to a safe nest while he lay in wait for a visual of Bertolino's sterling-silver Mustang. If all went according to plan, this final skirmish would put an end to the new interest in a cold case, and he could get back to business as usual.

Jack finished his plate of eggs, bacon, and fruit at one of the local diners in Wickenburg. The coffee was hot, the food passable, the waitress pleasant. He paid the check, over-tipped, and stepped out into the blazing morning sun. The town was compact, western-themed, filled with galleries, restaurants, and bars catering to the burgeoning tourist market. Upscale dude ranches and hotels skirted Wickenburg, and signs proclaimed you could rent horses by the day or enjoy a Western vacation with campfire barbecues and cattle drives.

The female security guard at the mobile home park had directed Jack to the Silver Point Gallery, where Cheryl Lee had been employed, and that was where he headed.

The gallery's rustic exterior belied the modern white interior filled with western sculptures, brilliantly lit with pin spots, looking more like a museum than a tourist trap. This was a high-end affair that dealt in fine-art pieces. Silver Indian belt buckles, pottery, oil paintings, sketches, and sculptures of cowboys, cattle stampedes, bucking broncos tossing their riders, and all things with a Western theme. Not Jack's style, but he could appreciate the talent of the artists.

A middle-aged woman with professionally styled shoulder-length salt-and-pepper hair, dressed in a dark green outfit with a starched blue blouse, sat behind a modern desk with a large computer screen and a handkerchief pressed against her face. She had clearly been crying, and she startled when Jack walked toward her.

"Hello," she said, trying to be polite, but dabbing bloodshot eyes that wouldn't stop flowing. "I'm sorry." She stood up, fighting for composure.

"I'm sorry to intrude," Jack said. "It looks like bad news travels fast."

"It's a small town, Mr. . . .?"

"Bertolino. Jack. I'm sorry for your loss."

"I'm Judy Cohen." She wiped her eyes again and held up a hand in front of her mouth until she caught her breath. "Cheryl Lee brought light to our little home. Never a harsh word. Who could do something like this? Why?"

"I'm hoping you can shed light on that," Jack said.

Judy gave that some thought, or maybe it was just the shock of Cheryl Lee's death. "Are you new to the department?"

"No, ma'am. Retired, NYPD."

"I thought … well, you look like a cop."

Once a cop, always a cop. "I'm working a case out of Los Angeles, Judy. Cheryl Lee was on my list to interview. I was the one that discovered her body yesterday."

"How awful that must have been for you. Well, how can I help?"

"Has Cheryl Lee been having trouble lately? Any threats? Any change in her behavior? Anything unusual?"

"No, not really. She was well liked. A happy person. She loved the art world. Cheryl Lee served as a docent more than a salesperson. She knew the history of all the artists, the local Indian tribes, and Wickenburg's storied past." Judy wiped her eyes again. "I'm at a total loss."

"Was Cheryl Lee seeing anyone?"

"You mean dating?" Jack nodded. "Nothing serious, as far as I know. Tried online dating a few years back, but wasn't comfortable with the experience. Nothing bad, but said it didn't suit her disposition."

"Okay then," Jack said, handing the distraught woman his card. "I'm going to let you go. Over the next few days, if anything comes to mind, no matter how trivial, please give me a call."

Judy regarded his card thoughtfully, walked to her desk and pulled a finely embossed card from a silver tray. "I'll think on it. Here's mine if you have any more questions. You never mentioned what the case was about."

"Cheryl Lee was a witness in a trial that took place twenty-three years ago in Los Angeles. Some new information came to light, and I just needed to ask her a few questions."

"Huh …"

Jack could see she wanted to say more, but was on emotional overload. He let his silence prod her on.

"She was very secretive about her past," Judy finally admitted. "But in these parts, nobody pries. Here in the desert, everyone has a history."

The sniper hadn't been surprised when he fielded the call alerting him of the investigation underway to prove Carl's innocence, or the call to arms alerting him the time had arrived to take action. He knew his past would come back to bite him one day. The murder lived with him, ever present in his psyche, like a dusty box stowed in an attic. But the impending situation forced him to think on his feet, take control of the situation, and juggle his tight schedule to make things right.

Now, with the body count rising, he sure as hell wanted this to be the end game. But what the fuck, he thought as a black dot on the horizon slowly grew in size. In for a penny ... His binoculars picked up the American sports car heading his way. With the Mustang's convertible top down he might be able to pull off a headshot. The body of the vic was a safer bet, but he didn't have a reputation for taking the easy way out of any situation.

The killer jacked the bolt, sending a round into the rifle's chamber, and concentrated on slowing his breath and lowering his heart rate. It was showtime. He had one shot. Two at the most. Lead the car by five degrees, allow three seconds for the round to reach its target, suck in a half breath, and squeeze the trigger on the exhale.

The gunman heard the rumble before he saw the cause. An eighteen-wheeler's air brakes squealed as it rounded a curve, traveling at a high rate of speed down the strip of blacktop in the opposite direction. He did a quick mental calculation of the distance and approximate speed of the two vehicles. If his math were correct, the behemoth could muddy his play. His pulse rose a notch.

The Mustang was five seconds from being a live target, and the eighteen-wheeler was thundering up the highway.

The gunman swiped a bead of sweat from his brow with the back of his hand when it became clear the big rig was going to block a clean shot of the Mustang. He tracked Bertolino's car and sucked in a breath as the orange cab of the big rig crossed his sight line and Jack's car disappeared from view.

The shooter adjusted. He squeezed off one round, jacked another and fired a quick second. One, one thousand, two, one thousand. The shots impacted the back end of the eighteen-wheeler, puncturing the truck's silver metal skin just as the Mustang cleared the rear of the truck and rocketed safely out of range.

"Shit!" he shouted, and immediately started breaking down his weapon.

Jack turned up the volume on his radio and took in the scenery, unaware of his close brush with death. He glanced in his rearview and saw the big rig's multiple red brake lights pulsing, and then the rear of the semi skidding dangerously across the broken white center-divider lines until the eighteen-wheeler raised a cloud of red dust and came to a chattering stop on the shoulder of the highway.

Jack, sensing trouble, eased his brakes, did a tire squealing U-turn and powered back toward the big-rig.

The driver jumped down, cursing as he left the harsh sound of an alarm from the cab. He strode the length of the semi-trailer. He stopped in his tracks when he approached the rear end. Two high-powered rounds had punctured the skin of his refrigerated semi-trailer, setting off the shrill klaxon.

Jack pulled in behind the eighteen-wheeler and introduced himself to the driver. The men gazed from the bullet holes to the red ridge in the distance. Jack could see that the height of the two holes in the side of the truck ran parallel to the front seats of his Mustang. The hair on the back of his neck snapped to attention. A fraction of a second had been the difference between life and death.

"The alarm sounded about an eighth of a mile back," the driver said, tamping down his anger and pulling Jack back into the scene. "Takes that long to stop this beast. But the shot could've been a ways back from there. Might take a while for the pressure change to raise the alarm."

Jack didn't agree. "I don't see any movement if the shooter was on the ridge."

"That'd be one hell of a shot. There are dry riverbeds between the road and that there hill, might've been hiding in one, hard to say. Your car wouldn't make it four wheeling. What's your interest?"

"The shot was meant for me," Jack said. He looked at the height of the Mustang again, with the top down. The first bullet would have blown his head off. The second was a body shot. "When did the alarm go off?"

The driver gave that some more thought.

"Right after we crossed paths," he finally said. It didn't make the man feel any better that he might not have been the intended target. "If so, it's your lucky day," he said, spitting a wad of tobacco he'd been holding in the side of his mouth, "But I'm sure as shit out of luck. I gotta call up the local police and my insurance company. I'm hauling six thousand pounds of frozen pork that won't make it to Denver in this condition."

The Ford Expedition eased down the dirt road that led from his sniper's nest on the ridgeline. He was careful not to leave a red contrail of dust telegraphing his location. Didn't want the police to pick up tread marks. He'd seen Jack execute his U-turn, but it was too late to complete the mission. Better to save the fight for another day.

He knew from his intel Jack was smart enough to put two and two together and would be on high alert. It added a complexity to the game he hadn't anticipated, but one that would now dominate the play.

Jack placed a call to Detective Don Harstad, who'd been assigned the Cheryl Lee Williams murder. Nice enough guy, straight shooter, said he was in his car and five minutes out.

Jack drove the short distance past the eighteen-wheeler's skid marks to where he thought the gunman had made the attempt on his life, and pulled onto the shoulder. He thought about powering up the ragtop, but then the sun hit his face and he decided the gunman had likely fled the scene. He powered his seat back a bit and waited.

Harstad's white Chevy Impala, with blue police side decals pulled up next to Jack. He got out of his car, looked at the skid marks in the road, shook his head. "Well goddamn Bertolino, you've been in town less than 24 hours and I've got myself a murder and an attempted murder. I don't know if you're lucky or damned, but I don't wanna to sit next to you in a barroom."

"Morning, Detective," Jack said and exited his car.

"Sitting with your rag top down. You got a death wish?"

"I'd be down on the sand next to my car but I hear you've got rattlers and scorpions."

"Can't argue that. Okay, take me through it."

"The bullets ripped straight through the skin of the big rig, so it's reasonable the shooter was perched parallel to where I'm parked. It was a straight shot from the top of the ridge."

Harstad pulled a pair of binoculars from his car. The detective scoped the ridgeline and then turned to Jack. "I take back what I said, you are one lucky hombre. What do you need?"

"My Mustang won't make the off-road trip, but I'm hoping you might know the back trails and maybe find something similar to the shooting site we found at Cheryl Lee's crime scene."

"I've got a Jeep at home. I can trade off my ride and take a look. A shooter who could send a bullet a half a mile and come inches from hitting a moving target had to be military or police trained. Something to think about."

"We're on the same page. If you could pull the rounds from the inside of the truck before the driver messes with the evidence, I'd appreciate it. The two bullets entered in a tight group, but there were no exit holes on the back of the eighteen-wheeler. I'm hoping they match the rounds used to kill Cheryl Lee."

"Already have Jake on it. He'll lock up the truck while the driver's filing his police report. We haven't found the round that killed her yet, but we're on the case. Are you heading back?"

"I've got a meeting with a judge, if you can handle it here?"

"I have your back, Jack. We'll stay in touch. If you discover anything that can help, call me anytime."

"Will do. Thanks, Don. Let's get this scumbag."

No argument from Harstad, as Jack slid into his Mustang, and headed down the blacktop.

It was too early to call Cruz, so Jack settled in and enjoyed the ride. The warm, cleansing breeze blowing across the open plain smelled of sage. It diffused the specter of Cheryl Lee's murder and his own brush with death.

Jack used the down time to mull over the case.

Who the hell had the most to gain from stopping the investigation was the question of the day. Keeping Carl in prison or, better yet, dead. Well, the killer, first and foremost. But the killer wasn't necessarily working alone. Whoever was behind the murders wasn't likely to stop now. And Jack didn't want the crime solved through attrition, where the last man standing was the guilty party.

Jack flashed on the grisly crime scene photos of Shelley Goldstein and then the cold-blooded murders of Gloria and Cheryl Lee. Jack added himself to the hit list and knew he wouldn't stop hunting until he'd run the killer to ground.

CHAPTER 13

Judge Bradley Cole was seated behind an imposing mahogany desk that shone as brightly as his bald head. The wall behind him displayed a personal photographic history, posing with presidents, governors, senators, and Hollywood celebs. A man on a career trajectory. His hair as a young prosecutor, thick and as dark as his feral eyes, but as his reputation grew, his hair took a dive in the other direction, thinning until it gave up the fight.

Commuter jets could be seen through triple-pane windows, silently landing at LAX. "So, you were there for the interrogation of Carl Forbes?" Jack asked.

"Memory serves, the arresting officers presented me with an airtight confession. Those boys were hungry, but it was all done according to Hoyle."

"And the eyewitness?"

"Well, that cemented it, didn't it?" A statement of fact. "I worked with the woman a few times. Now, we're talking twenty-three years ago. I'm lucky if I remember my wife's name."

"That must make your defendants feel secure," Jack said without sarcasm.

"I don't want defendants to feel secure. I'm not here to coddle them. I'm here to uphold the law. And I take umbrage to your tone. You're in my bailiwick, Bertolino." Niceties drained. His eyes bore into Jack. "Nobody likes to be second-guessed. I see you've been called to task a few times in your career."

Jack wasn't surprised the judge had done his research before taking the meeting. "Do you believe in coincidence?" Jack asked, changing tack.

"I believe in the rule of law. What are you referring to?"

"Bodies are stacking up. Gloria Millhouse was digging into the Carl Forbes case. She's dead now. The ex-wife of Kevin Cook, one of the arresting officers, a drive-by shooting put the fear of God in her. She won't testify if there's a new trial. Your eyewitness, her name was Cheryl Lee Williams."

"Was?"

"She was shot through the head yesterday. Single bullet, long-range." Jack gave that a beat to settle in. "Somebody took a shot at me from half a mile. If I were you, I'd watch my back. You may be on the shooter's list because whoever it is wants the case to disappear. And that is not going to happen, Judge."

The judge took a sip from a bottle of Fiji water and nodded almost imperceptibly before responding.

"Look, no need to worry about me, I can take care of myself," he said and pulled back his black robe, revealing a pearl-handled Colt .38 in a leather belt holster. "Thank you for the warning." The judge probed Jack's face and came to a decision. "Put your case together and we can reconvene. I had a reputation back in the day that I nurtured. I sleep well at night. I'd like to keep it that way. Oh, and send my condolences to Keith. This must be tearing him up."

"Will do. He's my next stop."

Jack started to the door, and turned on his heel. "Judge, was there any payment provided the eyewitness for testifying? I heard Cheryl Lee was afraid to take the stand, and then moved to Arizona before the verdict was read."

"It's possible. I'd have to dig through my files. Sometimes it was the only way to get a verdict."

Keith Millhouse stood rigidly at the eighteenth-floor window of his law firm's offices on Avenue of the Stars in Century City. If you suffered vertigo, this wouldn't be your office of choice. The Pacific Ocean shimmered like a silver ribbon in the distance. He turned to Jack, who was sitting in a comfortable tan chair covered in soft, buttery leather that exuded wealth. Trappings that no longer held meaning for the man.

Keith had just been given the news that in Jack's estimation, his only daughter had been murdered to stop her investigation. Jack was giving the man time to process the information.

"It almost makes me feel better, knowing," Keith finally said, not looking for a response. "This way I've got a place to focus my rage. When you take the killer down—and I have faith you will—my only concern is that you've mounted enough of a case to keep the bastard down. Incontrovertible evidence. I won't demean you with the cheap narrative where I ask to give me five minutes alone in a room with him, because I'd only need thirty seconds. Get him, Jack. Stay alive, but get him. Anything I can do to help, I'm at your service."

"Judge Cole offered to reassess the case if I can bring new evidence into play. If he becomes obstructionist, I'll give you a call. He sent his condolences."

Jack stood at the rear wall of glass in his loft in Marina del Rey, staring down at the FedEx trucks streaming in and out of their shipping center, always fighting the clock. Cruz was at his regular station at the dining table—computer, yellow pads, iPhone, all at the ready—bringing Jack up to speed. Jack tracked the flight of a seagull over the Fed Ex building on its way to the marina.

"Leslie dropped the jailhouse tapes off yesterday," Cruz said. "She was in the neighborhood. She's looking fine."

Jack let the comment pass. "Anything of interest?"

Cruz stifled his grin and continued. "Not much. The man knew where the cameras were located, and kept his body angled and his head low. A few three-quarter shots I've printed are the best I could do. I checked his name against the law firm's roster where he claimed to be a partner, and no such person exists."

Jack walked over and looked at the printed photos. "I'll have to take a trip to Victorville. Check on Carl while I'm there, and have a one-on-one with Larry the Rat in the hospital ward. He's a jailhouse liability now and might be willing to talk."

"I'd stay away from the window until you find out who took a pot shot at you, Jack. And I'd rent a new car for the duration."

"You read my mind."

"I'd ask for the cartel special." Off Jack's look, "Bulletproof," Cruz added, trying to lighten the mood and mask his concern.

"Did you check on that cop I got into the dust-up with on the training grounds? Joe Moran."

Cruz nodded, "I called the precinct. Somebody in the squad room said he was out of the office yesterday."

That got Jack's attention.

"I phoned again today and went directly to voicemail. Thought it'd be better not to leave a message."

"Smart."

"And I'll dive into the material you sent from Wickenburg."

"Hmmm. You should call it a day. I'm going to connect with Aprea, see if he's calmed down some. He might have a read on Moran."

CHAPTER 14

"Dinner's on you," Nick said, giving up nothing as he slid into the booth at Hal's Bar & Grill. "So, you're sure the bullets were meant for you and it wasn't some corporate sausage dispute?"

"Sausage dispute? That's a good one, Nick. I'm glad you haven't lost your sense of humor."

"Just saying."

"The cop from Wickenburg called. They pulled a slug out of a tree behind the shed at the Cheryl Lee murder scene. Back of her head was blown off. It was a .300-win mag. Used in M24s. Sniper weapon of choice for military and, uh, SWAT teams. Couldn't find a sniper's nest at the scene, too many off road vehicles, ATVs in the dry riverbeds beyond the trailer park. But it was a long-distance kill."

Nick listened, eyes narrowing.

"He did find a spot on the ridge at this morning's crime scene where he thinks the shots were fired from. He took photos of tread marks and sent them along. It was a good half-mile to the target. And yeah, I'm damn sure the bullets were meant for me."

"I had lunch with Brannigan yesterday," Nick said, tight. "He's in the office today, just to calm your mind. I'm sure it was killing you not to ask."

"Good to know your mind-reading skills are still sharp. Say, have you ever had any run-ins with Detective Joe Moran?"

"Oh, the hero that saved that infant's life? The one the mayor is giving a medal for bravery on Saturday? Oh, and did I mention, the commander's also getting recognized. He's one of three cops the Police Commission sent to the mayor for consideration for police chief. I'm afraid your sleuthing skills are showing some rust."

"How did he leap-frog past the assistant chief, Sheila Montgomery? I read she was being considered."

"Let me count the ways. The rank-and-file love him. He's one of them. Came up the hard way. Patrol, gangs, narcotics, when the LAPD wasn't the kinder, gentler force. And politics. The City Council loves a hero. The mayor loves a hero. Makes them all look good. Brannigan gets appointed chief, they get reelected. Oh, and he's a man."

Jack knew if Brannigan got the nod from the mayor, the last step in the confirmation process was a vote from the City Council. It was a definite complication, but wouldn't slow Jack down. He soldiered on. "Moran wasn't in the office yesterday, and possibly today. I'd love to find out what he was up to. One less rock to look under."

"You're on your own, Jack. I wouldn't share your personal information, and I ain't going there."

"Fair enough, but, if the rounds had hit home, and my carcass was getting picked over in the desert, you'd sure as shit ask some questions."

Nick sat mute.

"I had to pay a visit to Gloria's father and bring him up to speed. Tell him I believed his daughter was murdered out on Malibu Canyon. Gotta be tough losing your only daughter." Jack knew he was hitting below the belt, but desperate times… Nick's daughter was the love of his life. "Aren't you angry yet? Because I am. We've got three bodies and counting, Nick. Somebody's trying to shut down the investigation. And the attempt on Carl Forbes's life at Victorville wasn't a jailhouse coincidence."

Nick's scarred hands choking the life out of the cloth napkin gave him away.

"The killer's a trained shooter," Jack went on. "Sorry to ruin your appetite, but I've got more questions than answers, and now I've got a target on my back."

"Maybe you're in the wrong line of work. Too many opioids in your system."

"Cheap shot."

Nick flashed dead eyes, slid out of the booth and strode for the exit.

Arsinio magically appeared with a full glass of Cab and set it in front of Jack. Jack took a long pull, but the wine soured in his mouth as he watched Nick push through the door. He could almost see the heat radiating from his old friend's body.

Jack piloted his cabin cruiser past the light tower at Marina del Rey jetty, out into the Pacific, and pushed the throttle forward. Leslie stood by his side, a glass of wine in hand, letting the balmy wind take the sting out of her harsh day at court.

Jack let out a long breath, relaxing for the first time in two days. It wasn't the first attempt on his life he'd lived through, but once the adrenaline of the moment dissipated, it could leave the most battle-hardened warrior ragged at the edges. The vibration of the solid 260hp diesel engine as it knifed through the dark water and the smell of salt air were restorative. The multicolored computer-designed lights of the Ferris wheel on the Santa Monica Pier marked their heading.

Jack pulled back on the throttle and grabbed his glass of wine.

"You're trying to get rid of me already," Leslie said, playfully probing. Jack had told her it wouldn't be safe meeting at his loft until the case was closed.

"The last time I put you in harm's way," he said, "is the last time I'll put you in harm's way."

"God, Jack, you sound like a lawyer. No, like Bill Clinton. It depends what the meaning of 'is' is. Although, it does seem like a reasonable response." Leslie took a sip of wine, and Jack had the feeling she wasn't finished. "Did she call you?"

And there it was. "No, Angelica did not call me."

"Hmmmm." Leslie gave that some thought and let it go.

Jack questioned whether he'd made a mistake mixing business with pleasure until Leslie put down her wine and stepped behind him, wrapped her arms around his waist and pulled him tight against her body. Her scent, her breath on the back of his neck, and her hands sliding from his abs down below his waist vaporized any doubt. He pushed the throttle into neutral, spun around and wrapped his arms around Leslie, whose mouth found his. They locked in a lover's embrace and let chemistry rule the night.

CHAPTER 15

Retired Judge Walter Myers sat in a wheelchair by the lobby window, gazing out at manicured gardens in the Monteverdi retirement community in Woodland Hills. It was an upscale affair with apartments and villas, high-end fixtures, well-mannered wait staff, definitely for the well-heeled, Jack thought.

The judge, in his late eighties, appeared lost in thought. And then the man's head turned upon Jack's arrival, and his eyes focused, sharp as a bird of prey. Before Jack could offer his hand, a stylish woman walked by and said, "Hi, Judge, are you going to be at the mixer Thursday?"

"Of course, Elaine."

"I'll see you there," she cooed.

The judge smiled warmly and spun his chair to face Jack. They shook hands. His grip, dry and firm.

"Jack Bertolino," he said. His resonant voice must have impressed in his court of law. "I Googled you. Interesting career. To what do I owe the honor, and a call from the mayor's office, no less?"

Jack brought the wizened man up to speed on the case, sharing body count, possible motives, and a warning that he might be a potential target. He let him digest the explosive information. The silence was interrupted by yet another matron. "Hi, Walter. Oh my," she said giving Jack the once-over. "You didn't tell me you had a son."

"Just a friend, Janet."

Janet didn't want to interrupt but smiled coyly and said, "Bridge this weekend. Don't forget."

"I may be old, Janet, but I'm still of sound mind."

"Of course, Walter, or I wouldn't partner with you. Goodbye, young man."

The judge smiled again but didn't kiss and tell. "This isn't your grandmother's retirement community, Jack," he said by way of explanation. And then his eyes narrowed and he was all business.

"I never did like the case," he admitted.

"How so?"

"I pulled up the brief online when I received your call. I remembered feeling something was off. The defendant's attorney never gave me enough to question the verdict. He never put the defendant on the stand. He couldn't be faulted for that, but it didn't help his case."

"What was your take on the ADA?"

"Bradley Cole," he said with disdain. "Oily, political, but thorough. He wanted my job and wasn't shy about saying so. He made mincemeat out of the defense. The arresting officers, the eyewitness, the confession, all came together to build an airtight case. The guilty verdict was unanimous, and my hands were tied with mandatory sentencing. In those years, with murder one, I had no discretion. I had to give that young man the full ride."

"Well, someone is willing to kill to make sure the case isn't reopened," Jack said. "Somewhere along the line lies were told, deals were struck, and Carl may have lost twenty-three years of his life. And now Shelley Goldstein, Gloria Millhouse, and Cheryl Lee Williams have paid the ultimate price." Jack let the judge ruminate on that. "I've got plenty of suspicions and no proof. Nothing solid."

"Jack, I've got all my case files in the McGee's Self Storage building on Ventura Boulevard. Been paying the rent on the unit for years, just in case something like this ever arose." He pulled a set of keys out of his jacket pocket with an address printed on the key ring, and handed it to Jack. "I thought you might need these. The file boxes are stacked according to year. You'll have to do some digging, but if you think it will help, have at it."

"I appreciate it, Judge."

"And Jack, thank you for the warning, but it's you they'll come after."

"You're thinking it's more than one?"

"Gut feeling. That being said, stay vigilant."

"Thank you for your time."

"Call me, let me know how this plays out. I won't feel good if you can prove I had a hand in convicting an innocent man. But if the case is strong, send me a copy. I'll take a look, and when the court holds an evidentiary hearing, I'll speak out in Carl's defense."

"You've got a deal."

Jack had his cell phone out before the outer lobby door had whooshed closed. He told Cruz to meet him at the storage facility later in the afternoon. He'd hand off the keys, and Cruz could start the treasure hunt. Jack was feeling good, and if he was lucky, he could compare the DA's notes to the defense attorneys. See if the prosecution hid anything from the defense before the case went to trial.

Jack ducked in an alleyway when he saw Natalie, the councilman's assistant, bounding down the steps of City Hall, texting on her cell phone, oblivious to foot traffic. When she was safely past, he strode up the concrete steps toward Mark Corcoran's office. He was on Jack's list to warn of potential danger, but he wanted to take a look at a specific framed photograph hanging on Corcoran's wall. It hadn't meant much during his first interview, but after recent events he thought it might have some bearing.

The door to the office was open. "Councilman?" Jack said from the doorway, and when there was no answer, he walked past Natalie's desk and entered Corcoran's office. The wall behind his desk was filled with citations and the usual publicity shots. One photo in particular held his attention. It looked like a photograph out of *The Deer Hunter*.

Jack snapped a series of pictures with his cell.

Jack stowed his phone and studied the photograph. It showed the councilman as a young man, looked to be in high school, with five of his buddies. The photo had yellowed with age, the colors dulled, but the young men, all holding hunting rifles and beers, mugged for the camera standing behind an eight-point buck lying at their feet.

"Can I help you?" The councilman entered the room holding a mug of coffee, his face purple with rage.

"Councilman, I'm glad I didn't waste a trip. Your assistant wasn't in. I thought I'd wait a few minutes until one of you showed."

"Nothing's sacred with you people?"

"I'm on a mission of mercy, Councilman. Ratchet back the attitude."

"Talk."

Jack walked him through the shooting death of the eyewitness in Wickenburg, the drive-by shooting at Hanna's house, and the attempt on his own life. "Someone's trying to eliminate anyone who had anything to do with the case. Gloria Millhouse was the first victim. You're on my list, and you may be on the shooter's list."

That slowed Corcoran down. He took a seat behind his desk and a careful sip of coffee. He tried to recover, but the anger quotient was percolating just below the surface. "I'm protective of my personal spaces. I'm sure you can understand that."

Apologies were obviously not in the man's vernacular, Jack thought.

"I get it."

"Well, thanks for stopping by, Jack, and thanks for the warning. I'll take it under advisement. I've got a phone conference scheduled in five minutes, and I've got to go over some financials before it starts. Respectfully, call before you stop by next time."

"Respectfully, I'm on a murder investigation. I'll do what needs to be done, Councilman." Jack was about to step out of the office when he spun on his heel. "One more thing." Jack walked toward the wall, took down the photo of the deer hunters and placed it on the councilman's desk.

"I can see you're center stage. Who are the other young guys in the photo? This was high school?"

"Yeah, but what the hell?"

"You never sent me the list I asked for. Just give me the names, then I can put faces with names on the witness list. It's a part of the investigation. And let me know what they're doing now if you're still in touch."

Corcoran checked his watch, his face reddening again as he assessed the situation, calculating his political liability. Jack had the backing of the mayor, and Corcoran was a political animal. He let out a labored breath and, pointing with his finger, put names with faces, locations, and occupations, where he was still in contact.

Jack was caught in mind-numbing traffic on the 101 heading into the valley. He was inching past Hollywood and could see the landmark Capital Records Building. Just beyond that was the high-rise that Angelica Marie Cardona called home. His pulse ticked up a notch, thinking about their last day together on Kauai. The wave of emotion surprised him, but his car's Bluetooth ringing pulled him back to now.

It was Detective Don Harstad.

"So, let me get this straight, is this the same Jack Bertolino responsible for spoiling six thousand pounds of frozen pork?"

Country boys had a sense of humor too. "Depends who's asking."

"A badge-carrying, bonafide officer of the law who thinks he's suffering from frostbite. But I'm thinking the payoff might be worth the pain."

"I could use some good news."

"Yeah, but …" Harstad paused, stringing Jack along, enjoying himself. "You see, for you, it's a good news, bad news kinda deal. The good: the bullet I cut out of a frozen chunk of pork butt matched the rifling pattern of the bullet used to kill Cheryl Lee."

"That is good news. Well, not for Cheryl Lee."

"The bad, the shooter's still loose. And potentially good for a kill from half a mile."

"Point taken. Thanks, Don."

"Next time you're in Wickenburg, ring me up. I know where they plate the best Mexican in the state. We'll toss a few back."

"Done deal."

"And Jack, when you make the arrest, we get first dibs on hanging the son of a bitch."

"So, my district attorney will call your district attorney, and they can hash it out over eighteen holes of golf."

"Signing off, Jack."

The traffic loosened up as he passed Universal Studios fifteen minutes away from McGee's Self Storage.

Jack placed a call to Nick Aprea, who picked up on the second ring.

"Don't talk, just listen," Jack said. "The bullet that killed Cheryl Lee matched the rifling on the slug with my name on it."

Nick didn't respond right away. And then, "Brannigan gave Joe Moran a few days off. Said to be fishing in the Virginia Lakes region of the Sierras. Up around nine thousand feet. Off the grid, is what he said. He'll be back Saturday to receive his medal of honor. Off grid … just saying."

"Okay."

But Nick had already disconnected. What he'd begrudgingly shared, in his ham-fisted way, was that Jack should check out Joe Moran. Spying on another officer wasn't easy for the man, and it meant a great deal. It reminded him again of Angelica and then her father, Vincent Cardona.

Jack decided to pay Cardona a visit first thing in the morning. He was serving his prison sentence in the same federal pen as Carl and his failed jailhouse executioner, Larry Durkin.

Three jailhouse birds with one stone.

CHAPTER 16

An armed Bureau of Prisons officer unlocked the heavy metal door to the interview room for Jack. Carl Forbes was already seated at the table. Jack took the seat opposite and cut to the chase.

"Glad to see you're in one piece, Carl."

"I got lucky."

Lucky to be alive, Jack thought, but still locked up. "Talk to me about Cheryl Lee Williams."

"Right to it, that's good," Carl said. "I knew her, not close, but I mowed her lawn on occasion over the summer break. Never had any issues with her, no words, no nothing except working for pocket change. She was only a few years older, had a kid.

"Then, after Shelley Goldstein turned up dead, I saw her driving around the neighborhood with two cops. She said hi, and they drove off. A few days later she picked my mugshot out of a six-pack. That's what my lawyer was told. And then I got arrested and she fingered me in the lineup."

"What did you hear about her during the trial?" Jack asked.

"She testified against me. Pointed me out in court and said I was the guy she saw near where the girl was killed. Near where they found the body. I couldn't believe what I was hearing. I cried. Couldn't help myself. Felt ashamed. Then it finally struck me, I was going down for something I didn't do. It was a twilight zone moment. My mother cried out, and then Shelley's father stood up in the cheap seats and started screaming. I was a killer, I'd killed his baby, a killer who deserved to die. The crowd went wild, the judge banged that gavel, and I knew my sorry ass was in a sling. It was a pure nightmare."

"Is that the last time you saw Cheryl Lee?"

"She wasn't even in court when the jury read the guilty verdict. Mom said she'd moved. Mom said she was paid off. Or where else would she get the money to relocate?"

"What do you think?"

"That bitch was paid off. Nothing else makes any sense. Are you going to look her up? Maybe after all this time she'll tell the truth. That she mistook me for somebody else."

"I looked her up." Carl's eyes narrowed as though readying himself for the bad news Jack had come to deliver in person. The bad news he'd come to expect. "I was an hour or two late."

Carl raised his eyebrows in a silent question.

"She was dead," Jack said. "Killed by a long-range bullet. Same shooter tried for me the next morning. I got lucky."

That sucked the air out of the already stifling room as Carl mulled over the implications. One avenue of overturning his sentence was now buried along with Cheryl Lee.

"And you're still here? On the case? My case?"

"I'm here for the duration."

"Why?"

Jack took a moment before speaking. "Because I believe."

Carl's eyes, filled with emotion, shined. "Thank you, my brother."

Larry the Rat Durkin was handcuffed to the prison's hospital-room metal bed rails. He had IV drips running antibiotics and morphine into his arms. Mind-numbing, dueling beeps, echoed off the lime green walls. He appeared to be drifting in and out of consciousness. His midsection was wrapped in wide strips of wound dressings for the fiery burns meant for Carl.

The Rat's eyes blinked open as Jack approached, and he nodded his head to pull Jack closer.

"Fuckin' redundant," came out like a dry rasp.

"What?" Jack asked.

"Redundant. Look it up in Webster's. You'll see my picture, chained to this bed, in a fuckin' prison."

The Rat's eyes focused, trying to make sense out of Jack standing over him. "What the hell … who are you? Cop? You here to arrest me?" The Rat started laughing, but the laugh turned into a cough that racked his body. His face reddened with pain the drugs couldn't conquer.

"Ice … ice chips."

Jack would rather have drowned the Rat than make him comfortable, but what the hell? He pulled a cup of ice chips off the rolling tray table, and slid an ice chip through the Rat's chapped, bruised lips.

The morphine kicked in again, and the Rat drifted. His eyes rolled back in his head, then snapped open on a wave of pain. Jack wished he could transport himself away from the antiseptic stench to, well, anywhere else on the planet.

"Who are you?" the Rat asked as if for the first time.

Jack took charge. "Who paid you?"

"What?"

"To take out Carl. I don't want you. You already paid the price. I need a name. Who contracted you?"

Larry the Rat's eyes blinked and his face contorted into a pain-driven grin. "You can see I'm half dead here."

"So, unburden yourself," Jack said.

"Hah" turned into a phlegmy cough. "Unless you can up my morphine, get the fuck outta here. I'm half dead…and sure as shit not giving up the other half. Ice chip, copper."

Jack picked up the cup filled with ice chips and dumped it into the Rat's bedpan. He knocked on the door, and the BOP officer unlocked it. He stepped aside as Jack walked out. "Durkin's asking for a nurse."

"And I'm asking for a raise. Fuck the Rat."

Jack, not wanting to prolong the conversation, headed down the hallway, where he was met by another officer and escorted through another locked door.

Jack walked with Vincent Cardona around the tower in Victorville's central yard.

Cardona was pleased to have a visitor, making him more talkative than usual. Prison can do that to a man.

"It ain't like *Goodfellas,*" he said. "Money buys perks, but I don't cook in my cell. I'm not hurting, but hey, it goes with the life. What do you need?" he said.

There was no love lost between the two men, but they were attached by blood debts. Cardona, for providing information that led Jack to the man who had run his son down like a dog in the street in front of Jack's home. Jack, for rescuing Cardona's daughter, who'd been kidnapped and was being shipped to Iraq for a sheik's sexual pleasure.

Theirs was a messy relationship, but this was a messy case.

"I'm thinking, inmate Carl Forbes got a bad rap and has been paying for twenty-three years. Someone disagrees and is killing people associated with the cold case to make his point. They sent Larry the Rat to make the case go away permanently."

"You're breaking my heart. What's your involvement?"

"Young girl, a few years younger than Angelica, got pushed off Malibu Canyon Road."

"I read that story. Not an accident?"

"Not by half. Her father hired me to find the man who killed her. Law school student, working the case to exonerate Carl. I agreed to look into it, and the only witness that came forward twenty-three years ago to ID Carl was killed last week. I'm trying to get a line on who hired Larry Durkin, better known as the Rat. Is he one of yours?"

"No, he's a Polack."

"He's not talking. I need the connection. Nothing worth using on the security cameras. A man signed in with a false identity, but there had to be communication setting up the meet. I need a name. If the pay phones are monitored, it could've been a cell phone."

"There's good trade in burners," Cardona agreed.

"I'm flying blind, one step ahead of a bullet."

Cardona's eyes trailed a red-tailed hawk that soared overhead and then locked its wings like a fighter jet and dove toward a distant field and unsuspecting prey. Jack wondered if Cardona could relate to the symbolism.

"So, you want me to rat out the Rat."

"Like I said, I need a name."

"What's in it for me?"

And there it was. The Mafia handbook, page one. No surprise to Jack, who said, "What do you need that I can provide?" You gotta give to get.

"Stop by the Chop House. Have a steak. Angelica is holding down the fort, business is good, but keep an eye out. I need to know that she's good. That being said, how's your boy?"

"He's okay." Jack bristled at his son being dangled as bait, but he was the one who initiated the meet.

A unit staff officer pushed the metal door open to Cardona's unit and tapped his watch. The two men walked slowly across the only open space at the prison.

"I can do that," Jack finally said.

Cardona nodded. It was a done deal.

CHAPTER 17

Cruz waited with a small group of photographers outside police headquarters at 100 West 1st Street, in downtown Los Angeles. The press conference was scheduled for four o'clock, but Cruz was interested in getting an ID on Detective Moran's car. He wanted to check the front bumper for paint scrapes the color of pistachio, and compare the tire treads with the samples sent from the detective in Wickenburg. He had a press pass hanging on a lanyard around his neck, a gift from Leslie, compliments of the mayor's office.

A few black and whites rolled into the parking structure, and a line of personal cars exited as the early shift signed out for the day. Finally, a dusty Toyota Land Cruiser powered too quickly up the road. Cruz had a feeling this was his target and snapped close-ups of the massive front grill.

As the vehicle screeched to a halt, an arm snaked out, swiped his card, and raised the security arm, allowing him entry into the structure. Cruz's heart rate quickened as Joe Moran stuck his head out and gave a quick smile and wave acknowledging the cameras. This was his day. He was the man of the hour.

Cruz's lens moved from Moran's receding face to his license plate, then snapped off a series of tight shots of the mud-caked all-weather knobby tires as the Land Cruiser rolled into the parking structure.

Cruz forwarded the shots to Jack for backup, and hoofed it up the sidewalk and in through the glass doors to police headquarters.

Nick Aprea stepped out of shadow after Detective Moran slammed the door of his car and hoofed it down the stairwell. Nick walked up to the Land Cruiser, pulled out his cell, and started snapping photos of his own. Tire treads, mud splatters, looking for dents on the sides of the vehicle. The front fender was sprayed with mud, but Nick shot close-ups of every square inch, looking for any paint scrapes, dings, cracked turn signals, anything that might put the car at the scene of Gloria Millhouse's death. When he heard another car driving up the ramp, he walked stiffly away, distancing himself from Moran's vehicle.

He didn't find any clues by eyeballing the vehicle. There could be microscopic paint slivers, but he found himself relaxing some. Nick believed Jack was now on somebody's kill list, and Nick would do anything in his power to keep him alive. His good friend might piss him off at times, but he never made mistakes like that. Nick just wasn't sold on Brannigan and his team being involved. As he headed into police headquarters, He hoped his gut feeling about Brannigan wasn't self-serving.

Cruz stood off to one side of the media relations studio on the second floor of police headquarters, looking like just another photojournalist. Two local news crews with cameras were up front, readying for the press conference to begin. An array of microphones was bundled on the podium. The room was noisy and unruly as radio, freelance newspaper reporters, Brannigan's entire SWAT team, and well-wishers filled the room to the max. The crowd was already straining the air-conditioning unit.

Nick Aprea, wearing a black sports jacket, white shirt and loosened red tie that was hanging at an odd angle looked hot and uncomfortable standing behind the tight knot of young SWAT team members.

One of the detectives turned around, and his face split into a grin. His hand shot out. "Detective Donny Rice. I know who you are, Detective Aprea."

"Huh, pleased to meet you, Donny," as the two men shook.

"I want you to know," and he lowered his voice, "just between you and me..."

Nick raised his eyebrows in a get-on-with-it gesture.

"...That your career trajectory is on the ascendancy."

"Really? Sounds fancy."

"With your record, and the commander's support, you'll be riding the new wave."

"Not sure what you mean, Detective, but it sounds like a compliment."

"It really is."

Their conversation was thankfully cut off, Nick thought, when the door at the front of the room swung open. The police chief entered brusquely, followed by Mayor Henry Waltham, Councilman Mark Corcoran, Commander Terry Brannigan, and Detective Joe Moran. The men stood shoulder to shoulder on the raised platform.

Cruz scanned the room, looking for Jack. He hoped he wasn't caught in traffic. Just as the police chief tapped the central mike, and then raised it too close to his mouth, creating a shrill squeal, Jack entered and grabbed a spot on the opposite side of the room, not acknowledging his associate.

Jack's entrance wasn't lost on Nick, whose eyes narrowed as he turned back toward the stage.

"Welcome all," the police chief said graciously. "I'm going to make this short but sweet. We're gathered here today to honor two of our city's heroes. The police force has taken a lot of heat lately, in the news, and in social media, some of it deserved, some of it biased reporting." The room grumbled at the perceived slight and not too veiled reference to fake news. "But when two of our finest rise to the occasion, illustrating the best law enforcement has to offer, we have to take a moment to share our pride. And I want to thank you for coming today.

"Now, you all witnessed the armed standoff that took place on the streets of East Los Angeles last week. And you saw the life of an eighteen-month-old child being saved by the quick thinking and selfless action of one of our LAPD SWAT teams." The applause was started by the SWAT team members and picked up by the rest in the room. "Commander Terry Brannigan and Detective Joe Moran saved the child's life. Now the mayor has something for you both in recognition of your bravery under fire." As the chief moved away from the mike, he gestured the men to center stage.

The mayor took his place behind the podium as Brannigan and Moran stepped forward. "Gentleman, you are the best of the best. And you risk your lives every day when you put on a uniform. What you did on the streets of Los Angeles should not go unnoticed. You make us all proud."

The audience applauded, and Mayor Waltham beamed.

"These tokens of our appreciation therefore are for you."

Brannigan and Moran faced the mayor as plaques for bravery were handed to them. Camera flashes strobed, and the men accepted their honors. Brannigan thanked the mayor and patted his young charge on the back. The smile caused by a wave of applause stiffened when his eyes settled on Jack. The SWAT team followed his gaze, and the mood in the room momentarily darkened.

Cruz snapped photos, revealing the change in emotion, and highlighted the men on Jack's list of potential suspects.

Councilman Corcoran took control of the mike and, like the politician he was, made the event about himself. He thanked the mayor and his constituency, reminding them to vote for the change they were all hungry for. A change he would continue to deliver. And then thankfully, it was over.

Corcoran corralled Commander Brannigan for a photo-op and then the two of them leaned in for a serious discussion. Cruz snapped photos as Corcoran looked out over the crowd and caught Jack's eye. He gave him a slight wave as Brannigan turned to see who took the councilman's focus.

Brannigan narrowed his lizard eyes, and the cold stare told the story. Men like Bertolino would have a rough go of it when he was running the show. He turned his back on Jack and continued the dog-and-pony show needed to help grease the final vote for police chief.

The crowd started to dissipate as the film crews broke down their equipment and the news and radio reporters shouted a few questions.

Moran jumped off the stage, riding a high, and joined his boys on the floor.

Over back pats and congrats, Nick overheard him lean into Donny and say, "If fuckin' Bertolino gets in the way of the boss's promotion, there's nowhere he'll be safe."

By the time Moran glanced over his shoulder to see if anyone was in earshot, Nick had exited the room.

Moran's bravado aside, Nick wasn't sure how he felt about Brannigan running the third-largest police force in America. With the militarization of police departments around the country it seemed like a dangerous proposition. And the odds were good, after the TV exposure he racked up today, that Terry Brannigan was going to be Los Angeles' next chief of police.

Cruz walked past Jack without so much as a glance. They'd connect at Hal's Bar and Grill that evening to compare notes.

Jack was in the hallway, heading out, when his name was called. Mayor Waltham flashed his thousand-watt smile and waved him over, cornering him in an empty space near the elevators.

"So Jack, how's it going on the Gloria Millhouse case? Are you making any progress? I hear you're ruffling some very political feathers."

"It goes with the territory, Mayor. Lots of unanswered questions at this point, but I do believe Gloria was killed."

The mayor grimaced. "What else?"

Jack told him about Hanna, and then: "The eyewitness that helped convict Carl Forbes was killed a few days ago in Arizona. A bullet shot from long-range. The same shooter tried to take me out after I discovered the body. Same rifling on both rounds."

"Jesus, Jack." The mayor understood the implication and looked up as Brannigan walked out the door, surrounded by his team. Brannigan covered his surprise at catching the two men in intimate conversation, but his change in demeanor wasn't lost on the mayor, who never missed a trick.

"So, what's your take on Brannigan?"

Jack wouldn't talk about the man's record of violence until he'd gotten his hands on the results of the Pitchess motion, the official record of police brutality allegations leveled against the arresting officers.

Carl and Professor Anderson had petitioned the court for the file, but were in a holding pattern. Tommy made a few well-placed calls to expedite the process. The courts response hadn't been delivered, but their answer was expected any day now. At this point in the investigation the allegation against Brannigan was all hearsay.

"As soon as I have more answers, you'll be the first call I make," Jack said.

"Corcoran said you've been all over him, and he wants it to stop."

"Good luck with that."

The mayor wasn't expecting that answer, and his raised eyebrows asked the question, why?

"The councilman was one of the last persons to see Gloria Millhouse alive. Corcoran went to school with the victim of the original crime. He had a crush on the girl, and grew up in the neighborhood where she was killed. I think he knows more than he's letting on."

"What is it with you, Jack? I ask for a very specific favor, for a good friend and political supporter, and now it's looking like I'm being pulled into the middle of a shitstorm."

"With respect, sir, this isn't really about you."

"Okay, Jack. Point taken. Stay on it. Just know I don't want to be embarrassed. Don't withhold information. You know what's going on here?"

"Brannigan's on your short list."

The mayor's eyes probed Jack, searching for an answer, but knowing Jack wouldn't talk until he had his facts straight. "Okay, I'm putting my trust in you. You've got a great track record. Stay on top of it. But I want the truth. Nothing less. You've got my private number, use it."

"Deal, Mayor." Jack took his leave, walked past the metal detectors at the main entrance and got out of the building before he was subject to any more random exchanges. He'd never been high on corporate politics as he fought his way up the food chain at the NYPD. It wasn't a skill set he had any truck with, and it gave him agita.

CHAPTER 18

Jack stepped off the elevator at the Marina del Rey Ritz-Carlton just as a bellboy was pushing a brass luggage cart into Tommy Aronsohn's favorite suite. The room had a major view of the marina and its million-dollar yachts. The location always put Tommy in a good mood.

"I am definitely setting up an office out here. Look at that view."

"Promises, promises," Jack said. Tommy had been threatening to make a move West ever since he was struck with Hollywood fever on the set of Susan Blake's last movie. It had been a case Jack was working, and Tommy represented the actress for five minutes before getting the ignoble Hollywood boot in the ass when he wouldn't do her bidding. As much as Jack would enjoy having his old friend on the same coast, he wasn't holding his breath, knowing Tommy's wife, Elizabeth, would weigh in and put the kibosh on the move.

Tommy tipped the bellboy, who'd made short work of unloading his bags, and pulled the door closed behind him.

Tommy grabbed Jack in a bear hug and pounded him on the back. Jack was ready for it, but still winced. "Jesus, Jack, sorry. Still?"

"Whatever."

"All right, I won't push. So, what have you got for me?"

"I might have saved you some time with the court records. I met with retired Judge Walter Myers, who handled the case. He was willing to share his files. I'll have Cruz swing by and drop them off in the morning. Why don't you get settled, and we can meet at Hal's later and compare notes?"

"I'll make reservations, why don't you invite Leslie? Give me a feel for the political landscape. What's your take on Carl?"

"I think he was railroaded. I don't have the answers yet, but somebody's willing to kill to keep us from discovering the truth."

"Never stopped you before."

"Won't stop me now."

Jack felt comfortable for the first time since the case began. There'd been too many deaths, too much grief of the loved ones left behind, and too much prison energy. It was taking its toll. But now his oldest friend was sitting across the table in their booth at Hal's Bar and Grill talking with Leslie. Tommy regaled her with war stories of when both men were starting out in law enforcement. Jack was always caught off balance with the warmth Leslie radiated when she smiled. That same face put the fear of God into defendants and their lawyers when she wielded the full weight of the law. Cruz joined the party and pulled out the downloaded photos he'd shot at today's press conference on his iPad.

Arsinio, waiter extraordinaire, stepped up to their table and smiled as he took in the group. "It looks like old home week," he said, referring to Tommy's arrival and Leslie, dressing up the table again. He never forgot a name or a person's drink of choice. "May I freshen your drinks before taking your order?"

Jack nodded and ordered a plate of fried calamari and roasted cauliflower for the table.

Leslie looked at a photo of the mayor, frowning slightly as he watched Brannigan and the councilman locked in a serious conversation. She let out an abrupt staccato laugh. "I think the mayor may be having second thoughts about bringing you onto the team, Jack."

"He said as much today. But Keith Millhouse's law firm is a big financial donor, and the mayor's too political to risk losing their support. That being said, he doesn't want to get caught with egg on his face if he supports Brannigan for police chief and the case goes south on him. Floated the notion of keeping politics out of the equation, and by politics, he meant lay off Councilman Corcoran. Of course, he knew that wasn't going to fly and backed off. In the end, he just asked to be kept in the loop before he announced his choice."

Cruz swiped the screen to where Corcoran was making his pitch to the audience. The politician promised to deliver the goods if they delivered their vote.

"Look at the mayor now," she said. "The whole town knows Corcoran wants his job."

"And what does the mayor want?" Tommy asked.

"He's laying the groundwork for a gubernatorial run," Leslie said.

"Does he have a shot?"

"If he's not caught in a contentious battle to keep his job. And if he hires Brannigan, and Brannigan's past comes back to bite them both, then the opposition's negative ads would start playing twenty-four/seven."

Cruz swiped the screen and showed the sequence of Joe Moran's Land Cruiser pulling into the lot at headquarters. He narrated for the group: "The front bumper is dusty, but there're no apparent dents. We'd have to get up close and personal to look for paint scrapes. The dried mud on the vehicle is a light brown, and the hills outside of Wickenburg are brick red. I shot a close-up of the car's tire treads, and they don't match the set sent by Don Harstad, the detective handling Cheryl Lee's murder. Sorry, Jack."

"Hmmm. So, who else wants me dead? Who's got the most to lose?"

"It's all about the connections," Tommy said, and took a sip of his martini. "If Brannigan coerced the confession, who else gained the most from the successful prosecution?"

"The ADA," Leslie said. "He was on the ascendency and it made his career. Look for dirty tricks. Judge Walter Myers, who sat on the case, may have let himself off the hook today if his files are intact."

"I'll start tearing them apart tomorrow," Tommy said and devoured both olives on the toothpick.

"The entire SWAT team," Cruz added.

Jack knew where Cruz was going. "How so?" he said, giving the stage to his young associate.

"If Brannigan becomes the chief of police, who's he going to bring along? His trusted team. If Brannigan wins, they all win. He'll move them up the food chain, and that's why they're dangerous, Jack. And what did you tell me your uncle used to say when you were a kid: 'Don't poke a hornet's nest with a stick'? It's a little too late for that."

Jack couldn't help but smile. "Wise guy."

"Pot calling the kettle," Leslie said.

Tommy raised his eyebrows at Jack, who ignored his amused friend.

"Brannigan's high on the list for obvious reasons," Jack said. "He's up for a job that would put him in the national spotlight. I think Corcoran knows more than he's saying. He's worried about re-election and as Leslie just said, he wants the mayor's job. The first time I interviewed him, he said the last thing he needed was to be tied to a twenty-three-year-old murder case." And then to Cruz, "I want to track down the men in the photograph deer hunting with the councilman. Get their take on Shelley Goldstein's murder."

"I already blew up headshots from the photo and assembled a few notes."

"Good. You mentioned connections, Tommy. Brannigan and Corcoran. Why are they attached at the hip?"

"Brannigan needs the vote from the city council if he's chosen by the mayor," Leslie said.

"But look at the photo again. I'm picking up a strange vibe. They've known each other for twenty-three years, give or take. When Brannigan was asking the questions about the death of Shelley Goldstein, Corcoran was on the suspect list.

"If the killer isn't someone already on our radar screen, then he's not working alone. We need to find out who's leaking the information."

Jack glanced at Tommy, "I'll introduce you to Professor Anderson who runs Project for the Innocent. He's motivated and has the most history with the case.

"And I want to do whatever's needed to reexamine the DNA. Carl's was never found on the victim or at the scene. A lot's changed with the science and databases in twenty-three years. We might get lucky.

"Tommy, you and Cruz pick apart the judge's files, compare them to the prosecution's, the defense attorney's, and Gloria's, and you ..." Jack directed at Leslie, "I want you to stay clear of the case. For your own political well-being and your personal safety."

"Jack," she said, "I didn't know you cared."

"I'm serious."

"So am I."

Tommy faked a cough like a high schooler, eliciting a grin from Cruz, as Arsinio dropped off the appetizers. Everyone dug in. Workday was over, and the party began in earnest.

CHAPTER 19

Jack drove away from Venice, heading toward his building. Leslie wasn't keen on risking her life for a roll in the hay, and Jack wanted to get an early start in the morning. As he pulled onto Glencoe, he decided to drive around the block a few times and make sure no one was surveilling his loft.

On the second pass, Jack made a right and pulled behind a Ford Expedition parked in a lot a quarter mile away from his building with a clear shot of his fourth-floor unit.

Jack walked up on the vehicle's blind spot and knocked on the passenger side window with his Glock 9mm, loaded with a bullet in the chamber.

The black-tinted window powered down. "Nervous?" Nick Aprea asked.

Jack holstered his gun, and Nick took a pull from a silver flask Jack knew contained Herradura silver. He knew because he'd given the flask to Nick as a gift after he'd helped take down Arturo Delgado – a cartel boss who was out for Jack's skin.

"Slumming, or do I have something to worry about?" Jack said, sliding his weapon into his shoulder rig.

Nick handed the flask through the opened window. Jack took a healthy swig, and handed the flask back. Nick screwed the metal top back into place.

"This is where I'd set up if you were my target and I wanted to take you out at home. The building across from yours is almost too easy. The roof, or any unit on the third, fourth, or fifth floor. I'm not feeling it. I think this player likes the sport. Has a skill set. There's always the high rises that scumbag Delgado staked you out from. But that doesn't work for me either. After the shooter missed the first time, you're not likely to make yourself a target watering your tomato plants. I saw the lights in your unit come on with the timer. I'd stagger it some. Too predictable."

"Thanks, Nick. You wanna stop up?"

"Nah, gotta run. My wife still doesn't like you. Hasn't forgiven you for the bullet I took taking down the Dirks."

"Understandable."

"Hasta la bye-bye, and oh, I checked the rear of your building. There're three condos where a sniper could take you out while you're unlocking your door."

Nick's SUV shot out of the lot, doing sixty before he'd passed Jack's building.

Jack grinned. "You're the man, Nick," he said to the Expedition's receding taillights as he slid into his car. He circled the block in the opposite direction before rolling past his gates, and into his building and the protection of the covered parking. He'd stay vigilant until the killer was a distant memory—and Carl Forbes was a free man.

Jack poured himself a glass of wine and grabbed a stack of photos Cruz had taken of the deer-hunting picture, and blown-up headshots of each of the young men. Their faces were filled with testosterone, bravado, and the joy of the kill. On post-its, he'd penned the names the councilman attributed to each of his old buddies, along with a short bio if he was still in contact.

He pulled out the list of witnesses who'd been interviewed by the police and the DA's office twenty-three years ago. As he read Gloria's handwritten notes, he felt drawn to the young woman, her passion and singular intellect, and he also felt a slow burning anger.

Gloria penned her first impressions of each person interviewed. Only one man on the list, Chip Boyd, lived out of town. He'd been interviewed by the police and cleared. Per the councilman's recollection, his mother moved the family to Reno before the case went to court. Another sudden move out of the neighborhood. Gloria notated that Boyd hadn't responded to three phone messages. Jack didn't like loose ends and decided he'd interview him, one way or another.

As Jack drank some red, he wondered how to deal with Angelica Cardona. He wasn't comfortable showing up at the Chop House in Beverly Hills unannounced, but realized it might be the only way to get an unbiased read on how she was faring.

Jack hadn't talked to Leslie about his agreement with Vincent Cardona. Truth be told, he wasn't sure how he felt about seeing Angelica again. He knew he'd been headed for trouble when he laid eyes on her months earlier, but he wouldn't trade the time they spent together.

When Angelica walked out the door of their hotel room in Kauai, she asked Jack not to give up on her. Her father had just been arrested on money-laundering charges and second-degree murder. She ran back to L.A to protect her family's interests in the Chop House. Said she needed some time.

Jack told her she had a choice to make. Angelica could have stayed. She chose to go. Jack wasn't clear where their relationship was headed if she had stayed. An ex-cop in love with the daughter of a Mafia boss. What could go wrong with that?

He drained his wine, snapped off the lights in the loft, and stepped up to the blinds that covered the sliding glass doors leading to the balcony. He pulled an edge of the window covering back and looked out for an all-clear. Glencoe was deserted except for a few parked cars. Nothing out of the ordinary, and there was no movement on the roof of the adjacent building.

Jack walked into his office in the front of the loft and split the louver blinds with two fingers. Nick wasn't kidding when he said three buildings offered a direct line both to his doorway and into his office. Perfect for a sniper's nest. The view out the window had always been part of the comfortable neighborhood backdrop, but now it made him feel like a prisoner in his own home.

His back was killing him, and he downed a Vicodin. The bullet he'd suffered from a crack dealer in the Red Hook projects in Brooklyn was a memory that haunted him to this day. A buy-and-bust had been set up in one of the most notorious tenement complexes. Jack and his partner were undercover, with a backup team waiting in the wings. Jack had passed muster with the dealer, and now armed guards walked him and his partner past two angry, chained pitbulls that hadn't been fed in a few days to keep them hungry. The snarling dogs were more of a deterrent than an alarm system at protecting the apartment and the dealer's stash.

Jack and his partner were permitted entry into the second-floor, two-bedroom flat where the buy was set to go down. The dealer seemed a bit squirrely, but not enough to set off alarm bells. Once the terse social niceties were out of the way, Jack opened the briefcase of cash, showing good faith, and the dealer pulled the bag of rock cocaine from behind the couch. Yet when the time came to exchange money for drugs, the dealer took an awkward step back, almost tripping over the couch.

Two armed men charged from the far bedroom with automatics locked and cocked. Jack's partner blanched, pulled his revolver and shouted, "Police, down on the ground!" It was the wrong play, and the dealer and his two gunmen panicked and open fired.

Jack dropped to a crouch, pulled a .38 from his ankle rig and returned fire as bullets ripped through the apartment. The rest of Jack's team heard gunfire, overwhelmed the soldiers guarding the front door, and ran past the pitbulls into the building, taking the stairs two at a time. Jack shot both of the gunmen, who fell to the ground, and as he turned his weapon on the dealer, who was firing wildly at Jack's partner, one of the downed men raised his 9mm and shot Jack at point-blank range.

The bullet entered Jack near his naval, ripped through his body and exited his back. The round raised dust as it impacted the plaster wall. The shot was a clean through-and-through. It threaded the needle, missed major arteries and organs, and spared Jack's life by centimeters. A violent brush with death wasn't an event that was ever totally forgotten.

Jack's partner had screwed the pooch, giving up their cover before the backup team was in place. Jack beat the odds by coming out alive. And now, two o'clock in the morning, staring out his window in Marina del Rey, eyes raking the cityscape looking for a sniper, he could still hear the report of the 9mms and the choking smell of cordite that filled the room. Over and over he replayed the gunman's bullet ripping through his body. He collapsed to the ground, ears ringing, blood pulsing out of the wound with every beat of his heart.

Jack let the blinds fall back and sat down behind his desk. He wanted to call his son, but knew it was too late, and didn't want to scare him. His son was doing well after his own brush with death, and Jack was going to be damn sure the young man wouldn't pitch another game, or graduate from college, without his father in the grandstands cheering him on.

Sleep was out of the question. Staring down the long vacant hours ahead, Jack pulled up the photos of Cheryl Lee's banking statements on his computer and started searching for answers.

The woman kept immaculate records, and Jack had copies going back six months. On or about the fifteenth of each month a thousand dollars, even, was wired into her Wells Fargo account. It was an all-cash deposit without any way to trace the money's origin. The next account summary should be arriving in less than a week.

She collected eleven hundred dollars monthly in Social Security benefits, and after writing checks for utilities, park rental, car repair, insurance, and food, she barely broke even.

Jack pulled a card from his stack—Judy Cohen's embossed contact information for the Silver Point Gallery in downtown Wickenburg. He planned on calling Judy first thing in the morning.

Jack crawled into bed and dropped into a restless, troubled sleep.

CHAPTER 20

Jack shared an interesting phone conversation with Judy Cohen on the drive over the 405 into the valley. She reiterated that Cheryl Lee's work at the gallery was an avocation more than a job. More a docent than a salesperson. Judy paid for her gas and a credit card in lieu of a paycheck. And in the nine years Cheryl Lee worked at the gallery, she never ran up a bill of more than three hundred dollars in a month. She would occasionally sell one of the high-priced art pieces, and for that work she received a five percent commission, but there was no regularity to those sales and the checks were few and far between.

Jack called Cruz and asked him to trace the source of the monthly thousand-dollar deposits that were wired into her checkbook account. He was interested to find out if the money would dry up with her death. If it was generated from an annuity, the funding might continue and the payments would revert to her daughter. If the payments stopped, as Jack suspected, it might prove the person responsible for her death had also been her benefactor. And might have paid her for falsely accusing Carl Forbes and testifying in court, and continued to pay to guarantee her silence.

Cruz had culled the case files supplied by Professor Anderson, and was able to locate the court-appointed defense attorney who handled Carl's trial twenty-three years ago. His search led Jack to Rob Schneider, who had given up his law practice, but didn't turn his back on pro bono clients who needed his expertise.

Jack pulled his Mustang into the lot adjacent to a small neighborhood park in Van Nuys, where Rob Schneider's food truck sold hotdogs twelve-ways. The park was filled with families eating lunch, tossing balls, and relaxing on the grass or at one of the picnic tables scattered haphazardly around the park.

Schneider sat comfortably on a frayed aluminum tri-colored beach chair under a shady tree. His hair was too long and too unkempt for a man his age, but his brown eyes were clear and mellow, like a man who'd made peace with his life and accepted the curve balls the universe pitched that slid out of his reach.

Five men and two women with children in tow were chowing down on his fast food and patiently waiting their turn with the retired lawyer who meted out free legal advice. Jack bought a dog and a diet Coke off the truck, and took his place at the back of the line.

The hotdog was terrific and Jack tossed the wrapper in the trash as the last person stepped away from Rob Schneider, who smiled graciously. "Those doggies are skin on, nitrate-and nitrite-free, crafted from grass-fed beef," he said.

"Best I've had since moving west."

"What brings you here? You look like …"

"A cop," Jack said. "Retired. I'm here to talk about Carl Forbes."

Jack watched as Schneider's mind flipped through the thin Rolodex of his short career. "A major regret."

"How so?"

"Don't talk down to me," he said without animus.

Jack nodded, mildly impressed at the man's backbone. He offered his hand, "Jack Bertolino."

Schneider gave his name, leaned forward in his chair, and they shook. His grip was firm without attitude. "Are you working the case?"

"I am."

"Good. Damn it, very good. I heard about Gloria Millhouse. What a tragedy. I thought the case would die on the vine without her energy. I met with her and … have you met Professor Anderson over at Loyola?"

"I have, and he provided a copy of your files."

"Then how can I help?"

"I want your personal take on the case. What's not in your files? Did you feel Carl got a fair shake? Was he railroaded? Who should I be looking at? Who would you like to get on the stand and cross-examine again?"

Schneider didn't bat an eye. "The eyewitness."

"Cheryl Lee."

"She's the one."

"What about her?"

"She was too studied. She could cry on cue. The jury bought her testimony, but I was never sold."

Jack filled Rob in on the truth as he saw it of Gloria's death, Cheryl Lee's murder, Hanna's drive by, the attempt on Carl's life, and his own. The color seemed to drain from Rob's face, his mellow shattered.

"No one would be dying if Carl was guilty," he said in a whisper. "In trying to stop you from re-opening the case, the killer is giving you a road map for a circumstantial defense that might impel a judge to accept a writ of habeas corpus."

"It's already done," Jack said. "We'll use all of it in court."

"Good. Very good. As for your other question, I'd also put Carl's mother on the stand," he said, his voice rough, trying to recover. "I was advised by one of the partners at my firm that no one would believe the woman's testimony. It was a mistake. I should have gone with my instincts."

"Did you ever hear rumors about a payoff to Cheryl Lee? Moving money, whatever."

"I never received discovery regarding a payoff. If money had changed hands, and she was a paid witness, I would have used it against the prosecution. It was my first murder case and I was in over my head, but I would have jumped all over that. I did my best, but you can see how well it turned out. I left the law a few years later."

Jack felt for the guy, but didn't have time for a pity party. He had an innocent man he had to get released from prison.

Jack crossed the parking lot and his heart started pounding when he noticed a twenty-something banger slouched smugly against the hood of his Mustang. A tear drop tattoo under his left eye and jailhouse tats screamed gang affiliation. Two young soldiers stood behind the car, dripping with attitude, guns held loosely at their sides. The boss slowly revealed a 9mm pointed in Jack's direction and demanded, "gimme the keys maricon, and we won't have issues."

Jack saw only one way out of a bad situation. He pulled out his keys and stepped into harms way. His soldiers gave him the stink eye as he moved forward, but Jack noticed their boss's body was blocking a clean shot. He closed the distance in a heartbeat, and tossed the keyring, hitting the boss in the chest. The surprised gangster bobbled for the keys and was slow raising his 9mm. Jack's arm shot out, grabbed the barrel of the pistol and twisted. The men struggled for control of the weapon. The gun fired into the air.

Families in the park panicked. Their children screamed as they ran for safety. It was total mayhem.

Jack punched from the heels. He smashed his fist into the killer's face as he muscled the pistol free, whipping it across his temple cutting flesh, and knocking him against the car, and then down onto the pavement. Jack dropped to one knee and hammered the boss's face again with a hard right, knocking the wiry man out. Jack leaped to his feet with the gun trained on the two gangsters moving toward him around the car, and stopped them in their tracks.

"Don't even think about it," Jack hissed through clenched teeth.

The scene of stampeding families and cars barreling out of the lot was out of control. The Cholos looked from their fallen boss to Jack's resolve, and ran toward the street as a black sedan pulled up. The killers leapt in, and the car burned rubber leaving a contrail of white smoke as it powered away.

The downed man was bleeding profusely from his open wound. Jack kept the gun trained on him as he picked up his keys, and fought to slow his breathing.

Jack didn't notice a beat-up green Prius driving slowly as it passed the action. The driver, a man in his thirties with a wild mane of red hair, snapped pictures with his cellphone and continued down the road.

Schneider ran up, totally panicked. "Are you okay?"

Jack told him to call 911.

"Already done. They're on their way."

"Call again and tell them we need an EMT truck. One of the carjackers is losing blood."

Jack didn't know how he was followed, or if he was followed, but made a mental note to pick up a rental car when the dust settled.

The loud music and the buzz of alcohol-fueled excitement hit Jack as soon as the doorman opened the door to Vincent Cardona's Chop House in Beverly Hills. The piano player on the second floor was belting out a rendition of "New York, New York," doing his best Sinatra impression.

The downstairs bar had a few patrons waiting on reservations, but the upstairs room was where the action was. The bartender picked up a house phone as Jack hit the stairs. He was greeted by Frankie-the-Man, looming over him by the time he'd reached the top carpeted step.

"Jack, long time no see. Where you been hiding?" Frankie growled more than spoke. Weighing in at three-fifty, always armed and dangerous, he was Angelica's protector at the restaurant she was managing for her father.

"You're looking good, Frankie."

"Really? I'm just glad to be looking at this," Frankie arced his meaty arm, taking in the room, "and not a jail cell. Me and Peter lucked out, not being part of that unfortunate business the fucker

Rusty rolled over on the boss with." Frankie raised his eyebrows. "Not enough to indict."

"Any word where he is?"

"Feds got him hid somewhere, witness protection, whatnot. I hope he's in a desert somewhere frying his ass off. The douche won't be able to stay silent long. Not in his nature. He'll be scamming something or someone, and word'll get out—"

"Too much information," Jack said, cutting him off before the big man incriminated himself.

"Right, no problem."

Peter Maniacci was also running security, and he strode over with hand outstretched. He was scarecrow thin, sported stiletto-sharp sideburns, and a black sharkskin suit that did little to hide his .38 shoulder rig. Peter slapped Jack on the back and pulled his hand away like he'd touched a hot plate when Jack tightened. "Sorry, boss, good to see you. Does Angelica know you're here?"

"I was in the neighborhood, thought I'd stop by and say hello. How's she doing?"

"I think we'll let Angelica fill you in," Frankie-the-Man rasped as his eyes creased into a sly grin. The men followed Frankie's gaze as Angelica Marie Cardona walked across the room, a blonde vision with flawless alabaster skin.

The bar crowd and the patrons standing near the white grand piano parted as if for royalty. Angelica wore a wry smile, and a tailored pastel blue chiffon dress that accentuated her trim figure. She nodded to her men and then slid her arm through the crux of Jack's. She led him toward the bar, which was two patrons deep.

"You're looking fine, Bertolino."

"You take my breath away," was the only honest thing Jack could say. So much for keeping the visit professional, he thought, chiding himself.

Angelica was pleased. The end of the bar was magically cleared, and the couple slid onto the heavy leather-bound stools. "I bet you wish you could take those words back."

"Why?"

"Because it could complicate your life. Two glasses of Cab, Mel," she said to the bartender, who placed napkins and dark red wine on the bar in front of them and moved off. "Did my father send you?"

Jack narrowed his eyes as he looked into her azure blue eyes that she narrowed to mimic Jack's.

They both smiled, unable to break eye contact. "It's a hell of a gift you have." Angelica was twenty-four now, startlingly beautiful, and had the uncanny ability to read Jack's mind. She was always a step ahead, surprising for her age in the most amazing ways. "Business looks healthy," he commented.

"Anyone who says the restaurant business is glamorous has never been in the restaurant business. Are you hungry?"

"Not anymore."

"Hmmm."

"How are you?"

"Hungry." Angelica wasn't talking about food. She leaned in close. "Let's walk."

Jack and Angelica crossed Canon and made a left toward Rodeo Drive. Their shoulders touched comfortably like an old couple. The night was cool but not cold, with the light scent of jasmine hanging in the air. There's no way to describe Beverly Hills without including up-scale, and at nine o'clock on a winter's night, it was romantic, safe, and the streets were all but empty.

"How's your love life, Jack?"

Angelica always cut to the chase. "I'm not in love," he said. "Like, but not love. You?"

"I've only got eyes for yours truly."

Jack felt his heart rate spike before settling back down. "Tell me about your life. Is this like anything you envisioned?"

"It's full of surprises, Jack. First of all, I wouldn't be here if it weren't for you. You saved me from a horrible situation. If I'd ended up in a harem somewhere in Iraq, my guess is I would have taken my own life. So every day is a miracle. And this unexpected detour to dreams fulfilled is just that.

"My father would have lost the restaurant if I hadn't taken up the reins. I'm getting pressure to sell from the East Coast families, plus a group of investors who I'm sure are fronting for the East Coast families. They can't strong-arm a takeover as long as I'm at the helm."

"What does your father have to say on the subject?"

"He's leaving it up to me. Doesn't want me to sacrifice myself for his crimes. But I know he's happy I'm sticking it to Uncle Mickey. Dad said 'he'd rather burn the place to the ground than give it up to his fucking sister's rat-bastard husband.'"

"Your old man's a poet. Anybody on Mickey's crew giving you grief?"

"Once every few weeks John Franco comes in for a steak. But I have a large shadow these days."

"Frankie-the-Man," Jack said, glancing over his shoulder and taking in the length of Rodeo behind them before continuing their stroll.

"Afraid you're going to run into your girlfriend?" Angelica teased.

Jack filled her in on the case he was working, the target that was firmly on his back. "I don't want to put you in harm's way. You've got enough crosses to bear."

The two of them walked up Rodeo without the need to talk, just window-shopping and enjoying the intimate proximity of their bodies.

CHAPTER 21

Jack's flight from L.A to Reno was uneventful. A clear blue sky filled with white billowing cumulus clouds edged with shades of gray. The city's rough, windswept terrain reminded Jack of Steve Fossett, the first person to fly solo, nonstop, around the world in a balloon. Fossett was flying a single-engine, two-seater, outside of Reno, over the craggy remote mountains when he went missing. Thirteen months later, a backpacking hiker stumbled onto the crash site on the side of a lonely mountain.

Not a comforting thought, Jack decided as he tightened his seatbelt in preparation for landing. He knew that many people chose to disappear in desert cities like Reno where the action was loose and few questions asked. The art dealer Judy Cohen shared that nobody pries in the desert, because everyone has a history.

Jack was hoping to buck the odds and get a few answers.

In the rental place he found a black Mustang sedan, with eight cylinders under the hood and an exhaust system that growled. He tapped an address into the GPS system and powered out of the lot. Cruz had traced Chip Boyd's location from Gloria's list of witnesses and suspects' phone numbers. He plugged the number into the White

Pages Reverse Lookup, a site that could retrieve the caller's name, address, age, and carrier, even do background checks.

They learned Chip Boyd enlisted in the Army right out of high school. He served two tours of duty, one in Iraq and then Afghanistan, reaching the rank of sergeant. He mustered out in the early two thousands and now worked security at the Eldorado Resort and Casino.

Jack decided to appear unannounced on Boyd's doorstep. He'd left multiple messages and gotten the same result as Gloria. No response at all. That was not unusual. Not many people enjoyed being questioned about old cases. Better to turn a blind eye and hope the investigators got bored and moved on.

The GPS delivered Jack to a small bedside community a half hour from downtown Reno. Modest bungalows and ranch style homes. Old-growth trees, well-kept lawns and gardens, with the mountain range as a backdrop. Jack pulled to the curb in front of a blue house with black shutters and an inviting porch with a single red Adirondack chair.

As Jack stepped out of his car, he was greeted by a wave of dry heat and the smell of freshly mown grass. The driveway led past the side of the house to a detached garage. The neighborhood was quiet. Jack wiped a bead of sweat from his brow as he walked to the front door. A plastic ashtray perched on the arm of the chair contained the remnants of a cigar. It appeared Chip Boyd was a single man.

Jack knocked on the door. No answer. He knocked again and then rang the bell. A disembodied voice asked, "What can I do for you?" Not friendly, not angry.

Boyd's front door was hooked up to a Ring Doorbell System. Jack could now see the camera that was probably attached to the security lights that ran along the side of the house and the front porch.

"I'm Jack Bertolino. I've been leaving messages. I'd like to get your thoughts on the death of Shelley Goldstein. Girl you went to high school with."

"Why?"

"The case has been reopened, and in all honesty, this is just a matter of procedure. You didn't return my calls and I want to be able to cross you off my list."

"I'm at work."

"I just need a few minutes of your time."

Silence, the sound of a neighbor's dog barking. Then: "I work at the Eldorado. Downtown. I get a break at 1400 hours. Meet me in the No Vi Lounge. I can give you fifteen."

"Good, I'll see you there. Hey, how will I recognize you?"

"You're on camera. I'll find you."

Carl sat on the edge of his jail cell bunk as James, the unit staff person, opened a thick white envelope. Nothing was delivered to a prisoner in the federal system without a member of the staff opening the letter or package first.

Carl could see the return address – printed in a fancy font – was from the Superior Court of Los Angeles County. He knew what it contained; he'd been waiting months. It was potentially a giant step toward his exoneration. Carl's heart pounded and he was having trouble breathing.

Carl had applied for a Pitchess v. Superior Court motion. If the convict tried to get the court to re-litigate his case, he could submit the request to the courts in order to discover if any other complaints had been filed against the arresting officers.

He'd received three rejections before the court accepted his request, and now James held his fate in his hands. James knew the import and took his time rifling through the document, knowing Carl was twisting in the wind. "It still smells like smoke in here," he said, handing off the envelope.

"Beats the other odors."

"You got that right. Good luck, my man." James moved down the cellblock to his next delivery.

With trembling hands he pulled out the folded sheaves of paper and carefully hand ironed them on his mattress. He pushed his glasses back up against his nose and lifted the legal document. He tried to swallow, but his mouth was sandpaper dry. The printed words started swimming as tears rolled down his cheeks. Catching himself, Carl poked a finger under his glasses, wiped his eyes and continued. One page, and then he carefully shuffled the papers and started on the second.

Carl was soon spilling tears of joy. He had to be careful not to let them drip on his report. The legal document contained habitual reports of excessive abuse at the hands of Detective Terry Brannigan and Detective Kevin Cook. There were multiple accusations of physical and emotional torture in the interrogation room. They had been given written reprimands, but the squad captains appeared only too happy to turn a blind eye in order to close another case.

Carl set down the report, walked over to his steel toilet, and hurled his lunch. He wiped his mouth and said a silent prayer of thanks to God, to his mother, and to Gloria Millhouse, in that order.

He picked up the file again to make sure he'd read a specific paragraph correctly, and his red-rimmed eyes creased into a smile. Another case looked very similar to his.

The kicker—what Carl hoped could be the final nail in the prosecution's coffin—had occurred a year and a half before his trial. A young black man was accused of murdering a white coed. The arresting officers were Brannigan and Cook. The guilty party claimed the confession had been beaten out of him, and the eyewitness, a young female, was a bald-faced liar.

The hair on Carl's arms stood on end. He'd have to wait until he had computer time, but he felt certain when he pulled up the case in question, the eyewitness would turn out to be Cheryl Lee Williams.

Jack walked past a billboard that featured a picture of a cute blonde folk singer announcing: "Brooksie Wells sings the classics. Late-night."

The lounge was all but empty, the lunch crowd gone, and the bar had a few patrons sipping blue cocktails, the No Vi specialty.

Chip Boyd was leaning against the end of the bar, facing the door. His face was noncommittal as Jack approached. He had brush cut brown hair, the buffed physique of a gym rat, intense brown eyes, and military bearing.

"I thought you'd be wearing a red carnation," Jack said.

Boyd's eyes narrowed until he realized Jack was putting him on. He didn't look like he was fond of being put on, but relaxed some as they shook hands.

"You want a drink?" he offered.

"Some sparkling water."

Boyd grabbed the sparkling water and a Coke for himself, and headed toward a booth. "I work security here. Crazy hours, crazy patrons, good money."

"It's gotta keep you on your toes."

"No kidding. So, what can I do for you, Jack? Oh, I Googled you. Quite a career."

"I thought I was done after twenty-five years. It didn't work out that way."

"Never does, right?" Boyd wasn't looking for a response.

Jack pulled the headshots and the deer hunting photograph from a manila envelope and spread them out on the table. A picture of Shelley Goldstein to focus matters. Boyd flipped through the photos until he picked out the group photo and grinned. It faded as he picked up Shelley's picture. "She was a nice girl. Very friendly." He grabbed the deer-hunting photo again. "What a crew we were. Damn. We had some good times."

"Are you in contact with any of them?"

"Not really. Once I enlisted, we, uh, we all went our separate ways. I've gotten a few late-night drunken phone calls, you know, all nostalgia bullshit and no substance. Once the drunk wears off, there's no connection."

"Councilman Mark Corcoran seems to be doing well."

"Always figured him for success. Just had that vibe. Always in control, a real alpha dog."

That was the second time he'd heard that description used in reference to Corcoran. Carl's mother was the first. "Talk to me about Shelley."

"Not much to say. Mark was hot on her, I remember that."

Jack pulled a particular headshot out of the pile. "That's what this guy said."

"Fuckin' Tony. Man could never keep his mouth shut. Anyway, so, she was, you know, uh," he fluttered his hand in the air, "out of our reach. She threw a party for graduation. And we were all there, and damn, I'd never been to a house like that before. It was something. She had it all—and then she was gone. Crazy."

"Anybody else in the crew have eyes for Shelley?"

"No, the other guys were all hat no cattle, if you know what I mean."

"What was your take on Carl Forbes?"

"What's to say? Who knew he was a nutjob?"

"How so?"

Jack watched Boyd's body tense. "Are you fucking kidding me? He killed Shelley, for chrissake. The papers said it was awful. He fucking stabbed and raped her."

Jack switched gears, trying to keep Boyd talking. "You know they never found any of his DNA on her body?"

"No, I didn't know that. We all talked about it, the murder," Boyd said, sucking in a breath and calming himself on the exhale, "You know, after it happened it was all anybody talked about."

"What was the consensus?"

"Who knows? All over the map. Carl wasn't invited to her big graduation party. He wasn't part of the crew. Not a loner, but not in." Boyd took a sip of Coke, back in control again. "Maybe that set him off." And then as an afterthought, "And you know, being black and all that. Back in the day, couldn't have been easy."

"I know what you mean," Jack said.

"Anyway, that's all we could come up with at the time. Eh, we were young and stupid. What did we know?"

Jack wondered the same thing. What he did know was Boyd still had a charge when he spoke about the case. Twenty-three years was a long time to hold onto that level of emotion.

"My first time in Reno," Jack said, shifting focus. "I rented a muscle car and tore up the blacktop driving here."

"It's got its moments."

"What kind of car do you drive?"

"A four-by. I like to off road."

"A Ford?"

Boyd nodded.

"Me too, I drive a Mustang." And then changing course, "So, no connection, no communication with your pal Corcoran through the years?"

Boyd's brow furrowed.

"Because he was the alpha dog, your words," Jack said easily.

"Right. I've read up on him some. But again, no. He went to college, hit it big. I enlisted. Once you've been in combat, you see life in a different way. Different perspective. Hard to explain."

"I understand."

Boyd pulled out his cell and checked the time. "Hey, Jack, I gotta run. Anything else I can do for you?"

"What was your opinion of Terry Brannigan?"

"The cop ...? Eh, he was a cop," Boyd said as if that were explanation enough. "Not a bad guy, as I remember. Very thorough. I think he talked to everyone who was at the party. Made everybody nervous."

"Goes with the territory."

"Met with him and his partner a couple of times, and that was that." Boyd got to his feet and stretched his back.

"One more thing, where were you last Tuesday?"

"Why?" Not defensive, just perplexed.

Jack decided to drop the hammer. "Did you know Cheryl Lee Williams?"

"Yeah, she lived in the neighborhood. She's the one fingered Carl."

"She was on my list of witnesses. I stopped by to ask her some questions on Tuesday. Someone decided they didn't want her to be interviewed. Shot her dead."

"Huh," he said with no emotion, no eye blink, no nothing. "That's too bad." And then, "I was here, working the late shift."

"Anybody who can vouch for you?"

"Floor manager, name's Duke." Boyd turned crisply on his heel.

"Hey, Chip," Jack stopped him mid-stride. "Answer your phone if I call. Save me a plane ride."

Boyd's face creased into a tight grin. "No problem," and he strode out of the lounge.

Jack picked up the headshots one by one. He placed Shelley Goldstein's photo on top and stared at it. She was a beautiful young woman with a graceful, optimistic smile and everything to live for. Jack was angry by the time he slid the photos back into the manila envelope. Anger was his friend. He'd stay angry until he discovered the identity of the real killer.

As Jack headed to the airport, he called Nick, and filled him on the attempted carjacking in the park. Told him the cops were aware of the gang the cholos were affiliated with, and he was able to ID the two soldiers who got away from the CalGang data base. Attempted carjacking, using a weapon, and his gang affiliation, Renaldo Sanchez was looking at serious time. They're waiting on charges from the district attorney and keeping him in lockup until his bail hearing.

Nick asked, "Do you think it was related to your case, or just a straight up carjacking. Something's not ringing true to me."

Jack doesn't disagree. "I sussed out the play. They thought their three guns were enough to make me roll over. If I gave up the keys, I don't know if we'd would be having this conversation."

"Never stop trusting your instincts, Jack. Yours are top notch."

"Thanks Nick. I'll have more information when I'm back in town. I'll keep you up to speed."

Jack pushed the Mustang to a hundred just for the fun of it. He placed a call to Tommy's hotel suite, where he and Cruz set up shop, and had him put the call on speaker. He filled them in on his interview with Boyd and asked Cruz to check out the man's registered vehicles with the DMV. Jack had pushed Boyd as far as he could without shutting him down, but suspected the man knew more than he was letting on.

He'd interviewed the floor manager at the Eldorado, who corroborated Boyd's story. He was checked in, the night in question, but added sometimes his men swapped shifts. It was a pretty loose affair as long as the casino was covered. He promised to check the security cameras and call when he had an answer.

Jack signed off and pushed the pedal to the metal, the torque pinning him against the Mustang's seat, the stress of the day peeling away. Jack was headed back to LA, excited to see what secrets his men had uncovered in retired Judge Walter Myers' time capsule, the case files from Carl Forbes's trial.

CHAPTER 22

Jack pulled his new rental car up to valet parking at the Ritz-Carlton, got out, and took a ticket. It was a black BMW five series with tinted windows and a hard top. The car wasn't bulletproof, but it might buy him some time.

Tommy Aronsohn's suite had been turned into command central. Electricity sparked the air as the three men worked with purpose. Retired Judge Walter Myers' dusty boxes were stacked near the balcony window that looked out on the marina and acres of yachts, white sails, and darkening blue skies, in the early evening. The judge's files littered the rug. A tray of half-eaten crudités and sandwiches were set up on the dining table next to a silver bowl filled with melted ice, Coke, and sparkling water. Three heads turned as one as Jack entered the room.

"I invited the professor to join the party," Tommy said, glancing up from a stack of legal forms.

Professor Ted Anderson was on his feet, pacing, reading court documents. He was wearing thin-legged jeans and a vintage black Rolling Stones T-shirt with the hot lips logo. He smiled and fist-bumped Jack, who welcomed the man, knowing he could expedite the paperwork because of his deep knowledge of the case. Jack hoped the new revelations the team had uncovered would speed thing up before the body count rose.

Tommy and Cruz had conspiratorial grins on their faces as they let Jack catch his breath. "The floor manager at the Eldorado caught me at the airport," he said. "Boyd was all over their security screens Tuesday night. Put in a full shift. He moves back down the list. So, give me the good news." Jack grabbed a half a sandwich and took a healthy bite.

"The big news," Tommy said, taking a dramatic pause. "The LAPD paid Cheryl Lee two thousand dollars for moving expenses. That would be in exchange for her eyewitness testimony. It appears to be aboveboard, a reasonable expenditure, because in the court filing the woman stated she feared for her life and the life of her young daughter."

"Rob Schneider, Carl's lawyer, said the defense never got word of money changing hands," Jack said. This was the first anomaly found in their reams of paperwork.

"Exactly. The prosecution copied the court on LAPD's transaction, but at the evidentiary hearing the discovery never made it into the defense attorney's files," Tommy said. "And so, it was never brought up at trial, and that line of cross examination was conspicuously missing from the court records."

"A mistake?" the professor queried, but his tone and raised eyebrows let the room know he didn't think so.

"Giving the DA's office the benefit of the doubt, a big maybe," Tommy said, tapping his nose, "but it smells rotten."

"I'll drop in on Judge Cole, the ADA who handled the case," Jack said. "He promised to check his records and get back to me. Offered his help if we uncovered mistakes in the proceedings. Said sometimes paying a witness to testify was the only way to get a conviction. Not an easy admission for a political animal."

The professor's eyes were animated—he was clearly excited. A big change from the first encounter Jack had with the man. "So, Jack, I'm up to speed on the death of Cheryl Lee, the attempt on your life, the attempt on Carl's life, and the drive-by shooting at Hanna's house, that was either to intimidate a potential witness, or a failed murder attempt. Add Gloria's death to the mix, which could've derailed the case, and the failure of the prosecution, or the LAPD to share intel, and I think you're developing a persuasive case."

"Let's copy retired Judge Myers on what we've got to date. He said he'd take a look, and when the court schedules the evidentiary hearing, he offered to speak in Carl's defense."

"This is good," Anderson said. "This is so damn good. It'll take a few days to cull the rest of the files and create the document. Some of it is circumstantial, but gentlemen, we are definitely on to something. Good work all."

Cruz poured himself a Coke, dipped a stalk of celery into the ranch dip and crunched down. "Jack, remember you mentioned retesting the DNA? How do we put that in motion?"

"I've got the paperwork to petition the courts," Anderson said. "It may take some time, but we can get it done."

Satisfied nods of agreement from the group. Jack thought of something else and said: "When we discover who killed Gloria, it'll lead us to the killer of Shelley Goldstein."

The implied meaning knocked Anderson off balance. If the killer of the two women was one and the same, then Carl would be exonerated. The prof sucked in a breath. "Well, Gloria ... she'd be happy."

"Let's shut down for the day. Dinner's on me."

No argument from the men. They'd head down to the Cast & Plow for dinner on the outdoor patio with a great view of the marina. It was a productive day and Jack wanted to keep morale energized. A couple of drinks and a good meal would do the job.

Tommy pulled Jack aside as they headed for the restaurant. "I spoke with Geoff Franklin, the DDA at the district attorneys' office in Van Nuys. He's handling the carjacking case, and a good guy. Renaldo Sanchez didn't make bail. He's not going anywhere for the foreseeable future. Franklin said he'd keep me apprised of the case, and give me a call when they need you to testify."

"The team has enough on their plates," Jack said. "Thanks for the discretion. I need them to stay focused. We have a lot of moving parts, and I don't want to confuse the issue."

Jack's cell pinged and he read the text. Not a number he recognized but the brief content was pure Cardona. "Stop by."

A surge of electricity coursed down Jack's spine. The case was gaining momentum. He clicked off and shared, "We may be getting news on who set Carl up in Victorville. I've been summoned by Vincent Cardona."

CHAPTER 23

The sky was slate gray. The thick, low fog that rolled down from the hills and blanketed the high desert obscured the razor wire surrounding the penitentiary. It felt like Jack and Cardona were walking through a rain cloud. A slight damp breeze rose and fell, a distraction Cardona seemed to enjoy.

The guard in the gun tower kept a watchful eye, ready to shoot if necessary. Other than that, the yard was empty. Just the way Cardona liked it.

"If you give up control of the Chop House," Jack said, "you won't make it out of here alive."

"Did she say that?"

"Angelica?"

Cardona raised his eyebrows in a who-the-fuck-were-we-talking-about gesture.

"No," Jack said. "Not in so many words. But without skin in the game, New York will worry more than they already are that you'll roll over for time off."

"Fuck 'em. So, how's she doing? No bullshit, Jack."

"Angelica is a winner. She understands the reality and she's not willing to give an inch to your brother-in-law."

"Fuckin' Mickey." Mickey Razzano was the capo for one of the five New York families.

The men reached the far wall and started back across the yard. Cardona nodded his head like he was having a private conversation with himself. He finally decided to share: "I raised her right."

"You can't teach what she knows," Jack said. "It's a gift."

"Hey, fuck you, Jack, and your always gotta be right bullshit."

Jack grinned. He'd been called out for worse things. He remained silent waiting for Cardona to get to the reason for the visit. Cardona had other plans.

"You know, I never minded, totally, uh, you and her…"

"Good to know."

"Yeah, well."

"It was a long ride out here, Vincent."

"Fuck you."

The mist turned to a light rain. Cardona tilted his head back and opened his mouth. Jack wondered if the killer was losing his mind, if jail was going to be his downfall.

"We used to do this when we were kids," he said. "In this fuckin' place, simple pleasures, huh?"

"So?" Jack said, trying to hide his impatience. Cardona flashed his dead eyes, sucked in a breath, and walked away from the tower. Jack had to hustle to catch up.

"The guard in the tower, he can read lips. More than a few men got nailed with his skill set."

Jack gave Cardona some space. He'd get down to business when he was good and ready. He pulled the collar of his black leather bomber jacket tight against his neck, keeping the cold rain from rolling down his back.

"So, Freddie Triolo. A fuckin' pisan, no less. Has a storefront in Koreatown. Dirty accountant, lost his license. Now he's an advisor, investment counselor, the whole bullshit nine yards. A scumbag. Don't know the client."

Jack wanted more information and was clearly unsatisfied.

"Do some sleuthing, Jack, for chrissake. If I get more, I'll share.

Same deal. Keep an eye out for Angelica. Family's sacrosanct, but Mickey, I'm not so sure he wouldn't eat his young."

The door to Cardona's building squealed open as the unit staff officer stuck his head out, looking bored, and tapped his watch. His head snapped back out of the rain as Cardona and Jack changed course and disappeared inside the unit. The heavy metal door clanged shut in their wake.

The armed BOP officer locked the door to the interview room, giving Jack and Carl some privacy. Never leaving his position at the window in case Carl went postal on his visitor. The men sat on opposite sides of the long metal table.

"You're some kind of mind reader, Jack. I didn't get computer time till this morning, and this material was burning a hole in my pocket."

"What do you have for me?"

"Something that's been a long time coming. I've been filing for this here motion eight years. I'd all but given up. But working with the professor, and your friend Mr. Aronsohn, turns out the fourth time was the charm."

Carl put his hand behind his back and pulled a thick white envelope from under his shirt. Jack could see the return address was from the Superior Court. Carl was visibly moved, and his hands trembled as he handed over the documents. "They'd have to kill me before I'd let these papers out of my sight."

"What is it, Carl?"

"First step in proving my case. It's the list of complaints of police brutality filed against Terry Brannigan and Kevin Cook. These fools got a history of beating confessions out of men of color. And then there's, on page two, fifth paragraph down," he said, having memorized the placement. "A little something about Cheryl Lee."

Jack read the report and didn't get it at first. "This case looks a lot like yours." He checked the date. "About a year and a half earlier." Jack could hear Carl's labored breathing as he read. "I'm not seeing it."

"I got on the computer after chow and pulled up the record of the case. Brannigan and Cook were running the show. The defendant, a young black male, Tyrone Stevens, was found guilty of murdering a white co-ed. And here's the kicker. The eyewitness ... was Cheryl Lee Williams."

Jack saw right away how explosive this new information was. If Jack's team added this file to the two-thousand-dollar payment to Cheryl Lee in Carl's case – information withheld from the defense attorney – coupled with the damning report of excessive police violence, they'd have a reasonable shot at overturning Carl's conviction. Jack didn't want to get ahead of himself. There was still a lot of work to do, namely, find the killer, and Jack told Carl just that.

Carl took the news cautiously. "I can't let too much emotion in or it might kill me. Don't get me wrong, I'm on the moon. Just easing into what might be."

Jack knew he couldn't really understand what it would be like to spend twenty-three years incarcerated, and so he didn't make small talk.

"Let me get out of here with this, Carl. Keep things moving. This is good stuff, man. Congratulations. Should I give your mother a call, bring her up to speed?"

"Might give her a heart attack."

Jack grinned. "We'll wait until it's real."

"Don't get into an accident driving back."

"No worries. I'll photograph the documents when I get to my car and e-mail the copies to the office."

"Don't let me keep you," Carl said.

Jack gestured to the BOP officer looking through the barred glass window, and he opened the door. He fist bumped Carl who was trying to still his beating heart, nodded, and headed out.

So here was the deal, Jack thought as he drove down the CA-14. He didn't see the change from high desert, to mountains, past Vasquez rocks, to rolling hills, and then the I-5 toward the valley floor. He was weighing his options, playing out scenarios.

He knew in his bones Brannigan was dirty as sin. Jack felt certain he'd used Cheryl Lee early on, and then coerced another eyewitness confession out of the impressionable woman. Or had Cheryl Lee played Brannigan at Carl's expense, and then continued milking him until she became a liability? He'd probably never have a definitive answer to that question.

Vincent Cardona provided the name of the connection between Carl's failed executioner and the client. Larry the Rat was the killer, but how to nail the client? He didn't think there were enough specifics to sway a judge into signing off on a search warrant for Freddie Triolo's office, and if he delved into the gray area of sleuthing, as Cardona challenged, Jack would have to keep Tommy and the professor out of the loop to protect them.

There was a good possibility if he got inside Triolo's office, he'd uncover evidence that could tie him to Brannigan, the man who had the most to gain from shutting down their investigation. Corcoran, still high on Jack's list, was the incumbent in his district, but Leslie had said he was concerned about the election. Jack hadn't figured out the two men's connection, but something was there, rippling right below the surface.

If he confronted Freddie Triolo, he'd be showing his hand, and possibly put Triolo and the Rat in jeopardy.

It would make more sense to play down-and-dirty with a good old B & E – breaking and entering – and getting the facts. They wouldn't be any use in a court of law, but the information could be used to leverage one bad guy against another. And then his team could build the case backwards.

Jack decided to lay out the case to his men, with the new information Carl provided, and ultimately use Cruz's security system expertise and his own B & E skills to set the hook.

CHAPTER 24

The I-5 was a parking lot, but Jack wasn't feeling the pain. The music was mellow, and the case was gaining momentum. His cell phone chirped, and Jack tapped his Bluetooth. The jazz was replaced by: "Jack Bertolino? This is Ted Ward, at the *LA Times*. I was wondering if you'd like to comment on a story we're running in the morning paper."

"What's this in reference to, Ted?"

"I've been following the appointment of the new police chief, and new information has surfaced on one of the candidates."

Dread was all Jack felt. His stomach tightened as he waited for the shoe to drop.

"I've been notified that a case you're working intersects with the story I'm writing."

"What are the chances?" Jack said, dry.

"Universe works in mysterious ways."

"What do you have?" Not taking the bait until he knew for sure.

"Look, Jack, I'm aware of the case you're working with the blessing of the mayor. It involves the questionable death of Gloria Millhouse. I got a snapshot of you and the mayor talking, thick as thieves, at the press conference. And now I've got information that a Pitchess motion was delivered to a Carl Forbes up at Victorville. The information obtained would be good for the prisoner, but damning for Commander Brannigan's chances to take the top spot. It would likely be a career ender. Would you like to weigh in on the story before we go to press?"

Jack had to collect his thoughts. His entire case might blow up if he couldn't delay the article.

"Jack, are you still there?"

"I'm here, Ted. I'm stuck in traffic on the Five and you caught me off guard."

"Take your time. Your silence already told me all I needed to know."

"Don't push it, Ted. There are lives at stake here. You don't want to have blood on your hands."

That changed the tone of the conversation considerably. "Okay, you have my undivided attention."

"Am I your first call?"

"Yes."

"I don't want to do this over the phone. Here's what I need. Let's meet first thing in the morning. Wherever you want. Give me a few hours without distraction, and I'll give you the entire story, as it progresses. It's bigger than one man's promotion. And all I'll say now is that there's already a body count involved. That will sell newspapers. It might even get you a publishing deal."

"I've already written the story. I'm editing as we speak."

"It's your call. I'll deny any knowledge of the case if you go to print without giving me some time. If you made the call, you know who I am. I deliver. When it all plays out, and it's moving quickly now, you can be at the back of the line or in the epicenter with the exclusive."

"You've piqued my interest."

"Do the right thing."

"Let's meet at Phillipe's, at one. Give you time to get your ducks in a row. Don't burn me, Jack."

"I'll see you then." Jack clicked off, silently cursing. He'd have to make a move on Freddie Triolo's place tonight before Brannigan got wind of the shit storm headed his way and cleaned house. He called Cruz, filled him in on the unexpected wrench in the works, and told him where they'd be meeting in Koreatown. "And Cruz," Jack said, "bring your equipment."

Nick Aprea was sitting in an 80's era, beat-up blue Chevy Impala in a low-rent section of East L.A. The small stucco ranch houses that lined the street had barred windows and doors, and the cars parked curbside were sun-damaged. It was pushing eighty degrees in the car, and with the heat, and mind-bending boredom, Aprea's eyes started to blink closed. One of the gangbangers he was chasing had a family that lived on a corner lot, and Nick was going to call in the troops if he showed. It was a reasonable assumption after the banger skipped bail. They all returned home after a few weeks on the run.

His cell jarred him awake, and he saw it was Jack calling. "What do you need?"

"Did I wake you?"

"I'm chasing down Manny Rodriguez, and I've lost five pounds sitting in this shithole of a car. I'm in a foul mood."

"I'm not gonna make your day."

"Christ, what do ya got?"

"I'd give Brannigan and his crew a wide berth because the shit is about to hit the fan. The Pitchess report just came down, and it's damning for the commander. Torture, forced confessions, physical abuse, going back twenty-plus years." Nick didn't respond and Jack added, "Two grand was paid to Cheryl Lee for her testimony in the Carl Forbes case."

"So?"

"That piece of information was never delivered to the defense. But here's the kicker. There's a similar case, a year earlier, same scenario, young black kid, murder, rape, same arresting officers… and the same eyewitness. Cheryl Lee Williams."

"Huh."

"It gets worse. Somebody leaked the Pitchess motion to an *LA Times* reporter who's going public with the story. My guess, Brannigan is going to be out of contention for chief."

"Son of a bitch. What did the mayor say?"

"He's not in the loop yet. I've got a few things I need to handle before I make that call. But by tomorrow it's going to blow up."

Nick let that information swirl around. "Thanks for the heads-up. Sounds like you're on a roll. Watch your back."

"Later." And Jack clicked off.

CHAPTER 25

Jack sat in the booth of a twenty-four-hour coffee shop in the low-rent district of Koreatown. He was eating a cheeseburger, a choice that appeared to be the lesser of many evils on the menu. Sometimes Jack got it wrong. The odor of grease was cloying, and it would take more than bleach to eliminate the smell from his clothes: black shirt, black jeans, and black running shoes. The coffee shop was located a few blocks south of Freddie Triolo's storefront in a tired L-shaped strip mall on Beverly Drive.

The mall was situated on the outskirts of the trendy section of Koreatown, where new high-rise loft buildings and condos, bars and restaurants, had sprung up like mushrooms. Gentrification hadn't settled in the outlier areas, though, and that worked for Jack.

It was almost midnight and Cruz was doing surveillance, waiting for the last retailer at the location to close up shop. Triolo had left work at six on the nose.

The men had done a drive-by down the alleyway behind the strip mall earlier. They discovered the alarm and cable hookup on a telephone pole across from the building. Cruz pulled up specs of the alarm system online. The system ran to a high-end camera package and the alarm that protected Triolo's unit. Nothing Cruz couldn't manage. He grew up learning the trade at the feet of his father, who founded Bundy Lock and Key. He learned from the best.

The money spent protecting the rundown office impressed Cruz, and he told Jack there had to be something of value inside. The lock on the back door would be Jack's job. Cruz had the higher level of expertise, but he couldn't be in more than one place at a time.

Cruz texted Jack 999, the alert signal. Jack paid his bill, grabbed his bag of tools, and walked out into the cool night air. The traffic was light at this time, and Jack took the long way around the block to enter the back alley.

Cruz, also dressed entirely in black, was perched on the pole, removing the metal casing that housed the alarm system. He was all but invisible as he hand-signaled Jack a five-minute warning.

It was quiet. The sound of sporadic cars was followed by the siren of an EMT vehicle screaming down Beverly. A red, white, and blue light pierced the darkness on either side of the strip mall as it raced past.

Cruz gave a thumbs-up, and Jack advanced to the reinforced back door. He slid in thin metal prongs from what looked like an electric toothbrush. The work was made harder wearing latex gloves, but the device did its thing. It whirred, the tumblers fell, and in twenty seconds the door swung open. Jack stepped in, mini mag light in his mouth, and locked the door behind him.

The plan was to be in and out in fifteen minutes. Triolo's office comprised three rooms. Jack entered through the back storage area. He gave it a quick once-over, saw nothing of interest and opened the door to the office proper. A small vestibule with an empty desk and two folding chairs awaited him. And then door number three. Also locked.

Jack worked his magic and entered Triolo's private office. No windows, no artwork, just faded institutional green walls. A large metal desk held a printer, yellow pads, a half empty snow dome, and an inbox-outbox for bills and correspondence. Of special interest was the large desktop computer and two tall industrial file cabinets. All locked. Jack cursed out loud.

He eased the well-worn mahogany chair back and took a seat. Turned on the desk lamp, being careful of light bleed under the doorjamb, which might alert a security guard of the intrusion, and started his search.

He powered up the computer, and the iMac requested a password. Unless Jack got lucky with his search, it was a dead end. He looked under the keypad, where people often taped their password, but no luck.

He pulled the center drawer open and rifled through an array of pens, receipts, post-its and paper clips. Again, no key to the computer files. He pulled out each side drawer, finding nothing of interest. In the bottom drawer, he found a fifth of Canadian Club whiskey—and a thick binder. The leather cover was worn and brittle. He pulled it out, it had some heft to it. It was an accounting ledger. No names, just numbers and dates. All written in fine cursive.

Jack powered through the journal and discovered entries going back twenty-plus years. He pulled out his cell and snapped photos of the ledger at breakneck speed.

Cruz checked his watch from his vantage point on the telephone pole when he heard a sound down below. He grabbed tight to the pole, trying for invisible.

An elderly man dressed in pajamas and slippers, being all but dragged by a muscular Doberman, stopped directly beneath Cruz. The dog took a steaming piss on the pole, and the gentleman took a hit off his vape pen. The smoke smelled like pot, and Cruz prayed it would calm the dog.

Cruz's heart pounded. He knew damn well if he was caught on the pole, break-in-tools on his belt, with Jack involved in a B&E, he might end up behind bars.

He hugged the pole tighter as the gentleman enjoyed his clandestine date with his pot pipe. "Hah," the man said out loud, grinning, and dragged the thick-necked beast back to home base.

Cruz let out the breath he'd been holding and understood why he wouldn't trade his life for anything in the world.

Jack was in the zone. He spun the computer around, looking on the back for a possible passcode, and came up empty.

He rifled through the yellow pads, finding more accounting figures in pencil but nothing that seemed to relate to the case. Jack was looking for payments or anything that tied Triolo to Brannigan, and he was getting frustrated.

He spied an old Rolodex on top of one of the file cabinets. He turned the dial, snapping the worn cardboard cards in a circle until he found B. And there, on a stained card, was Brannigan's name and contact info. Three penned numbers had been crossed out, and one remained with an address. Jack photographed the card and continued his search. It connected Brannigan to Triolo, but not in a definitive fashion.

One of the yellow pads had an interesting scribble: "stop $ at 27689***B." Jack's neck hair stood on end. He couldn't be positive, but it sure as hell might be tied to Cheryl Lee. He'd call Detective Harstad in Wickenburg and have him contact Cheryl Lee's daughter. Ask her to check the new bank statement that should have arrived and see if the money trail ended with her mother's death.

As he was sliding the yellow pad back onto the pile, his eyes fell on the snow dome. Inside the glass ball was a plastic cutout of the New York skyline with the twin towers sticking up above the evaporated water level. He picked up the object, shook it, and then looked underneath the black plastic base. Taped to the bottom was a series of letters and numbers. The Scotch tape had yellowed with age, but the code was readable. Jack input the series into the computer, and the old Mac sprang to life. Jack slipped in a thumb drive and downloaded the contents of Freddie Triolo's files.

As the wheel spun, he looked through the file cabinets, but he found nothing worth copying. He finished putting the office back in order. Once the download was complete, Jack shut down the computer. He put the mag light in his mouth, texted Cruz 999, and headed out.

Mayor Henry Waltham's private cell phone rang eight times before a light was switched on. His wife, Alyssa, angrily stripped off her blackout sleep mask. "Henry, pick up the damn phone … Henry!"

The mayor rolled over in bed, wearing his own sleep mask. He reached out an arm blindly and fumbled around until he retrieved his phone. "Who? Damn it, Jack, when I said twenty-four/seven, it was a figure of speech. What time is it?" he asked, pulling off his mask.

Jack was on his boat, moored in the marina, with a glass of red in one hand, the phone in the other, and a satisfied look on his face. "Two AM. Sorry to bother you, Henry, but we've got a problem."

"Good Lord, Jack. I don't like the sound of that. Let me move into the living room so the wife can sleep. She's hell on wheels if she doesn't get seven hours."

Alyssa slapped her husband's arm. "Shut up, Henry."

Henry slid his legs over the side of the overstuffed bed, slipped his feet into sheepskin slippers, and shuffled out of the room. "What do you have for me, Jack?" Henry snapped off the light in the bedroom, leaving him to make his way down the hallway in ambient moonlight.

Jack filled the mayor in on the Pitchess motion, Brannigan's history of violence, along with Cheryl Lee's earlier collusion and the money paid to her. To top it all, the leak to the *LA Times* reporter and his threat to publish. "We may have a few hours, maybe more. I think I've held him off until midday. We're having lunch, and I've offered him an exclusive if his story doesn't go to print before that."

"What does your gut tell you?" the mayor asked.

"If you get ahead of the story, you'll make a few enemies, but come out of it unscathed. You say new information turned up that needed to be shared with the general public, that sort of thing."

"What does it do to your case?"

"Puts it in jeopardy. Definitely be blowback. Won't help that Brannigan will get hammered in the press, and he'll know he's under increased scrutiny in the Gloria Millhouse murder. He'll fight back, and things will get ugly."

"*Get* ugly? I just gave the man an award for valor. It's already ugly."

"And it appears, so is his history, Mayor. You can't afford to be tied to that."

Mayor Waltham poured two fingers of aged scotch into a crystal glass, took a thoughtful sip, and sat down in a well-worn leather chair. "What was your take on the reporter?"

"Hard to say. If it doesn't hit the stands in the morning, our lunch is at one. I'll call as soon as I nail it down."

"If I'm behind the curve on this, it will appear I'm complicit in a cover-up."

"And that will cost you more than votes."

"What about Carl Forbes?"

"I'm not sure it will hurt him. The number of allegations against Brannigan speak for themselves. Hard to defend his record. I doubt he was planning to testify in Carl's defense, no matter what line of goods he tried to sell Gloria."

"All right, Jack. Give me a few hours. It would be better for both of us if the reporter toes the line. But I'm not sure it's a gamble I'm willing to take."

"Let me know if you decide to blow the lid off. And I'll call when I have something definitive."

"Thank you for the heads up."

Jack set down his phone and took a deep sip of Cabernet. The clanking of lines against aluminum masts and the sound of water lapping against the dock were calming.

Cruz would get on the computer files first thing in the morning, and Tommy and the professor would use the new information to move the case forward. But Jack knew once the paperwork hit the courts, the damning information against Brannigan would leak and explode in the press.

CHAPTER 26

Jack set up the cabin cruiser's coffee maker, powered up his computer and searched for Ted Ward's byline at the *LA Times*. His article had been posted. It recapped the upcoming race for police chief, but didn't mention the revelation of the Pitchess brief. Jack was impressed by Ward's honesty and hoped he'd play ball.

If the Mayor decided to call a press conference to get ahead of what could be a damaging revelation, he would make sure Ward still got the lead and an exclusive on Jack's case. On second thought, if the mayor gave Ward an exclusive, he could control the timeline, alert Brannigan, let the press go wild, and leave Jack out of the mix altogether, preserving his case. He decided to run that by the mayor before his lunch with the reporter. It never hurt to have ammunition to sweeten the pot.

"Mayor Waltham has agreed to give you the exclusive. It's a win-win," Jack said to Ward as they sat in a wooden booth at Philippe's in downtown Los Angeles. "The mayor, who was in the dark regarding Brannigan's sealed history of violence is willing to give you the story. And in doing so, control the timeline and, between you and me, save face. You'll break the news, and I'll make sure you stay one step ahead of the insanity that sure as hell is going to follow publication."

Ward tried to remain cool, but couldn't hide his growing excitement. The twenty-seven-year-old reporter was tall, nail thin, and his modern Tom Ford glasses couldn't hide his world-weary brown eyes. He wore a blue button-down shirt over tan slacks along with worn cordovan loafers.

Jack had done his research and knew Ward was a journeyman who had been around the block – the courthouse was his turf – but hadn't broken through the ranks of the crime beat. This could be his breakout story, a career maker. Ward's head nodded as he took two huge bites of his lamb French dip sandwich, one of Philippe's specialties, and washed it down with Coke.

Jack knew the young man was hooked and almost felt guilty. Almost being the operative word.

"We've got a deal," Ward said, as if he were controlling the negotiations. "When do I get to see the mayor?"

"Finish your lunch and we'll head over to his office. We're filing some preliminary paperwork with the courts regarding the evidentiary hearing in the next few days, and we want delivery timed to come on the heels of your breaking report. Because you're not the only reporter in town with sources keeping a watchful eye for the next big story."

"Works for me. And Jack … you will never regret this decision."

Famous last words. Jack slathered spicy mustard onto his sandwich and took a bite. He could only hope that Ward would keep his word and the case wasn't about to blow up in his face.

After lunch, Jack dropped Ted Ward off at City Hall. He made the introduction to Mayor Waltham, who graciously greeted the young man. He headed back to the loft, where Cruz was mining the download from Freddie Triolo's computer for gold. Jack wanted to provide a firewall between Tommy, Professor Anderson, and the break-in.

Jack's cell chirped and he fielded a call from Detective Harstad in Wickenburg.

"How's the detection business?" Harstad said with a light drawl.

"Things are starting to get interesting."

"Well, don't let me stop the momentum. I dropped by Cheryl Lee's double-wide, and her daughter Chelsea was there. Nice enough person, but if I'd lost my mother, I wouldn't be moving into her house before the old woman was buried. But that's just the way my mama raised me. Chelsea let me see the recent Wells Fargo statement, and missing was …?"

"A thousand dollars."

"I knew you were good. And hey, put a smile on my face. But the daughter was none too happy about it. Knew her mother's finances to the penny. Already spent the extra grand. Greed is very unattractive. Any hoo, I took a picture and sent the copy to your e-mail address."

"That's good news. I think we have the middleman involved in wiring the funds. I just need to connect a few more dots and find out who's writing the checks."

"Someone with knowledge of the murder. You go get 'em, Jack, make me look good. I'd like to put this heifer to bed. If you need backup, you won't have to call twice."

"Good to know. We'll talk soon."

Jack pulled to the side of the road and texted Cheryl Lee's bank statement to Tommy and Cruz. Tommy could add the new information to the case file's money trail. Now, added to the two-thousand-dollar payment at the time of the trial, the years of a thousand dollars a week drying up days after her death would paint a damn good picture of a conspiracy to stop the reopening of Carl Forbes's case.

If they could connect Brannigan to Triolo, it would break the case wide open.

Jack stopped by Jersey Mike's and picked up an Italian sub for Cruz. He drove around the block twice, checking any rooflines and parking lots with a direct shot at his building. When he felt all was clear, he hit the remote and powered through the gates of his building and down into the underground parking structure.

Upstairs, Jack tossed the Italian sub to Cruz as he walked past. "You read my mind, thanks," Cruz said, unfurling the sandwich and taking a bite.

"Any word from Tommy?" Jack pulled a Vicodin from a bottle in the cupboard and chased it with two Excedrin.

"He's working with the professor, who's crazy for the Ritz-Carlton. I think we'll have to put him on the payroll. They're coming up with wording for the judge. Hey, great news about the missing thousand dollars."

"Now we just have to find out who was sending it."

"Hmmm," Cruz said taking a mouthful of his sandwich.

So far Jack had been delivering all the news. "Okay, what've you got, wise guy?"

Cruz lifted one finger to wait a second, finished chewing his food, and then washed it down with some bottled water. "Good sandwich, Jack."

"Cruz."

Cruz snorted a laugh. "So, I went into Triolo's computer files and there's tons of work there. We might need a forensic accountant to make sense out of what we've got. I get the feeling we may be dealing with offshore accounts, but I don't really know. I was a little bummed. And then I looked at the photos you shot of the ledger you found in the desk drawer."

"Yeah?" trying to keep the impatience out of his voice.

It only made Cruz laugh again. "Okay, so I tried to read them, but they were too small and again, so bummed. Then I transferred them to my computer, increased the font size, and guess what?" But Jack wasn't playing. "We hit pay dirt!"

"How so?"

"That notation you pulled from the yellow pad. Didn't make any sense when I first read it. But as I skimmed through the ledger, there were no names. Only files with different numerical headings. All inked by hand. Old school. Like an old accountant would do. And did I tell you last night? This guy is even older than you are."

"Cruz ..."

"So, halfway through the ledger I hit on a new account."

"Okay?"

"27689***B. There were multiple pages of those numbers and asterisks ending with the letter B."

Cruz had Jack's full attention now.

"The file started in 2000."

"That's twenty-three years ago. When Carl was jailed." Jack's heart rate ticked up a notch. These were the moments he lived for.

"The payout was monthly. The amount started at three hundred dollars, and every few years the sum ticked up. Five years ago, Triolo started wiring a thousand a month." Cruz handed Jack a printout of the last page of the file. "Look at the date it ended. Instead of the thousand-dollar payout, Triolo wrote Void."

"The day the account was voided," Jack said quietly, "was the day Cheryl Lee was shot dead."

"Sad but true," Cruz said. "But we've still gotta tie Brannigan to Triolo."

"Glass half full, Cruz. If we can trace a call from Brannigan to Triolo's landline the day Cheryl Lee was killed, we might have him. At least have enough to scare Triolo into rolling over on Brannigan."

"Gallina and Tompkins?"

"Nick. He's got a friend at the phone company. If we start with the trace, we can backtrack and get Gallina to apply for a search warrant to make the arrest stand up in court. And if we're lucky, we might be able to get Judge Cole to agree to sign off on the search warrant."

"And guess who could be sitting in the courtroom when the jury comes back with a guilty verdict?"

"Carl Forbes."

"Should we call Tommy and the professor?"

"No. We keep it close to the vest. But hell, that's some damn good work, Cruz. Let's go after the trace."

CHAPTER 27

Jack placed a call to the Pacific Division Station and caught Nick at his desk.

"What kind of hell are you dredging up today, Jack?"

"Always a joy, Nick. How'd it go with Manny Rodriguez?"

"We caught him in his mother's house, sitting at the kitchen table in his skivvies doing laundry. Grabbed him without a fight."

"Sounds good. Look, I need a favor."

Jack gave him the iceberg tips of the new damning information. "Once the story breaks, Brannigan'll circle the wagons and make sure there are no loose ends that could come back to haunt him. I need the information before the mayor makes the announcement, or the ledger and files will disappear, along with my case against him."

"How'd you come up with the ledger?"

Jack was ready for that, and he said lightly, "That's a good question."

"For who, Jack?"

"If I violate the trust of a CI, I'll lose street cred."

"Bertolino, you're talking to me."

"And you know who you're talking to. There are lives at stake, and this could break the case wide open."

"It could also be a career ender."

"You will always have a job with me."

Nick let that nugget slide. "I can't promise. E-mail me the names, dates, and numbers of the principals, and I'll do what I can on the QT."

"Thanks, Nick."

And Nick hung up.

Jack found Judge Bradley Cole seated at a table in the Lunch Stop, a small café in the Airport Courthouse. The judge was rubbing his bald head with one hand, eating a tuna on toast with the other, while he read a court brief. He looked up as Jack threw his table in shadow and frowned.

"Jack, take a seat. You want something to eat?"

"I'm good. I just need some information."

"You were on my call list. This case I'm working is a waste of time. The defendant is representing himself. Never a good move. I think he's bipolar, and his outbursts are scaring the jury. I want to get it over with and stop wasting the taxpayers' money."

"Cheryl Lee Williams, Judge?" trying to get the man on track.

"I went over my files with a fine-tooth comb and found the police report delivered by the arresting officers, Brannigan and Cook. Their work appeared to be by the book. They mapped out the eyewitness's story and it appeared, as she did when I interviewed her, to be credible. In fact, she was compelling. Good on the stand. I found that some of her personal information had been redacted from the file because of the violent nature of the crime. The woman was afraid for her life and the life of her newborn daughter if she testified. It's a step that's often taken, and it seemed reasonable."

"And the monetary payment?"

"It's in my file, two thousand dollars. I thought it excessive, but the LAPD was footing the bill. The defense never brought it up. It wasn't for me to do his job for him. I took the win."

"Were Brannigan and Cook at your office when you coached Cheryl Lee?"

"Sure, they all came in together."

"And the files were stored ...?"

"They filled two boxes and were kept in a utility room next to my office."

"So it's possible, while you were interviewing Cheryl Lee, one of the detectives could have walked into the other room and redacted the payment to Cheryl Lee in the defense's file?"

"It's possible. Look, I'll give you this much. You asked the last time we spoke if I believed in coincidences. I gave that some serious thought, and I don't. And with the body count you described, the only reasonable inference is that someone is trying to stop the investigation. What I'm having trouble with is questioning Brannigan's motives for hiding a cash payment on a case that's twenty-three years old. There's no way to prove it. The statute of limitation has run out. And the man's on the mayor's short list for Police Chief. I really don't need the heat if your instincts are wrong."

"With respect, Judge, I think it was Gloria Millhouse who suffered the heat. I believe Brannigan and Cook coerced the confession from Carl and paid for eyewitness testimony."

Judge Cole ran his fingers across his shiny bald scalp as if he were hand brushing phantom hair. He was clearly on the fence, an unapologetic political animal. If Cole were playing Jack, if he was complicit in altering the evidence in the original case and now the cover-up, more lives would be destroyed.

Jack decided to take a leap of faith. "I have some politically explosive information that's confidential, and I need your word it won't be shared until the story breaks."

"Go on, I'll respect your request."

"We received a copy of Carl Forbes Pitchess motion."

"Brannigan and Cook's personnel records?"

"Will be made public in the next few days. It shows a history of brutality, sadism, emotional and physical abuse allegations, endemic in their careers with the LAPD. There are too many reports to question their credibility. And you just said you don't believe in coincidences."

"That's right."

"Brannigan and Cook were the arresting officers on a case that was adjudicated a year and a half before Carl's. Similar circumstance, young black defendant, white female victim. A murder, rape case. There was another similarity. The eyewitness who delivered the guilty verdict to the prosecution … was Cheryl Lee Williams."

That took the air out of the café. The judge took a sip of his now lukewarm coffee, folded the court brief he'd been reading and gazed at Jack.

"Have you spoken with Judge Myers?"

"He's willing to testify on Carl's behalf when the court schedules the evidentiary hearing. It would help to have you on board."

Jack witnessed the judge doing a balancing act on a moral tightrope. Jack decided to go all in: "Cheryl Lee had cash wired to her bank account for twenty-three years, from the day Carl was convicted to the day she was killed. Then the payments magically dried up."

"Brannigan?"

"It's looking that way."

"It would help if you had proof."

"It's coming, Judge. I may have to reach out to you."

"I'll withhold judgment on that. But copy me on your bullet points, and when the time is right, I'll compose a letter stating my support for re-examining the case."

"You're doing the right thing," Jack said. "We'll be in touch."

CHAPTER 28

Jack was in his loft standing at his stove, warming olive oil before dropping in the garlic. He poured himself a glass of Cab, hand crushed tomatoes, tore a handful of basil into rough pieces, and added it to the sauce along with some salt and red pepper flakes. He took a moment to appreciate the scent.

As if on cue, the four phones in the loft rang as one. Jack checked the digital time on the microwave: 7:30. "Nick," he said, happy for the diversion, hoping he'd delivered. "You still on the clock?"

"I thought you needed the information ASAP. I texted you the info. Delete after you download."

"Nick ..."

"I know, I'm the bomb."

"The case is picking up, and this could make a big difference. I've gotta run. I'll let you know how it turns out. Dinner's on me when I come up for air."

"Don't let me keep you."

"Later."

Jack turned the sauce down a notch to a low roll, poured another glass of wine, and checked out the pilfered phone numbers. It was a slim day for the slimy accountant: very few calls and very little activity on the date in question.

Then he hit the jackpot. His night was definitely looking up. Two phone calls matched Brannigan's number from the Rolodex Jack had found in Triolo's office. It was a different number from the one reported on court documents or the LAPD's contact sheet.

A call had been placed to Triolo from Brannigan's phone at 5:45, minutes after Cheryl Lee was killed. A half hour later, the accountant returned the call.

The calls traced to Brannigan's phone showed more activity. Around the same time period, one call was received at 5:30. Then again at 5:43. The calls lasted less than a minute. The following day, a call from the same number was placed at 11:15 AM. Just about the time the sniper shot up the big rig outside Wickenburg, in a failed attempt to shut down the investigation, and Jack for good. That number wasn't on anybody's list—it appeared to be generated from a burner. Also, less than a minute in duration.

Jack called Nick again to find out if his people could triangulate the location of the mystery number.

Nick agreed to give it a try before banging the phone down.

Jack filled a large pot of water and set it on the stove, turning the gas to high. He decided to cook spaghetti and pulled out enough for one. As he was reaching for his wineglass, the phones rang again.

"Ted Ward," Jack said. "How did it go with the mayor? And what are we looking at for a timeline?"

"Mayor Waltham loves to talk. He's a great interview. We got along famously. And as for the timeline, it's the reason I'm calling. He's afraid of a leak, and he really wants to get ahead of the story. He's calling a press conference for tomorrow afternoon. I'm in El Segundo finishing the story. The header will read, *The Mayor Drops a Bombshell and Lieutenant Brannigan Is Left Out in the Cold*. Waltham will be standing in front of the cameras at the same time my byline hits the internet. It'll give the mayor the morning to have a conversation with

Lieutenant Brannigan. He apologized if it messed with your timeline, but was sure you'd understand."

"It squeezes me," Jack said. "I'm not thrilled about it."

"So, when can we talk? This is going to set off a firestorm, and you're going to find yourself in the middle. I want to be there with you."

"I'll make good on my promise. I've got some things that just hit, so let's talk after the press conference. If something breaks before, you'll be my first call."

"Okay." Ward didn't sound convinced, but he signed off.

Just as the water was starting to boil, the phone rang again. Nick sounded mellow now, and Jack was pleased.

"The calls were triangulated, placed from a small town outside of Phoenix."

"Wickenburg?"

"The same. Home of the deceased, Cheryl Lee Williams. Damn, Jack," Nick said.

"You pick the restaurant."

"Yeah, yeah, Bertolino. I've gotta get home. Let me know how it works out."

Jack smiled as he hung up the phone. The new information tied Brannigan to Triolo. But more important, it connected Brannigan to the killer.

Jack covered the sauce and turned off the heat. He cut the gas under the boiling water and set the spaghetti pot in the sink. He called Lieutenant Gallina, who picked up on the eighth ring.

"What?"

"I get you at the wrong time, Lieutenant?"

"What do you want? My meatloaf's gonna dry out."

"Turn off the heat and throw it in the fridge. Dinner's going to have to wait. I need your full attention." Jack proceeded to lay out the case against Brannigan, his connection to Triolo, the timing, and location of the calls surrounding the shooting death of Cheryl Lee, and the attempt on Jack's life. The report of violence against Brannigan that was going to hit the airwaves in less than twenty-four hours.

"We need a search warrant for Triolo's office before the paper hits the stands and the shit hits the..."

"And who do you think we can get to sign off on what appears to be a fishing expedition this late in the day?"

"I met with Judge Cole this afternoon at the airport courthouse."

"I know Cole. He's a tough bird."

"He's been fully briefed on the case, and he's predisposed to be supportive. Fill him in on the new intel regarding the phone calls. You just have to approach him with your natural charm and wit. On second thought, maybe it's a job for Tompkins."

Gallina ignored the dig. "Let me see if I can get him on the horn. We're going after a cop, Jack. A fucking hero cop. Jesus, this better not come back to bite me in the ass."

"I can have the mayor call if we need his support. I'll ring your partner and bring him up to speed. We'll need more manpower if we get the okay."

"Jack, just sit tight. As far as I'm aware, you're still not wearing a badge. I'll call *you*."

The lieutenant hung up. Jack drained the pot of water, and set the sauce on a folded towel in the fridge. He called Cruz and brought him up to speed. They made plans to rendezvous at Triolo's storefront.

CHAPTER 29

Lieutenant Gallina stared mournfully at his plate of gray meatloaf, mashed potatoes, and green beans, an unhappy product of the twenty-four-hour greasy spoon in Koreatown. Jack had a half-eaten grilled cheese sandwich that he thought was the better part of valor.

The diner was the only game in town as they waited for Tompkins to arrive with search warrant in hand. Judge Cole had risen to the occasion, and if Jack had any lingering doubts about the judge's complicity in altering evidence in the original case, it was a distant memory. This was vindication in spades.

Triolo's office had been cordoned off with yellow tape, and uniformed officers stood guard at the front and back entrances.

"You're gonna pay for this meal tonight, but I'm gonna pay in the morning," Gallina said as he guided a forkful of meat through the congealing gravy. "The mashed potatoes are from a box, the green beans from a can," he complained, wiping a gravy drip off his white shirt.

"Didn't know you were a gourmet."

"There's a lot you don't know about me, pal."

Jack chuckled, excused himself, and walked out on the street. He was two blocks from the strip mall that housed Triolo's office. Cruz was in the shadows down the block, keeping a watchful eye on the proceedings.

Jack dialed a cell number. Ted Ward picked up on the first ring. "Where are you?" Jack said.

"Almost back from El Segundo, flying down the 405."

"If you want an exclusive, keep driving." Jack gave him the address in Koreatown where the search warrant was being served. "Bring a camera, but no contact or shots of me. I'll fill in the blanks tomorrow."

"I've got my Panasonic in the trunk. Thanks, Jack. This is fucking great."

Jack walked back into the diner and finished his grilled cheese, knowing it was going to be a long night. He was crossing his fingers that the ledger was still waiting in the desk drawer. Jack's cell pinged, and he read a text from Cruz: "Triolo's here."

Jack paid the bill and followed in Gallina's wake. The man was surprisingly fast for a slightly overweight, out-of-shape forty-something man. Tompkins pulled into the lot when they were half a block away. They could hear Triolo's shrill voice before they saw the man.

"The fuck?" A wiry, white-haired, hawk-nosed man in his sixties was red-faced, shouting at the uniformed officer blocking the entrance. "Lemme see the fuckin' paper or get the hell out of my way."

Detective Tompkins unlimbered his six-foot-three frame from his unmarked car and walked over to the riled Triolo. He stared down at the man, who looked like he was headed for a stroke, and said in a stern voice, "I got your papers right here. Now shut the fuck up, or I'll lock your ass in the back of my car until we're done here. Should only take four or five hours, your call."

Jack hung back while Gallina came forward and said to Triolo, "You might as well hand over the keys so as we won't have to break your door down."

"Motherfucker," Triolo muttered as he struggled to separate the front door key from the ring.

"I'll need the key to your office as well," Gallina said with a smirk he couldn't control.

"How the hell do you know I lock my office?"

"I'm a detective, I detect. It's what I do."

Triolo pulled a second key off the ring and handed it over.

Tompkins unlocked the front door, turned on the overhead lights, and headed for the office. He keyed the room open and gestured to his partner.

"Now step back. Go get some coffee or whatever," Gallina said to Triolo.

"Shit! I'm calling my lawyer. He'll have something to say about this."

"They usually do," Gallina said. As Triolo pulled out his cell phone, Gallina grabbed the device out of his hand. "That's in the warrant too."

Before Triolo blew up, Gallina turned his back and entered the office, closing the door behind him.

Tompkins was in the office for no more than sixty seconds when he stepped back into the small vestibule. He signaled through the glass window toward Jack, who stood curbside. He raised something into the air, and Jack let out the breath he was holding. Tompkins had the worn leather-bound ledger.

Jack crossed the street, and found Cruz in the shadowed doorway of a dry-cleaner with a hidden view of the proceedings.

An old Toyota Camry skidded to a curbside stop, and Ted Ward jumped out, opened his trunk, and strode onto the strip mall's parking lot, snapping photos of Triolo, the cops, and the graphics painted on the glass window in black. Being a smart reporter, he edged over to Triolo, who clearly was the aggrieved party, and started a conversation.

Triolo's shrill voice floated in fits and starts across Beverly and the lookie-loo traffic that was slowing to a halt. "Communist county … search warrant … illegal … Mother …"

Jack was enjoying the show. He'd briefed Gallina about the ledger and monies paid to Cheryl Lee. Gallina wanted to ask how he'd come upon the intel, but was smart enough to hold his tongue. It was a narrow warrant and limited the search to the files, Rolodex, electronics, yellow pads and ledgers. The items were carefully documented, carried out, and placed in the rear of a police van that had arrived on site for that purpose.

Jack pulled Tompkins aside and told him to check the Rolodex for Brannigan's number. "Also, it would be a wise move to have your IT crew triangulate that number with the calls received on Triolo's landline."

"Why would I want to do that?" he asked.

"You might find they match the time Cheryl Lee Williams was shot dead." Tompkins didn't ask how he knew this, but merely walked back into the office.

Jack was about to step into the pool of light created by the street lamp when Cruz tapped his shoulder and started snapping pictures with his cell phone.

SWAT Detective Joe Moran, driving his Toyota Land Cruiser, powered up the street. As the traffic slowed to a horn blaring halt, he snapped a few shots of his own. Focusing on the damning inventory being loaded in the van. His face, an angry mask.

Triolo glanced at the Land Cruiser, and a flash of recognition crossed his face. His expression darkened. As he knew damn well, the information contained in the objects the police were confiscating could mean a jail cell was in his future.

Mayor Waltham and his wife were both dressed to the nines and holding court at a Democratic fundraiser at Wolfgang Puck's restaurant in the Hotel Bel-Air. He grimaced when his cell phone vibrated. He discreetly checked the name and politely excused himself, leaving his aged porterhouse behind.

He headed into the hotel lobby. "This better be good, Jack."

"Judge Cole's search warrant was served, and we have to run it by the DA's office, but I think we've collected enough for an indictment. We should have an answer sometime tomorrow."

"Ah, Jesus. It's got to be airtight."

"It will be. But, Mayor, it's time for you to cut bait."

"Did you just go country on me?"

"And just a heads-up," Jack said, ignoring the jab. "Brannigan's already in the loop. My guess, he's rallying his troops as we speak."

"Shit."

"Detective Joe Moran, one of your newly decorated heroes, did a drive-by while the cops were loading up the evidence van. Interesting how he knew about the raid. Snapped a few photos. That means he's involved somehow in what looks more and more like a conspiracy to obstruct justice."

"It's always bad to worse with you, Bertolino," Waltham said without attitude. "I tell you what," he went on, feeling his political genes take control. "I'll reach out to Brannigan tonight, tell him I was just brought up to speed, and hoped I was misinformed. And I want you to have that reporter, Ward, contact Brannigan first thing in the morning. Tell him he just got off the phone with the mayor, and ask him if he'd like to make a comment. The kid might get lucky, but it also might knock Brannigan off his game. Then tell Ward to run with the story. Don't wait for me. It'll go viral and we'll be guaranteed a full house. I've got the press conference set for four-thirty, in time to get coverage in the evening news. We might even make the nationals. Keep me informed, Jack. Must run, thanks."

CHAPTER 30

"What happened to innocent until proven guilty, Mayor?" Commander Brannigan was sitting on his living room couch in his T-shirt, drinking a beer. His voice was calm, disarming. It caught the mayor off guard, but then again, he knew the commander hadn't been surprised by the call. Brannigan had time to prepare.

The mayor was lounging on the overstuffed leather chair in his den. He was still wearing dress slacks, but his starched white shirt was open at the collar. "You know better than that," he said, his voice measured. "You're a political animal. I couldn't have been more surprised, and hoped it wasn't true. But as soon as the story breaks, my hands are tied. There's no easy way to say it, but you're out of the running."

"You're making a mistake here, Henry. Take a deep breath, and see how it plays out before jumping to false conclusions and making statements you can't take back."

"What I can't do is rewrite your history, Brannigan. I feel terrible about this. You were my guy. You should've been more forthcoming during the vetting process. Would have saved us both the aggravation.

If I were you, I'd get a good lawyer, or a PR firm, because the press is going to swarm and blowback is headed your way."

"I don't know the man. This Italian guy you're talking about," Brannigan said, hammering the *I* in Italian. "How are they tying us together? Don't take this the wrong way, Henry, but I think you're the one who's going to need a PR firm. And if you drag me through the mud, you'll need a lawyer for the civil suit I'll file for defamation of character. You're backing the wrong horse here."

"I'm sorry you're taking this so badly. I know in the end, you'll do the right thing and maybe come out of this whole."

"Really? Whole would be your continued support for police chief?"

"That's off the table."

"Hmm. I appreciate you giving me a heads-up."

"Well, we go way back."

"And don't forget that."

"I'm not sure I'm comfortable with the subtext, but I'll say good night."

The mayor hung up, and Brannigan sat deathly still. His only reaction to the call was the vein in his temple that was swollen and pulsing. He took a swig of beer and checked the charge on his cell phone. He had to think through how he was going to redirect this shit storm.

Freddie Triolo was alone in his office. The door was open because there was nothing left to hide. It seemed like the police knew exactly what they wanted when they violated his privacy. How the hell did that work? He was bone tired and took a long pull of the Canadian Club, re-corked, and slammed the bottle down on his desk.

There was nothing to tie him to Brannigan, and that's exactly what he'd told the commander, who took the news surprisingly well. Brannigan's name wasn't on any of the documents, and his advice to Triolo was to sit tight and he'd work the cover-up, if one were needed, from his end.

The power of being a cop, Triolo thought. Still, he felt violated, and he wasn't sure he fully trusted the commander. He took another shot of whiskey straight from the bottle, then decided to check his file cabinets. He worked up a manic head of steam as he opened and slammed the near empty four-drawer cabinets that had held years of records. He was almost on his knees as he pulled the bottom drawer out—and didn't immediately register the twisted manila rope that had been looped over his head.

Triolo's head jerked up as he sensed a presence. He raised a hand blindly and grabbed the rope. He squealed in fear.

The slight man was straightened as the noose lifted his body. It ripped tight, pinning his fingers to his neck.

He never saw his ski-masked assassin. The killer spun and yanked Triolo off his feet. His short legs kicked like he was running in place. One arm flailed but found no purchase. The killer bounced Triolo off his back, muscling the manila rope tighter, until it broke through the skin of his slender fingers and skinny neck, tighter, and tighter again, until Triolo's legs fell limp.

The killer dropped the little man onto the dirty rugged floor, righted the desk chair that had been knocked over, and swung the length of rope over the sprinkler system's rusted pipe. He pulled hand over hand until Triolo dangled three feet off the ground. He tied the rope to the leg of the desk, overturned the chair again, making it look like suicide, and exited the office out into the back alley.

Leslie Sager was naked and angry. She straddled Jack, who wore a surprised look on his face.

"You decided to wake me from a beautiful sleep, have your way with me, and then share you've not only been in contact with Vincent Cardona, you had a meeting with his twenty-three-year-old daughter."

"She's twenty-four."

"Jesus, Jack."

"It's the first time you and I've spoken in a few days. It got away from me."

Leslie spun off the bed and grabbed her favorite robe out of the closet. Walking to her balcony, she looked out toward the Pacific. She took a deep breath of the cool air before stepping back into the room. "You went to Cardona for a favor, and now you owe the mobster."

"That's about it."

"What the hell were you thinking?"

"That I needed a leg up on the case. The righteous bust today never would have happened without his intel. It seemed like a fair trade."

"Sleeping with his daughter?"

"Leslie?"

"God, you're infuriating."

"I didn't sleep with her. I checked on her. That was our agreement. And I'll have to do it again."

"You see? You are so naïve. They never stop once they have their hooks in you. You got lucky the first time—hell, the first two times. Don't let it go to your head."

Leslie poured some wine into her empty glass and took a long pull. It calmed her down some.

"Do you want me to leave?"

"Yes … no, you just piss me off so."

"I've been known to have that effect on people. But there is an upside."

"And what's that?"

"Angry sex. I hear it's pretty good."

"Huh …" Leslie gave that some thought, took another sip of wine, looking at Jack over the rim of her glass. "I am angry."

"I'm a little ticked off myself," he said.

Jack pushed himself up on his elbows, his unblinking brown eyes getting lost in Leslie's blues. Leslie walked back toward the bed and deposited her glass on the nightstand. Their breathing grew shallow even before their bodies touched. Leslie dropped her robe and slipped under the white silk sheet. "I'm really angry," she said with a whispered urgency.

Jack didn't have to be asked twice.

A perfect day, ended on a high note.

And then Jack's cell phone rang.

CHAPTER 31

Jack made a hard left off Beverly and pulled his rental car into the strip mall, thick with flashing lights, police cars, a medical examiner's van, and unmarked vehicles. Tompkins was sipping a Starbucks as Jack hurried to the accountant's front door.

"The lieutenant wanted you to see for yourself. They haven't touched the body, ME's waiting until the crime-scene crew arrives."

Jack walked through the small vestibule to Triolo's office. Gallina was gazing in, lost in thought, dead on his feet.

"A suicide?" Gallina said. "Looks like he maybe changed his mind. I hear that happens a lot. His fingers are caught in the rope. They bled, the neck bled." He looked very dissatisfied. "I don't know. It looks too violent for suicide."

Triolo's body weight had cracked the fire alarm's rusted pipe. A fine mist was spraying the room. Triolo was drenched from head to foot, his hair and clothes plastered to his scrawny body. The rug, which hadn't been washed since it was laid down, was a soggy mess that smelled of pizza and sewage and dog. Triolo's body swayed and twisted from a draft coming in from outside.

"So much for using Triolo to roll over on Brannigan," Gallina said. We may be fucked. Ideas?"

"I got a call from Cruz, who took shots of Triolo raging in the parking lot while you were executing the warrant. Something about him looked familiar. Cruz had worked with the security video from Victorville. Trying to ID the sham lawyer who contracted Larry the Rat to kill Carl Forbes. It sounds more complicated than it is. Triolo was playing the lawyer, and he had his head tilted away from the camera. Thought he was smart."

"So?" Still not getting it.

"Cruz was able to push in on his ear. It was a definitive match. So, we have that, and Brannigan's tied to the killer, and Triolo, through the phone call placed minutes after the shooting death of Cheryl Lee Williams."

Gallina gave that some thought. "Still, not enough to hang the case on."

"Not yet, but with the Pitchess motion, and Brannigan getting convictions in two different cases using Cheryl Lee as the eyewitness, we've got enough to squeeze him. And you'll never have to call him sir."

Gallina shook his head, too tired to follow Jack's train of thought.

"There'll be an announcement coming tomorrow," Jack said. "He won't make the cut for chief. Let the accountants dig into Triolo's files and the ledger. My guess, they'll find offshore accounts tied to Brannigan, and we'll have enough to hang him."

"Couldn't happen to a nicer prick," Gallina said.

It was eleven o'clock when Jack woke up in his own bed. Thank God he e-mailed the crew to let him sleep in. But they all knew he would've been in a foul mood with only three hours. He made a pot of coffee, tossed a bagel into the toaster, woke up his computer, and pulled up the *LA Times*. Ted Ward's story was the lead. The writing was concise—and damning.

He'd gotten a statement from Commander Brannigan, per Mayor Waltham's request. Brannigan proclaimed his innocence and promised there'd be hell to pay for tarnishing his name. He believed in the rule of law, and the courts would be the final arbiters, not unnamed sources looking to curry political favors and votes.

At first it appeared Brannigan was righting the ship. Showing the public persona he'd polished coming up through the ranks of the LAPD.

And then Ward threw a wicked jab. He asked about the nature of a phone call placed between the commander and the accountant Freddie Triolo minutes after Cheryl Lee Williams was killed. The question was met with a moment of silence.

Ward rocketed an uppercut. "She was your eyewitness in a cold case, wasn't she? The Carl Forbes case that's in the process of being re-litigated?"

"I seem to remember her name."

With Brannigan on the ropes Ward went in for the kill. "If my sources are correct, the Forbes' case wasn't the first time Miss Williams testified for you. She was also your star witness in the Tyrone Stevens' case a year or so before Forbes. Any comment?"

You could feel Ward's joy as he wrote, "The commander cleared his throat, said, 'Excuse …' and clicked off."

Ted Ward and the *LA Times* win with a knockout.

Jack was satisfied with Ward's reporting. He didn't draw conclusions, just stated the facts. Facts that caught Brannigan off-guard and forced him to shut down, letting the readers to fill in the gaps. The tease would also give the mayor wind at his back at the afternoon's press conference. He could act devastated by the breaking news and take the high road, making a swift decision to eliminate Brannigan from the race for police chief.

Brannigan's choice to cut off the interview cemented his fate, making him appear defensive and diminished. Not the tower of strength you'd want running the third-largest police force in the United States.

Jack knew it would also make Brannigan deadly.

Jack placed a call to Leslie, who picked up on the first ring.

"How's your back?" he asked, smiling.

"Why, Jack, I'm not sure what you mean. Although your early

morning theory about conflict and pleasure proved quite invigorating."

The way Leslie said invigorating got Jack's blood pumping, but this was a business call. "Do we have enough for an indictment?"

"You're no fun," she said, brought back to earth. "Not yet. Still dotting the I's. DA's position is the preponderance of evidence is circumstantial. Without having Triolo to roll over on Brannigan, it's a hard sell."

Jack wasn't surprised, but he wasn't happy. "What about the ME's report?"

"Still waiting."

"Can you give me a heads-up?"

"I think I already did. Or are you just using me for political advantage?"

"Hah. Never crossed my mind."

"So, Jack, who leaked the information about the phone calls between Brannigan and Triolo to the *LA Times*?"

"I wouldn't know. Ted Ward appears to be well connected. A good reporter never gives up his sources."

"Right," Leslie said drolly. "Gotta run, Jack. I'll be in touch."

Mayor Waltham's press conference went off without a hitch. The major networks were all in attendance. Waltham's approval rating spiked eight percent. His countenance appeared gubernatorial and increased his chances in the upcoming race.

Brannigan wasn't around for comment. He was cloistered in his den with reporters and camera crews standing guard on his front lawn, waiting for a sighting.

"Put an end to this prick," Brannigan snarled, pacing like a man possessed.

Councilman Corcoran pushed himself up from behind his power desk at City Hall. As he quietly closed the door, he glanced at the photograph with his old friend's deer hunting. "We're too late."

"I want it done."

No response.

"Are you questioning me?" Brannigan said.

Corcoran snapped, "I'm not committing suicide for you or any man. Are you listening? Just because you screwed the pooch with Bertolino, don't come down on me. You might need a job someday."

The silence on the other end of the line made Corcoran's throat constrict. The man he was talking to had a violent history. He picked up his stained mug, fought to still the slight quake in his hand, and took a sip of cold, bitter coffee.

"I'll get it done," Corcoran finally conceded, "But this is your play. We're better off covering tracks than making new ones. You can only shut so many mouths before they come screaming back from the grave."

CHAPTER 32

"Did you move in?" Jack asked Professor Anderson, who was sporting a Neil Young T-shirt and skintight jeans. He was pacing in Tommy's suite like a man on a caffeine high, but Jack soon found out it was adrenaline fueled.

"Good one, Jack … Tommy's a silver-tongued genius."

Tommy raised both hands, palms up. "It's a gift."

Cruz barked a laugh and drained his bottle of Coke.

"Word was just handed down from the DA's office and the courts," the professor said, barely able to contain himself. "We're approved to retest the DNA samples from Shelley Goldstein's body and clothing. I'm having them shipped to the lab we've been using, and then we're off to the races."

"Sex offenders' database?" Jack said.

"That's our first stop."

"That's some damn good news. How long will it take?"

"A few days to cull the DNA samples. Then we start our database search. Fingers crossed, gentlemen."

"What can I do to help?" Keith Millhouse asked holding his cell phone to his ear, as he watched waves curl and dissolve to sea green foam from his patio.

"You've already done it," Jack said over the car's Bluetooth. "Your reputation opened doors and loosened lips. Judge Cole wouldn't have been so forthcoming if Gloria wasn't your daughter. We never would have gotten the search warrant. I just wanted to bring you up to speed."

"Appreciated. Do you think Brannigan killed her?"

"I'm not there yet. I know he was complicit in the false imprisonment of Carl Forbes. Gloria thought so, too. I know he had something to gain from quashing the case." Not jumping to conclusions was the right play here. "I don't have enough factually to tie him to your daughter's death, but he might be calling the shots. That's one of the tracks I'm following."

"Thanks for the call, Jack." Keith sounded weary.

"When I have more, you'll hear from me," and Jack signed off.

Jack tipped the doorman and entered the Chop House in Beverly Hills. It was nine-thirty: prime time. Peter Maniacci stood guard at the downstairs bar. He waved Jack over and leaned in close. "That prick John Franco is upstairs again. Second time this week. Runs up a big bill and walks out the door like he owns the place."

"Where's Frankie the Man?"

"Upstairs keeping an eye out. We don't need no more trouble on the home front, but I know Angelica is feeling the pressure."

Jack headed up the carpeted stairs. The piano player was belting out a Broadway medley as Jack raked the crowded room. Drinks were flowing, the bar standing room only, and the booths and tables were full. Jack headed to the back, where the kitchen entrance was located.

Angelica stood blocked in the hallway beyond the swinging kitchen doors. The man crowding her was John Franco. A middle-aged, suave Italian, with slicked-back hair, wearing a custom-tailored suit.

Angelica's beautiful face was an angry mask of resolve. Franco was violating her personal space and accentuating his speech with a jabbing finger.

Jack cut across the room and thumped the man on the back, causing him to straighten. "You want to step back, get out of the woman's face?"

Franco glanced over his shoulder and said, "Get the fuck out of here," like he was talking to a jamoke.

"One of us is on his way out."

Franco coiled and spun, leading with a blistering haymaker. His jacket fanned open revealing a Colt .38 in a shoulder rig.

Jack grabbed his fist like he was fielding a fastball and plucked the man's snub nose with his free hand. He muscled Franco's hand back until his wrist threatened to snap. Frankie-the-Man bounded toward them. "What's the play here, Franco?" the big man rasped, his voice like broken glass.

Franco's body uncoiled and Jack released his grip, never breaking eye contact. The gangster's narrowed eyes demanded blood. He fought the urge to rub his wrist, which was painful and swelling.

"C'mon, the house is full. We don't need the trouble," Frankie said, meaning, *you* don't need the trouble.

The confrontation had happened so quickly, the play was lost on the crowded room of diners.

"Franco was just leaving," Angelica said. "Dinner's on me, our conversation is over."

"Just trying to lend a hand."

"Don't bother. We're done talking, you hear me? Finito," she said.

Jack dumped the bullets from the revolver into his pocket and handed the weapon, barrel first, back to the wise guy. He snatched it out of Jack's hand and flashed a tight grin. "You, my friend, are a dead man."

"What part of finito don't you understand?" Jack said lightly.

Franco's head bobbed. "You haven't seen the last of me."

Jack and Angelica watched as Frankie-the-Man escorted Franco back to his table, where he flicked his hand angrily in a c'mon gesture. His date jumped out of the booth and played catch-up as Franco strode stiffly across the room, past the white grand piano toward the carpeted stairs.

"Never a dull moment," Angelica said, trying to pull herself together. She slid her hand through the crux in Jack's arm and walked him down the hallway into the private office.

"He offered me an ultimatum," Angelica said, pacing in the small, well-appointed office like a panther. "We could partner up, the smug bastard said. I'd be the face of the Chop House; he'd be the silent partner. Said he already ran the idea past Uncle Mickey, who wasn't against the move."

"You think that's true, or was he just testing the waters?"

"I don't know what to think. But I'm going to need some more men to make sure there are no more surprise visits."

Jack didn't know what to say. He wasn't surprised by the attempted takeover. Mickey Razzano and the New York family had tried to take control the semi-legal way, sending a group of investors with their lawyer mouthpiece. Now they were pushing, trying to muscle their way in. A Mafia takeover.

Angelica was caught in the middle. Trying to keep the business alive for her father, and now trying to stay alive. Jack didn't want any part of the internecine warfare, but he wouldn't turn his back on Angelica.

A knock on the door stopped their conversation. Frankie-the-Man stuck his melon head in. "Sorry for not being there, Angelica. Won't happen again."

"No worries. We need to have a meeting before we close. Let the crew know."

"Will do." The big man looked contrite as he quietly closed the door.

Angelica walked over to Jack and slipped into his arms and they embraced. Her body was vibrating; Jack could feel her heart beating against his chest and tried to calm the adrenaline flowing through her body and taking him over.

This was mafia business, and more trouble than he'd signed on for. But when Angelica raised her head and searched his eyes, he pulled her tighter, lifting her into a kiss.

It was close to 2:00 AM by the time Jack pulled into the driveway of his loft building. He'd circled the block twice and hadn't seen anything unusual.

The man who sat crouched in the weather-beaten green Prius with dark-tinted windows wasn't sure what kind of car Jack was driving. His Mustang hadn't left the building in days. He swiped a thick shock of red hair out of his eyes and snapped a series of shots the second time the black five series BMW drove past and made the right turn into his building.

A few minutes later, the light from the elevator shone on the fourth floor. Using the telephoto lens, the camera followed Jack as he walked down the open-air hallway, keyed his door, and entered his unit.

The man in the Prius tapped out a quick text, and forwarded the photographs of Jack and the BMW. He waited until the lights went out in the loft before driving away.

CHAPTER 33

It wasn't easy spending time with Larry the Rat, but Jack put up with the antiseptic smell, the man's scab-ridden attitude, and the overall cloying environment of the Victorville Penitentiary's medical ward because he wanted to tie the Rat to Brannigan through his now dead mouthpiece Freddie Triolo.

The man was still on heavy opioids to deal with the excruciating pain from burns and skin grafts, but finally his eyes blinked open again.

"Do you remember me?"

Larry tried to focus. "Yeah, I fucked your mother while you shot the video."

"Here're the pictures I wanted you to see," Jack said, ignoring the taunt. He pulled up the photo of Triolo walking through the metal detector, entering the prison. "This was Triolo *before*." His face was partially obscured from the camera.

"This man told you he was a lawyer, a week before you tried to fry Carl Forbes. That didn't go too well for you, I notice."

"Blow me."

"And this is what he looks like now." Jack showed him the photo of Triolo hanging from the rafters in his office.

The medical examiner had weighed in on Triolo's cause of death. He ruled it a murder because the top three vertebrae were ruptured in a way his ninety-eight-pound body could not have caused, even if he'd changed his mind at the last minute and struggled until he was asphyxiated. Triolo was dead before he was hung, to make it look like suicide.

Jack held the picture at arm's length, then moved it close to the man's nose.

"So what? I've seen worse," the Rat croaked through cracked lips.

"So, what I need you to explain is the deal you struck that day. How it was structured. What was your end? And did you know the man who sent the mouthpiece?" The Rat was looking queasy, and Jack drove his point home. "When I asked you before, you said you were half dead, or some bullshit like that. If you talk, I'll make sure you're moved to a protected ward, and you'll live to enjoy another Thursday mac-and-cheese night. If you don't, you won't make it through the week. You see, the cop that set you up is cleaning house. You're a loose end. All the pain you've been suffering is just a prelude to hell."

The Rat's eyes drifted, as if he were struggling to formulate an answer but losing his train of thought. He whispered something inaudible. Jack leaned in closer.

The Rat tried to spit in Jack's face. His mouth was too dry to succeed, but his breath was enough to make Jack gag.

Jack fought the urge to launch his fist and signaled to the guard instead. He'd have Tompkins trace the telephonic timeline with Brannigan and Triolo after he met with the Rat and plotted Carl's death.

Jack decided to pick Carl's brain while he was at the prison, and the warden was happy to comply. Jack pulled out the headshots Cruz had blown up along with the original photo of Corcoran and his buddies, deer hunting.

"What can you tell me about this guy, Chip Boyd."

"Like what?"

"Where was he in the hierarchy of his crew? Any feelings you can remember. Was he a regular guy? Likeable, whatever comes to mind," Jack said.

Carl slid Corcoran's photo next to Boyd's. "He was second banana. Tried to out–Corcoran Corcoran, but didn't have it in him. I think it probably pissed him off. He was too standoffish. Wasn't the smartest, wasn't the coolest. Didn't have that, you know, ease that came natural to Corcoran. Everyone wanted a piece of that boy."

"Did that piss you off?"

"I wasn't, uh, never gonna be buds with their crew. So, maybe a little. We were all hormonal as get out. All anybody talked about was sex. Nobody was doing much, just a lot of talk."

"Corcoran?"

"If anybody was getting something-something, yeah, then it would've been Corcoran."

"Shelley Goldstein?"

"He didn't mouth off like the rest. If he did, I never heard. I spent years in here trying to put him in the hot seat, but could never really figure out the angle."

Jack brought Carl up to speed on Brannigan, the DNA, and the momentum the case was taking on, and then signaled to the guard.

He glanced back through the bars and caught Carl permitting himself a tentative smile. Unwilling to let go. Too easy to get sucked in, and then get hurt. Protecting himself was too ingrained, too deep in the muscle to let go until things got real. Jack understood.

Jack checked his watch as he was led into the open central yard. Vincent Cardona stood under the tower and signaled Jack over. The two men started walking the perimeter without the preamble of social niceties. This was an unscheduled visit, and Cardona read Jack's discomfort.

"What?" he finally said when he was far enough from the tower guard that their lips couldn't be read.

"You've got trouble on the reservation, and I'm afraid your daughter's caught in the middle." Jack went on to describe the events as they played out the night before. "I can't tell you how to run your life, Vincent, but someone needs to reach out to Mickey Razzano and have him call off the dogs. John Franco is going to be a thorn in your side, and he doesn't look like he'll go gently into the effing night unless it's in a pine box."

Cardona belched behind his meaty fist, his eyes angry slits. "I've got to think on this. Thanks for the heads-up."

"Don't take too much time. Angelica needs support, now. I can't be there twenty-four/seven. I'm up to my ankles in cockroaches."

Cardona nodded, and signaled to the guard on the door. Jack took his leave and headed into the building, leaving Cardona to worry about the danger he'd created for his only daughter. The love of his life.

Once free of the oppressive walls, Jack jumped in the BMW, keyed up Miles Davis's *Kind of Blue* and did a gravel-spitting exit from Victorville Penitentiary, leaving the prison in his rearview mirror. There wasn't much traffic and he powered down the windows and opened up the Beemer, enjoying the car's responsiveness and the fresh air.

He pushed the car to eighty on the four-lane highway and felt like he was doing thirty. He glanced in the review and saw two rice rockets heading in his direction. He didn't give them more than a second's thought until he looked up again, and the bikes were closing the distance. The fools had to be doing ninety.

At the same time he was approaching Vasquez Rocks, a place that always put a smile on his face. The symmetrical rock formations jutting out of the red sand had the feel of a Martian landscape. The area had been used for multiple Hollywood film shoots because of the rocky terrain.

Jack's smile faded when he saw a bright flash of sunlight, like the reflection from a mirror—or a rifle scope—piercing the daylight from the highest ridge. His eyes flicked to the rearview. The motorcycles were closing in. The situation immediately dire.

Jack eased his foot off the gas and let the car slow some.

One of the bikes was about to crawl up the car's trunk, and Jack saw a glint of silver as the ski-masked biker pulled out a 9mm.

Jack stomped on the brakes.

The motorcycle smashed into the bumper.

A high-powered round punctured the hood of his car from the ridge atop Vasquez Rocks.

The ski-masked biker went airborne and slammed down on the hood of Jack's car, cracking the windshield with his helmet. Scrabbling to hold on, the man locked eyes with Jack.

His motorcycle raked the side of the car. The engine whined as it bounced head over tail on the concrete surface, creating a shower of sparks as it slid driverless down the road. The gas tank ignited. The cycle exploded.

The second biker couldn't brake in time and rocketed past.

"You mother fucker," Jack yelled as he pulled hard on the wheel, tossing the biker off the car's hood onto the highway.

Jack barreled across the freeway's shoulder and raced down a slight incline, fighting to keep the car from rolling over. The shocks bounced on rocks and chaparral as a second high-powered round punctured the roof.

"Shit," Jack screamed. He felt a jolt of pain as the third bullet raked his upper arm, sending a shock wave through his body.

He fought to keep the BMW on track as he muscled the car toward a copse of trees and out of the shooter's sight line. When he came close, he pumped the brakes and the car went into a power skid. The axle cracked and the sound of metal wrenching was ear-splitting. The front wheel folded in on itself as the car's bumper cut a trench in the rocky soil. The car came to a teeth-rattling stop as it smashed into several trees.

The airbag exploded. White powder billowed in the driver's compartment. Jack shook off the impact and cleared the bag. He had to move fast. He hit the OnStar button and yelled 911 as he leapt from the vehicle. He pulled his Glock from the leather shoulder rig he'd secured under the front seat, and jacked a round into the chamber.

An SUV raced past the black smoke billowing from the burning hulk of the motorcycle on the highway above, and skidded to a stop out of Jack's sight line.

Jack charged deeper into the overgrowth, his gun cocked and

loaded. And then he heard tires squealing away. The SUV driver not bothering to check on the accident or his condition.

He pushed through the tree line running as fast as his legs would carry him, heading for the sniper on Vasquez Rocks. His heart was pounding, his hearing acute. By the time he got to the base of the rocks, he heard an engine turn over. Jack sprinted around the biggest outcropping of rocks, leading with the barrel of his gun, and stopped short.

A rooster tail of dust obscured the vehicle in the distance as it vanished around a bend in the service road. Overcome with panic-fueled adrenaline, Jack doubled over at the waist, sucking big gulps of air.

When it was clear nobody was following, he hiked back to the BMW, spoke to the OnStar rep, and explained the situation. He asked her to alert the first responders that he was licensed to carry, had a loaded weapon, and had been the victim of an armed attack.

Jack leaned against the totally trashed BMW and tried to control his breathing. He was light-headed, his back a molten sheet of pain. He grabbed his throbbing arm and pulled back a bloody hand. His sleeve was drenched in blood. His eyes raked the landscape as he heard the distant approach of sirens.

CHAPTER 34

Jack was standing on the side of the I-14 when the first black and white arrived with red, blue, and white lights flashing. Jack gave the young cop the Cliffs Notes version of the attack, and the officer went down the embankment to check out the bullet-riddled BMW.

They were soon joined by another cop car, a fire truck, and EMT vehicle. The fallen attacker was nowhere to be seen, just the burnt-out skeleton of the downed motorcycle.

The paramedic made Jack sit on the side of his emergency vehicle while he cut off his shirt, cleaned and wrapped the deep bloody gash the bullet had opened in his upper arm.

"You're going to need stitches. This is too much for me to handle here. We'll take you to Sand Canyon, where they can make you whole."

The first responding officer walked back up the hill and said, "Jesus Christ, you're lucky to be alive."

Jack nodded and said, "I need to get up on the ridge and check out the sniper's nest."

"Not until you're sewn up," the young cop said. "I don't want anybody bleeding out on my watch."

"Let me call Lieutenant Gallina, LAPD, and get the L.A. crime scene crew up here," Jack said. "They're up to speed on the case and know what they're looking for. Good guys."

"I've got no issue with that. I'll call my boss, secure the area, and your guys can take it from there."

"Thank you." Jack got on the phone and set things in motion. He also placed a call to Cruz and Tommy, who offered to pick him up at urgent care and drive him back to the marina. Once Jack was comfortable the crime scene was under wraps, he took a ride with the paramedic to get stitched up. Happy to be alive.

Jack sat in his favorite booth at Hal's Bar & Grill. Nick Aprea sat opposite and tossed back a chilled shot of Herradura Silver, then bit into a bitter wedge of lime.

Jack had showered, shaved, and was wearing a black T-shirt. His upper arm was taped and wrapped in a gauze bandage.

Arsinio placed a Stoli martini with three olives in front of Jack and another shot of tequila. Nick remarked, "With those pain meds you should probably eat more than fuckin' olives."

"I'll take a cheeseburger, Arsinio. Thanks." And then to Nick, "You should probably eat more than lime wedges."

"Point taken. Make that two, my friend."

"I'm glad you're in one piece, Jack," Arsinio added before disappearing into the kitchen. Never one to intrude.

"Ditto," Nick said nodding his head, satisfied with his response.

"Let me get this straight. You heard Detective Joe Moran threaten me if I screwed up Brannigan's chances for police chief. I did, in fact, screw up Brannigan's chances, and all you can come up with is, ditto?"

"I'm a man of few words." Nick took a lick of salt, tossed back the shot of booze before biting down on a lime wedge. "If we were sure Moran was involved, I'd hunt him down myself."

Jack knew he's just gotten the answer as to why Nick had been doing recon outside his loft building earlier in the week, and why he didn't fight him when asked to triangulate the phone calls to Brannigan. "I've got Cruz going down the list to find out if anyone on the SWAT team was hospitalized today. Broken bones, whatever. That motorcycle wasn't the only thing that got bent out of shape. Because if it's someone on their team, they'll be circling the wagons."

"It's getting tougher to get that info, with all the urgent care hospitals in the area. If there's cash on the table, doctors fighting insurance companies are more willing to turn a blind eye and not report accidents."

"Did you run into Brannigan today?"

"I called and got the cold shoulder. Go figure. But in a few days they're doing their bimonthly training exercise. We could pay them a visit. Show up early, see if anybody's limping onto the shooting range, or MIA."

"Brannigan may be indicted before then," Jack said. Then he glanced up and his face creased into a smile.

Leslie stood beyond the booth, having heard the last bit of conversation. "He doesn't know it yet, but he's being brought in for questioning tomorrow." She waited for Nick to be a gentleman and slide over, then took the seat across from Jack, where she could get a good look at the battered warrior. "Jack, Jack, Jack. What was Tommy's plan?"

As if on cue, Tommy walked up the aisle, and Jack moved over to give him a seat. "Tommy," Leslie went on, "I thought you were going to set Jack up solving white-collar crimes. I liked that plan. It was a good plan."

"He went rogue on me," Tommy said. "I'd like to say I wish I was with you in your latest skirmish, Jack, but what I saw of your car, I'd be a dead man. But hey, you don't look half bad." Tommy took an exaggerated look at Jack's bandaged arm. "I take it back, you look like hell."

Jack enjoyed the banter, but kept everyone focused. "We'll know sometime tomorrow whether the lead pulled from the BMW matches the rounds that killed Cheryl Lee."

"I'm having second thoughts about breaking bread with you in public," Nick said. "You've become a human target."

"Brannigan's the nexus," Jack said. "Let the forensic accountants do their work and tie one or more offshore accounts to the commander and we've got him. I still don't understand his connection to Councilman Corcoran, but they're attached at the hip. I know it."

"It will be interesting to see how he responds to Brannigan being defrocked," Leslie said.

"I'm gonna sic the *Times* reporter on Corcoran. Ask for a statement. Rattle his cage."

Arsinio dropped off Leslie's and Tommy's drinks, and the table toasted to cage rattling.

Jack and Leslie strolled toward her car, past a group of tourists window-shopping and taking selfies of the high-end retail shops on Abbot Kinney.

"Do you want to follow me home?" Leslie said.

"Not tonight, the pain pills are kicking in. I'm going to crash on the boat for the next week or two, because I must have been tracked from the loft this morning. I'm not spending time there until this is settled."

"Okay, I understand." Leslie opened the door to her Lexus and turned to Jack. Her eyes probing. Not angry, resigned. "You saw her again."

Jack was tired, he wanted to evade, but after coming close to death for the third time in as many weeks, he couldn't summons the energy. "Last night. There was an emergency at the Chop House. I found myself in the middle of it. Not my finest hour. You were right. I asked for a favor from Cardona and now I'm in his debt."

"Oh, Jack. What are you going to do?"

"Hopefully, the right thing."

Leslie stepped close and feathered a kiss on his lips. "You take care."

Jack had an uneasy feeling as Leslie slid into her car, turned over the engine and motored down the boulevard. There seemed to be finality to her goodbye. He felt empty and at a loss for words. He needed sleep and made a mental note to call Ted Ward.

First things first, though. Once Jack showered on his boat, he put on a pair of sweats, sat in the director's chair on his deck and dialed a number in Reno. "Duke," Jack said to the floor manager at the Eldorado. "Sorry to bother you, but I've got a question."

"Hey, night owl, what can I do you for?"

"I'm trying to run down Boyd and he's not answering his cell. Could you have him call me when he's off shift?"

"Would if I could, but he called in sick. Got another man to cover, so he's not in any hot water. Said he'd be in tomorrow night. Is he in trouble?"

An alarm bell went off in Jack's mind. "No, nothing important, just a loose end I'm hoping he can help me with."

"If that's it, I'm signing off."

"Thanks, Duke. I'm gonna look you up when I come to town. Drinks are on me."

"I'll take you up on that."

Jack hung up, and sent a text to Cruz. He wanted him to dive into Chip Boyd's background. He also wanted to meet for breakfast and needed Cruz to drive. Jack's arm throbbed, but that didn't hurt as much as his back. He downed another Vicodin.

Jack was concerned he wouldn't be able to sleep with the adrenaline rush of the day. But with the slight roll of his craft, the comforting smell of salt air, and the rhythmic tapping of taut lines striking aluminum masts, he passed out before his head hit the bunk.

CHAPTER 35

Councilman Corcoran pushed through the doors at City Hall and marched down the concrete steps to street level. His brow was furrowed, his body rigid. He slid on his sunglasses, only to find himself blocked by Ted Ward.

"Councilman Corcoran, Ted Ward, *LA Times*. I'd like to get your reaction to Commander Brannigan losing his bid for police chief?"

The councilman started walking, with Ward on his heels. He spoke in clipped tones over his shoulder. "I'm very disappointed. The man's an American hero."

Ward kept pace. "Have you heard the rumor he's about to be indicted? He's a suspect of interest in the recent shooting death of Cheryl Lee Williams."

Corcoran stopped in his tracks. "I don't deal in rumor, only facts. I know nothing about the case. Now, you'll have to excuse me, I'm running late."

Ward pressed, "Cheryl Lee Williams was an eyewitness in a twenty-three-year-old murder trial."

"Not ringing a bell."

"Funny, you were on the list of suspects the commander submitted to the DA's office and the defense attorney back in 2000. Brannigan was one of the arresting officers. He questioned you himself."

Corcoran straightened his sunglasses, stalling for time. "Oh, that's right. That's right. Jesus, that's a long time ago," the councilman said like it was just coming back to him. "It was a terrible tragedy. Happened close to home. Everyone in the neighborhood was questioned. I was never called to testify."

"So you do remember? What are the chances you'd become a political ally of the detective who questioned you in the rape-murder of Shelley Goldstein? One of your classmates. And how could you forget Cheryl Lee Williams, the eyewitness who testified against the defendant Carl Forbes and put him away for life? She was also from your neighborhood."

"Sorry." He flashed a studied smile that never reached his eyes. "I have no further comment." The councilman juked past Ward and headed for a Town Car that had just pulled up.

"How about Gloria Millhouse?" Ward hammered, "A young woman who died under suspicious circumstances. She was in your office a month ago. Asked for your help re-litigating the case against Carl Forbes. You were one of the last persons to see her alive."

Corcoran jumped into the back of the black Lincoln and slammed the door as the car pulled silently away from the curb.

When Ward was sure the conversation had been recorded, he looked up from his micro-digital recorder and nodded. Jack gave him a thumbs-up as he rolled by in the passenger seat of Cruz's Mini Cooper. Cruz followed the Town Car at a discreet distance.

"I spoke with Gallina's tech crew that worked the scene yesterday. He said the VIN number had been filed off the headstock tube on the frame of the motorcycle. The license was charred but readable. Reported stolen six months ago. There's no way to trace the bike to its owner," Jack said.

"What about prints on the Beemer's hood?" Cruz asked.

"He came up with some partials he's running through the system.

Didn't sound optimistic. Let's hope Ward put the fear of God into the councilman. It'll be interesting to see who he goes running to."

Jack didn't have long to wait. The Lincoln Town Car pulled to the curb on Figueroa Street, in front of El Compadre Restaurant, across from the Staples Center. Downtown modern chic mixed with old world charm and classic Mexican cuisine. Accents of brick, cement, dark wooden tables, dim lights, and Mexican artifacts. Perfect for a meet.

The driver jumped out and opened the car door for Corcoran. Simultaneously, the thick glass door of the restaurant banged open.

Out stepped Brannigan, flanked by a smug Gallina and a stoic Tompkins.

Brannigan's furious eyes raked over Corcoran, still in the back seat of the Lincoln, without registering recognition. Then he spun on Gallina and Tompkins with a finger jabbing in their faces, threatening their careers.

He strode down the block toward the only car parked in the red zone – Gallina's government issue – drawing the officers' eyes away from the councilman.

The three cops jumped in the vehicle, doors slammed, and the unmarked car rattled away, driving toward headquarters.

"Slick move," Jack said.

"Who do we follow?"

"We know where Brannigan's headed. I think the councilman just lost his appetite." And then Corcoran surprised them. He jumped out of the Town Car and walked into the restaurant.

"Looks like someone else was joining the party," Jack said. "Why don't you sit at the bar, order something to eat and check things out? We might get lucky."

Cruz started to get out of his car.

"Hey, give me the keys."

"Really. With your track record?"

Jack's eyes narrowed, couldn't really argue the point.

Cruz barked a laugh and tossed his boss the keys. "Gotcha."

He waited on the sidewalk until a small group of people were about to enter the restaurant. He glanced at Jack over his shoulder, walked in as if he were a member of their party and split off at the maître d's station.

Jack felt pride watching Cruz's gambit. He was a natural. The kid had great instincts for undercover work that couldn't be taught. Jack slid behind the wheel, pushed the seat all the way back, and turned over the engine. He drove down the road, executed an illegal U-turn, and parked a few stores down and across the street with an unobstructed view of El Compadre's front door.

He pulled his camera from the back seat and checked the charge. He was good to go. He hoped the rest of Brannigan's crew was inside. He was looking for a head count and physical bodily damage of any kind.

The man who'd planted himself on Jack's windshield might have been wearing a ski mask, but Jack would never forget his eyes. If he were still alive and on Brannigan's team, he would take him down.

Jack slouched in the seat and waited.

A lot of detectives Jack worked with in New York balked when they were assigned surveillance duty. Hours on end, sitting in a car, a van, or standing out on icy Manhattan street corners. Coming up empty, pissing in a can, eating stale pizza.

But it suited Jack. He liked being in the hunt. It gave him quiet time to assess the case. Progress made. Moves on the chessboard. He came up with some of his best ideas in the front seat of an undercover car.

Jack's ex-wife, Jeanine, accused him of volunteering for the duty when he was a young undercover detective. She was right, he now admitted. And it had destroyed their marriage. But Jack had the sickness, full-blown back in the day. Married life couldn't compare to the adrenaline rush of infiltrating a drug cell or a money-laundering operation.

His biggest regret in life was how much of his son's life he'd missed. All the firsts. First steps, first words, first T-ball game. He was still working hard to repair the damage. It was going well and their relationship had come a long way in the past year.

Jack's cell pinged, a 999 from Cruz. Go time.

Jack brought up the camera and let the auto focus zero in on the front door of El Compadre. He started snapping photos as a few of Brannigan's men spilled out and said their goodbyes. They were subdued, all business. Hard young men with killer instincts and sniper expertise, trained by one of the best.

Detective Joe Moran peeled off from the other three and walked in Jack's direction. He slouched down in the seat until Moran was a half a block past his location. Jack texted Cruz, "Uber it to Tommy's. I'm on Moran." He executed a U-turn and followed Moran as he strode into a car lot. Jack pulled to the curb and waited until the detective rolled out in his Land Cruiser and headed down Figueroa Street.

Because of the oversized tires on the Land Rover, Moran was easy to track without getting too close. He jumped onto the 110 and drove north on the 101, exiting at Silver Lake.

The tail became more of an issue when Moran pulled off Sunset and headed into the hills above Hollywood. Jack lost the Land Rover on a series of tight switchbacks. He was just making the decision to call it a day he saw the taillights of Moran's car pull into the detached garage next to a rustic bungalow.

Jack pulled out his phone, and as he drove past the driveway, he blind-snapped three quick shots and continued up the road. He glanced in the rearview. He saw the garage door roll down but no Moran. There must be a side door, Jack thought as he made note of the street's name and the address of Moran's house. Jack took the next left and followed the winding road that looped back down the hill.

Cruz's Mini was the perfect car for the hilly roads of Silver Lake. It was the first time Jack had been in the area, and he liked it. Eclectic homes, artsy feel, good views. If his stitches hadn't started itching and his arm throbbing, he would've enjoyed the drive home.

By the time Jack handed the keys to the valet at the Marina del Rey, Ritz-Carlton, it was time for dinner. Jack had skipped lunch and needed a glass of wine and a Vicodin. Now.

Tommy was on the phone and Cruz was working his laptop when

Jack entered the suite. Tommy waved and Cruz looked up from the screen and grinned. "How did you get these pictures?" Cruz spun the laptop so the screen faced Jack.

"I shot on the fly as I drove past. I didn't want to get made."

The traffic had been so dense on the I-10, Jack could have texted a hundred photos to Cruz's phone.

"I transferred them to my computer and brightened the backgrounds. Check the second one out."

The first photo was dark and blurred. Jack could make out the back of the Land Rover but little else.

The second photo got more interesting.

"Look over on the right side of the garage," Cruz said.

The image was still a bit dark, but the object appeared to be a motorcycle. The same make and model as the one Jack tangled with at Vasquez Rocks.

Tommy hung up the phone and walked over to peer at the photograph.

"Looks like the same bike," Jack said. "It was coming up on my left, fast, but they sure as hell look alike."

"How do we prove it? We can't go up and ask him," Cruz said.

"No, but—cover your ears," he told Tommy, who waved him off. "We take a ride to Silver Lake when we're sure Moran's at work. If the VIN numbers have been filed off, we know we have the right bike. We take a picture, send it to Gallina and let him get another search warrant and drag Joe Moran in for attempted murder."

Jack tossed down his Vicodin and Excedrin with bottled spring water. "I need a glass of wine. Is anybody hungry? We can get caught up on our news downstairs."

No argument from the team.

"Hey, Jack, how'd you like the car?" Cruz said.

"Loved it. Great in the hills."

"Good, gimme the keys," he said, mock serious.

"It's in one piece," Jack said, grinning and handed him the valet card.

"That's the way I'd like to keep it."

Tommy laughed as they headed to the restaurant.

Jack sat on the deck of his cabin cruiser, glass of Cabernet in hand and punched in Lieutenant Gallina's number. The midnight blue sky was a shade lighter over the horizon, caused by the light bleed from Fisherman's Village on the far side of the main channel.

Gallina picked up on the eighth ring. "What?"

"Long day, huh?" Jack said.

He was told in no uncertain terms that the interview with Brannigan had been a bust. "He denied any knowledge of Triolo. And if he ended up in the man's Rolodex, we better arrest everyone listed, because he had no recollection. He'd rubbed shoulders with plenty of low-lifes in his career and wasn't a bit concerned." Gallina coughed in annoyance. "Cocksucker demanded a union rep and dummied up. We had to comply. It took a few hours to corral the rep, who was a real douche, and by the time the two of them met and ended up on the same page, we had to cut him loose. Walked out of the interview room like a bantam rooster."

"He's a piece of work," Jack said.

"We're close," Gallina said. "I know he's dirty. But we need more to indict. You've built a beautiful case, but it's just too circumstantial. As for his past history with violent arrests, well, it was par for the course back in those days. Terrible but true. And the statute of limitations have kicked in, making it a moot point."

"The DA signed off on his release?" Jack said, unable to keep the frustration out of his voice.

"Are you listening to me? We don't have enough to indict," Gallina said sliding into the snarky attitude that made Jack want to slap him. "There just wasn't enough to hold him at this point."

"I might have something for you in the morning."

Momentary silence as Gallina rolled that notion around. And then: "I'm loath to admit it, but I'll take any help I can get. The body count is really pissing me off. I agree they're all tied together. I just can't prove Brannigan's running the game."

"Can you e-mail me the list of men on Brannigan's team? The whole nine yards."

"I look like a secretary?"

"I want to find out who's MIA. Hopefully sporting broken bones."

"Done. I'll have Tompkins check from our end, see if anybody was a no-show this morning.

"Good."

"You're welcome," Gallina said, and the line went dead.

Jack took a long pull of wine. He was staying ahead of the pain with the meds, but sleep wouldn't come easily until he discovered the missing link.

He thought about calling Leslie but decided some time off was the best plan. His mind drifted to Angelica and he dialed her number, hanging up before the call went through.

It reminded him to keep an eye out for John Franco. He'd poked the hornet's nest the other night at the Chop House and had to stay on high alert. The last thing he needed was trouble with Mickey Razzano and the East Coast families. Mobsters weren't the sharpest tacks, but hell if they didn't have long memories.

He drained the wine. In the morning he'd find out if Moran was on call and then he'd rent a new car and take another trip to Silver Lake.

CHAPTER 36

Jack was now driving a black Camaro with tinted windows and ten thousand miles on the odometer. Cruz was riding shotgun.

"Are you sure you signed the damage waiver?"

"No one likes a smart ass," Jack said, not looking over.

"Just saying."

"What we're doing is a quick in and out. I'll sit out front and run interference if any is needed. We know Moran's at the precinct. What we don't know is if he has a roommate."

"I ring the bell. If no one answers, I walk around to the side door of the garage. Fifteen seconds is all it'll take," Cruz said, bragging. "Shoot photos of the bike, concentrating on the headstock tube on the frame where the VIN number should be. Take a shot of the license plate and slap the GPS locator on the bottom of the rear fender. In and out in less than three minutes."

"That's the plan," Jack said. "I checked, and the house across the street is cantilevered over the hill. There's a carport and a front door, but no windows with a direct view. That shouldn't be an issue."

"I'm pumped," Cruz, said, finishing off his Egg McMuffin, balling up the yellow wrapper. He pulled the case that contained his tools from the back seat. It looked like something chefs carry their knives in.

"I'm going to pull directly in front. If there are any issues, the car will partially block the side door of the garage."

"No worries."

The Camaro's engine hummed as it climbed the hills above Silver Lake. Jack pulled onto Moran's street and slowed as he made the ascent. It was a sleepy neighborhood. Jack spotted the bungalow on the right and pulled to a stop.

Cruz got out of the car and walked casually up onto the porch. He rang the bell and waited. Nothing. He rang one more time, stepped off the porch and walked up the side of the house like he belonged.

Jack kept a watchful eye as Cruz picked the lock with amazing speed and closed the door behind him.

Jack saw no movement in the house, but a jogger appeared on the crest of the road above, running in his direction. Jack stepped out of the vehicle and messed with the side mirror.

The man slowed to a stop. "Having car trouble?" he asked, keeping his legs pumping so they wouldn't cramp.

"No, damn rental car. I can't get control of the power mirror, and driving these hills I need all the help I can get." Jack adjusted the mirror manually. "I should be good to go. Hey, hell of a workout you're getting," Jack said as he stepped farther into the road, drawing the man's gaze.

Cruz stepped out of the garage and then snapped back.

"I'm training for the LA Marathon," the man said.

"Impressive, 10k's my limit." Jack checked his watch and turned to get back in the car. "Good luck to ya."

"Thanks, and to you." The man continued jogging down the hill.

Jack turned over the engine and revved it loudly enough for Cruz to hear.

Cruz locked the door behind him and strolled to the car. As soon as he slid in, Jack pulled away from the curb.

"No VIN number," Cruz announced. "There was another set of plates up on some pegs. I'll bet the plates he's using are stolen," Cruz added, a little hyper, fueled by the B & E adrenaline rush. "Slapped the tracker on, so we're good to go. And it's a clone of the bike you wrecked. Kawasaki Ninja. A road rocket."

"Smooth work."

Cruz nodded his head, grinning. "I got clean pictures of the lot."

"Okay, copy me, Tommy and Nick," Jack said, feeling a familiar buzz of electricity on the back of his neck. Another potential break in the case. Gallina had texted Jack first thing in the morning. Nobody from Brannigan's team called in sick. It didn't mean someone else wasn't logging in for him. The SWAT team was a loose crew unless they were training, or all hell had broken loose and they were called to a standoff or hostage situation. Jack wasn't convinced Gallina's intel was correct. Whoever had been thrown from the hood of the BMW didn't walk away without a scratch.

Jack had studied the photos he'd taken of the men standing in front of El Compadre and his guy wasn't there.

Jack and Nick were parked on Sunset Boulevard in Silver Lake. They'd watched Detective Moran drive by in his Land Cruiser at the end of his shift and roll up the hill toward his house.

"What if he's in for the night?" Nick said.

"It's his partner. He'll pay a visit."

"What if he takes a different route?"

"It's a loop. One way in, one way out. Speaking of, how'd you get out of the house?" Jack said.

"I told Lynn I was cheating on her. She said no problem as long as you aren't hanging out with that Bertolino prick."

"Fair enough," Jack said.

The computer beeped, and the men tensed. Joe Moran came down the hill on his Kawasaki, wearing a black helmet, black leather jacket, and skintight black leather pants. He made a right turn and powered away from the men. Jack waited for a set count, pulled away from the curb and followed.

"I might be able to squeeze into leather pants like those," Nick said. "I just don't know if I could get out of 'em."

"I'm thinking that ship's sailed."

"Don't take this the wrong way, pard, because I'm comfortable in my own skin … but fuck off."

Jack grinned.

Nick checked the computer screen. "What's the range on the GPS?"

"We're pinging off satellites. No real limit. When he stops, we'll find him. My guess, if his partner's injured, they're keeping him somewhere local. Tompkins rubbed shoulders with Brannigan's team today. Everyone was there except Donny Rice, Moran's partner. Said he was out to lunch. Tomkins didn't want to press and step on our play. Sent the personnel info of the entire team. I saw the graduation photos from the academy, and Donny's our man."

"I met him at the awards ceremony. Said when Brannigan was chief, I'd be riding the wave, or some crap like that. I knew he was a bad actor."

The computer dinged, and Nick told Jack to make the next left. They drove for fifteen minutes. "The icon stopped up ahead, on the right."

Jack slowed and pulled into the parking lot of Glen Oaks Urgent Care. They saw Moran stow his helmet and walk into the facility, carrying a bag from McDonald's.

"I hated the hospital food," Nick said approvingly. "I would've killed for a quarter pounder with cheese. He's looking out for his partner."

"He's a saint," Jack said.

"Just an observation."

Jack parked a few aisles behind the motorcycle, walked over to the Kawasaki and started snapping photos. He pushed in close on the right-hand side of the bike's headstock frame. The VIN numbers had been filed off, just like the one Jack wrecked at Vasquez Rocks. Then the stolen license plate and a full body shot of the motorcycle. Same make and model of the wreck that sent Detective Donny Rice into urgent care.

The men sat for a half hour before Nick grumbled about getting hungry.

Jack didn't respond. His eyes were intent on the exit. "Look there. Showtime."

Moran exited the building, mounted his bike, and snapped on the headlight. They could hear the engine's high-pitched whine as Moran shifted gears, driving out of the lot.

Jack texted Gallina and Tompkins that their target might be en route. He'd monitor Moran's location on the GPS system. When it became clear Moran wasn't coming back to Glen Oaks, he nodded to Nick, who stepped out of the Camaro. The big man stretched and headed into the building.

Jack could see Nick flash his badge to the nurse at the admittance desk. He sweet-talked her a bit and then walked down the hallway, disappearing from view.

CHAPTER 37

Nick Aprea stepped into the hospital room and pulled back the curtain. Donny was lying on his back, his leg elevated with a pulley system. A plaster cast ran from his foot to his hip. He had three IV drips feeding him intravenously, along with monitors beeping softly. His eyes were closed, and his lids were twitching as if he were having a nightmare. Little did he know what was in store, Nick thought as he pulled out his cell phone, snapped a few pictures and sent them to Jack.

Donny's eyes blinked open, and as they focused, Nick said, "What the fuck happened, Donny?"

The officer looked confused. He hit the button on the side of the bed that raised him up slightly. "Hey, Aprea, what the fuck are you doing here?"

"Stifle the attitude. You think I want to be babysitting your ass?"

Donny groaned as Nick examined the chart. He'd been admitted using an alias, Earl Wilson. His leg was broken in four places and put back together with eight titanium screws. His shoulder was a mass of bloody bandages. His leather jacket had shredded when he hit the pavement at fifty miles an hour and slid.

"How's the pain?" Nick asked, feigning sympathy. He was staring at the man who tried to kill his friend.

"It's a ten."

Nick walked around the bed, pushed back the saline drip, the antibiotic, and squeezed the bag of morphine, sending a shot of white lightning into Donny's veins.

"Thanks, dude," Donny said, feeling an immediate wash of relief.

"What the fuck happened?" Nick asked again. "IA is jumping all over my ass because of my relationship with Brannigan."

"Thanks, dude," he said again, his words starting to slur. "I was coming up on the passenger side ... dude slammed on the brakes, and I thought I was dead, rolled and broke four bones in my leg, tore up my shoulder, need skin grafts...hear the dude is still alive."

"It was a cluster fuck," Nick said.

Donny's heavy-lidded eyes were blinking like a junkie's now. He started to nod, then shook his head awake. "We were just supposed to keep the car locked in. Deliver a clean hit, and we're gone."

"That's what Moran said."

"Right. Bertolino went nuts on us and I took the hit."

Nick eyeballed the half of a Big Mac that sat uneaten on the rolling tray next to the bed and fought the urge to grab it.

"Moran was supposed to be here," Nick said conversationally.

"Just left."

"Well, I've got the night shift. You get some shut-eye and we'll get you back in the field."

"I didn't fuck up."

"No one's throwing blame. You're a good soldier. Brannigan sends his best. He's got his own issues."

"That asshole Bertolino."

"What a dick, right?" Nick said, fighting another urge. To grab Donny and hurl him onto the floor.

Jack sat in the Camaro listening to the conversation and smiling, knowing the conversation was being recorded. He forwarded the photos of the Kawasaki and the patient to Gallina, who was staking out Moran's house. Also to Tompkins, who was standing outside Judge Bradley Cole's house, waiting to show him the damning evidence and have him sign off on a second search warrant. Moran was in for a big surprise tonight. It warmed Jack's heart.

"Where's Moran?" Donny asked, stoned.

"I'm supposed to take over for him."

"Why?"

"Nothing, relax."

"What the fuck? Why?"

"I'm going to let you in on a little secret. You see, shit like this happens—and don't take this the wrong way—but you're a loose end. They're going to figure out you're MIA and put two and two together. Donny, there are lots of bodies stacking up, and you're in the middle of the conspiracy. People get scared, they cut their losses, you know? You, my friend, have become a loss leader."

"So, why did Brannigan send you?"

"He's the boss. Calls the shots. But who can you trust? You roll over, ten other lives are destroyed. But you get to fight another day. Get my point?"

"I didn't have nothing to do with that chick in Arizona."

"You're still involved."

"Get me outta here."

"No can do, Donny. I dance to the commander's tune."

"Fuck, this is bullshit."

"You're telling me."

Donny drifted again, and then: "Why are you here?"

"Trying to keep you alive."

"Oh." Donny's eyes closed. When they opened again, he went to lift his arm, which slammed back down. He was being restrained by Nick's handcuffs that secured both arms to the metal rails of his hospital bed.

Jack received a text from Detective Tompkins. Judge Bradley Cole signed the warrant, and Tompkins was heading over to Moran's place to meet up with Gallina. As soon as Nick coordinated the incarceration of Donny and his transfer to a hospital facility near police headquarters, they'd take a ride back to Silver Lake and throw salt on the wound. See how Moran liked being in the hot seat. See if he was cool under fire.

The icon on the GPS system dinged, alerting Jack. Moran's bike had come to a stop on Sunset Boulevard, a half mile from his house. Probably at one of the local bars for a few drinks, Jack thought. This could time out well. He punched a text into his phone and hit send.

Nick was on his cell in the hallway when he heard shouts emanating from the room. "Yo, Donny, keep a lid on it." Nick shouted as he hung up and walked back in.

"What the fuck? What the fuck is this all about?" Donny yelled, red-faced.

Nick answered by quietly reading Donny his rights. "You're being arrested for the attempted murder of Jack Bertolino. You'll also be tied to a conspiracy to kill Gloria Millhouse, Cheryl Lee Williams, Carl Forbes, and Freddie Triolo."

Donny's mouth was too dry to respond.

"Cat got your tongue, wise guy? Lots of people don't like cops. We get a bad rap, you know. But nobody likes a dirty cop." Nick came in close, like a patient father. "You need help, and I can put in a good word with the DA. He's gonna want something in return. You know how it goes. But remember, the sooner you share, the better the deal. The longer you wait, the longer you'll serve."

"Take off one of my cuffs and hand me my phone."

"In your dreams," Nick said as he bagged the phone, wallet, and keys to Donny's apartment. "Everything you own is evidence now. Your life is over."

"So, Brannigan didn't send you?"

"No, Einstein. But he'll find out I was here and take you down. My guess, you won't make it to trial."

A knock on the door stopped the conversation. Two uniformed officers stood sentry in the hallway. Nick walked out and shook their hands. "Nobody in, nobody out."

CHAPTER 38

Jack and Nick drove past Moran's Kawasaki, parked curbside in front of the Eight Ball Pub on Sunset Boulevard. It was a classic dive with vintage neon beer signs blinking through dusty windows, inviting thirsty men to stop by and take a load off. Nick texted Gallina and Tompkins, alerting them to Moran's location.

Jack headed up the slope and pulled his car past Moran's house. The two hoofed it back down, joining Gallina and Tompkins on the porch. The only light was the ambient glow of a street lamp a few doors down.

The lieutenant stepped up to Jack, "I know you think I'm a tight ass, strictly by the book kinda cop. I don't take offense anymore. We've shared too many successes together."

Jack accepted the olive branch. "You afraid he's going to jackrabbit?"

Gallina shook his head. "Got it covered. Just let me know when the scumbag starts to move and I'll call in the troops."

"Sounds like a plan."

Nick's cell phone beeped, and he pulled up the GPS app. "Moran's on the move."

"Let me know when he's on the hill."

"Now," Nick said.

Gallina spoke into his cell, once and then again. They could hear the sound of the motorcycle powering up the incline.

"Now," Gallina shouted, a second time.

As soon as the Kawasaki came into view, blinding headlights lit the entire road from above as an LAPD tow truck rolled down the street, stopping on the edge of Moran's property, blocking his egress.

"Now," Tompkins said into his cell.

Moran braked sharply, revving the engine in neutral. His head swiveled as he took in the men standing on his porch.

"Fight or flight," Nick said his face splitting into a wolf grin as two black-and-whites, bar lights spinning, came to a tire-squealing stop on the butt of the leather-geared detective, who was lit up like a Hollywood stunt man. Moran engaged the motorcycle and drove gently up his driveway. He dismounted his bike, threw the kickstand, and peeled off his helmet like he was amused.

"Got him," Gallina said with more energy than Jack had ever witnessed in the man.

Joe Moran sauntered up to his front porch where Jack, Nick, Gallina, and Tompkins stood.

"So, what did I do to deserve the entourage?"

"Good one," Gallina said, enjoying the moment. "You still think you're important, huh? A hero? Well, you got one point right, with that entourage bullshit. We're going to surround you. But we're going to be a constant source of irritation, because you're a fraud. A killer. And there's nothing you can do about it. Life as you know it is over. Give me the keys to your house, your motorcycle, your vehicle, your phone, and your garage."

Moran was about to crack wise.

"Now!" Gallina shouted, stilling the crowd of police that surrounded them.

"Lemme see the papers," Moran said, his bravado holding tight.

Tompkins walked up and shoved the search warrant into Moran's face, forcing him to stumble off the porch before catching his balance. He was about to charge, but Tompkins c'mon-do-it grin stopped him in his tracks. He followed him down the steps, handed off the warrant, and snapped his fingers.

Moran pretended to read while he rifled his tight pants pocket and pulled out a ring of house keys. He shoved his other hand into his back pocket and pulled out the keys to his motorcycle.

"You carrying?"

"No."

"Your jacket."

Moran shrugged out of his leather jacket with studied ease and handed it off. Tompkins rifled through the pockets and came up with a burner phone and his private cell.

"Hand me your throw-down, wise guy, grip first."

Moran bent over, pulled a .38 out of his ankle rig, and handed the gun to Tompkins, who added it to the evidence pile.

"What the hell's this all about," Moran said, trying to conjure some semblance of dignity.

Gallina ignored the question as Tompkins opened the front door, switched on the porch lights. He fumbled a bit before the house was illuminated in light.

A few of the neighbors appeared from their homes in bathrobes and sweats, tossing questions at the uniforms who were protecting the property's periphery.

Ted Ward pushed through the growing crowd, his camera ready to document the arrest.

While the LAPD tow truck operator rolled Moran's bike onto the bed of his truck and secured it with chains, Gallina Mirandized the detective and handed him off to the uniforms.

Ted Ward closed in on the black-and-white and started shooting photos of the arrest. "Detective Moran," he shouted as the uniformed officer walked him toward the police car. "*LA Times*, would you like to make a statement, Detective?"

Moran flashed killer eyes at the reporter as the officer held his head down and pushed him into the caged back seat of the cop car.

A red-faced Gallina charged down the lawn. "Who the hell called the *Times*?" Then he barked at a young uniform, "Can you protect the scene, please? Keep everyone back, including the press."

"Would you like to make a statement, Lieutenant Gallina?" Ward said, snapping a photo. Gallina snarled and walked up the path to the open front door, where the search of Moran's house, garage, and property began in earnest.

Jack strolled across the yard, ignoring the reporter. He locked eyes with Moran as he passed the police car. Jack flashed a satisfied grin: he was still alive. Moran, fired back with his best dead-eyes, knowing he was in for a world of hurt.

Jack leaned over the tow truck's bed and grabbed the GPS rig from beneath the Kawasaki's rear fender. Moran wouldn't be riding his bike anytime soon.

They had him for attempted murder: his partner, Donny Rice – who Nick had on tape – implicated Moran in the attempt on Jack's life. Plus, using stolen plates and illegally altering the VIN number on his motorcycle in his conspiracy to murder Jack Bertolino. They also had Nick Aprea's signed affidavit stating he overheard Detective Joe Moran threaten, at the mayor's press conference, that if Bertolino interfered in any way with Brannigan's bid for police chief, there would be no place on the planet he'd be safe.

He was also tied to a conspiracy to commit murder in the Freddie Triolo case. Gallina now had the photos of Moran doing a drive-by of Freddie Triolo's office while the search warrant was being executed. Jack knew that when they locked down the exact timeline, they'd discover the call Moran made from his burner, and the photos of the evidence being placed in the police van, had been sent to, and received by, Commander Brannigan.

That was the same night Triolo was found dead, hanging by his neck. The coroner's report labeled it a murder. Triolo was killed in an attempt to distance Brannigan from the man who had sent monthly payments to Cheryl Lee Williams for twenty-three years. Every month like clockwork until the day she died. The timelines were already locked down, supporting the original charges, and were the reason Brannigan had been pulled in for questioning.

Jack still had to find a direct link between Brannigan and the murders. But there was no question in Jack's mind that Donny Rice and Joe Moran were following orders and it was Brannigan who called the shots. He just had to prove it.

Jack and Nick stopped in at the Eight Ball Pub to check out the joint and toss a few back in celebration of a productive day's work. Then Nick received a page calling him back to headquarters to take care of the paperwork generated from his arrest of Donny Rice.

He was feeling no pain when Jack dropped him off, and Jack was damned relaxed himself. The job wasn't done, Carl was still in prison and Gloria's killer still on the loose, but the noose was tightening around Brannigan's neck and Jack wanted to be there to throw the sack over his head and pull the lever.

The traffic was light on the I-10. The sound system was banging out Mumford and Sons when the Bluetooth rang, letting Jack know Angelica Cardona was on the line.

Jack turned down the volume. "I hope you've got good news."

"Where are you, Jack?"

"Getting off the 90, heading for my boat. What's up? You sound stressed."

"John Franco showed up again tonight. He's dangerous. Frankie-the-Man is on me like a shadow, and Peter ran interference. I don't feel safe going home alone, and I can't abide him sitting outside my door all night. Do you want some company?"

"No question."

"I'm leaving the car here. Peter's offered to chauffeur. I'll bring the wine."

"Tell Peter to drive safe, eyes in the back of his head."

"See you soon. And Jack, thank you."

Jack was showered and shaved, but the adrenaline rush of the day had worn off. His back was throbbing, and the stitches in his arm were raw and angry. He chastised himself for not staying ahead of the pain, and washed down his Vicodin and Excedrin with bottled water.

He put in a call to Ted Ward and filled him in on the details of Moran's arrest and the connection to Donny Rice. Ward got photos of Rice as he was being wheeled out of the urgent care facility and transported to his new hospital room with an armed guard.

The young reporter was very grateful and thanked Jack, promising once again that he wouldn't disappoint. So far, the man had kept his word.

Jack was sitting on the deck of his cabin cruiser when Peter Maniacci's black RAV4 pulled to a stop by the chain-link fence. Jack walked up the dock and opened the gate.

He stepped back to let Angelica pass. Bussing his cheek, she handed off a bottle of Benziger Cab. "Make yourself comfortable," he said, "I'll be there in a few minutes."

Jack walked around to the driver-side window, which powered down. Peter looked dead on his feet. Five o'clock shadow, bloodshot eyes, and worry lines on his forehead. Running security at the Chop House was taking its toll.

"I took a crazy route through Beverly Hills, then up Coldwater to Mulholland. Stopped at a turnout until I was sure there was no tail."

"Good work."

"Don't know how it's going to play out with Franco. We're gonna have to move on him sooner or later. He's pushing too hard, bringing it on himself."

"Too much information. It's a 'family' thing. That's where I draw the line."

"I don't know. From where I'm sitting, you look fully engaged. Keep an eye out."

Peter put the car in drive and headed out of the parking lot. Jack stood in the shadow of the marina's laundry building. He thought about what Peter had just said. Hard to argue the point, but with Leslie still in the picture, and with Angelica's new complication, Jack wasn't sure how to proceed. What he didn't want was for anyone to get hurt. When he was positive Peter hadn't been followed, he walked down the dock to his little slice of heaven.

Angelica was clearly stressed. The tension she was wrestling with was obvious. Jack opened the wine and poured two glasses. He decided to let her talk when she was good and ready. Angelica was a smart woman and didn't need to be prodded. A little down time was in order for them both. Jack was learning to grab these quiet moments whenever they presented themselves.

His meds were kicking in, and the wine cut the edge off the day's activities. He watched a gull soar silently past, powerful white wings against the black sky like an apparition. The air was thick with salt and moisture and the tension of the day dissolved.

"This is where you tell me I'm in the wrong line of work," Angelica said, leaning back in the canvas chair, staring up at the field of stars. "I know why I got into the restaurant business. I just don't know how to get out."

Jack took a sip of wine, and when she didn't continue, he commented, "It's time you had a come-to-Jesus talk with your father."

"He texted this morning. Thanks for bringing him up to speed. He's reaching out to Mickey, but there's no way my uncle will fly out for a sit-down at the penitentiary. The Mafia's funny like that. When he responds, it'll be me he's talking to. And Jack, my head feels like it's going to explode."

"You know, with a good night's sleep you might find some clarity. Why don't you lie down? We can hash this out in the morning."

"I knew there was a reason I fell in love with you," Angelica said. She flashed a tired smile and started down the teak steps into the boat's cabin, letting Jack off the hook on the love statement. She turned as Jack stepped into the cabin, "I know I'm just one big complication. You're a good man, Bertolino. Thanks for being there."

The ambient light emanating from the wall sconces created a soft amber glow. Angelica dropped onto the bunk fluffing the pillow behind her head.

Jack pulled his Glock from his leather shoulder rig and slid it behind a pillow on the padded foldout bench that turned into a second bed. He settled in, sipping his Cab until he heard the soft purr of Angelica in REM mode. Jack wished her sweet dreams.

CHAPTER 39

Leslie texted Jack first thing in the morning. She had read Ward's exclusive in the *Times* and knew Jack was the man responsible for two arrests. She was in the area, picked up some lox and bagels, and was on her way over to the Marina. Jack hadn't responded to the text, but she chalked that up to a shower, or sleeping in, knowing he was out late. This was definitely out of her box, but she decided to surprise him.

Jack turned the wheel of his boat and straightened when he was in the center of the channel, heading for the main waterway. He took a pull of the steaming coffee and glanced back at the empty slip as Angelica stepped onto the aft deck.

Jack's heart skipped a beat when he spotted Leslie standing at the chain-link security gate. The painful look of surprise on her face tore into him like a thunderclap. The sea of masts instantly blocked her image as his boat headed for the main channel.

Angelica poured some coffee and stepped close to Jack. "I think someone sent you a text while you were in the shower."

"I'll check it later," he said quietly, feeling a pang of guilt. Knowing he'd just stepped into a worst-case scenario.

Leslie stood rooted in place as she watched the stern of Jack's boat disappear from view, not quite prepared for the level of emotion she felt. It confused her. She'd pushed him away after their last dinner. She'd gotten too possessive after he was honest about seeing Angelica at the Chop House. He told her there'd been an emergency, didn't try to hide it.

When they first met, Jack was sitting in a jail cell having been arrested for murdering a female confidential informant he'd run working narcotics with the NYPD. The arrest was without merit, and Leslie forced the arresting officer, Lieutenant Gallina, to withdraw the complaint and offer the offended man an apology.

Their attraction was undeniable. When Jack told her he didn't fall into bed or love easily, she was sold. It was her decision to break up the first time. They'd been around the block a few times.

Oh, what the hell, they didn't have an exclusive relationship. It was her big idea to float friends-with-benefits. It was supposed to be a fluid, chemistry reigns sort of thing. She just never admitted to herself how far she'd fallen.

Leslie passed a dumpster on the way to her car and tossed the bag of bagels. A hungry pack of gulls squawked and swooped down landing in the dumpster. They tore into the bag in a feeding frenzy as she drove out of the lot, swiping angry tears.

Jack and Angelica cruised as far as the jetty before executing a slow U-turn and heading toward Fisherman's Village, where Frankie-the-Man was waiting to drive Angelica to Beverly Hills. They were taking extra precautions to keep Jack's whereabouts a secret. It stoked his anger, but after two attempts on his life, and the sniper's range at a half mile, it was the only move that made sense.

CHAPTER 40

Tommy looked up from the *LA Times* as Jack entered the suite. He'd been glued to the story of the arrest, and he recited Ted Ward's headline with a satisfied expression. "*A Hero's Fall from Grace.*"

Ward had been careful not to include Jack in any of the photographs his editor had chosen to lead the story, and although Gallina thought Jack was the leak, he was too pleased with another notch on his belt to complain. He was still pissed he had to cut Brannigan loose. If this rattled his cage, so be it.

Cruz was on his laptop and Jack tossed him the GPS rig.

"Thanks, boss."

"A thing of beauty."

Tommy asked him if he'd heard from Leslie. Said she called earlier and reported that the Rice arrest was righteous, the tape made it a slam-dunk. They were still going over Gallina's report on Moran, but it looked like there was enough to indict. "Surprised she didn't call you first."

"Women," Jack said, acting totally mystified.

Tommy's eyes probed his old friend. "Did you step in it, Jack?" he said knowingly.

"Let it go, Tommy."

"Right, what'd you do?"

"You're worse than my ex."

Cruz kept his eyes lasered on his computer but was all ears, enjoying the exchange.

"She caught you with Angelica," Tommy said, folding the newspaper and placing it carefully onto his desktop. When Jack didn't immediately protest: "Hah! Gotcha."

"Hey ..." Jack barked, trying to sound angry and failing. "God, you piss me off. I'm surrounded by people who can read my damn mind."

"One of my many gifts. I used it often when I had a defendant in the witness chair. They never knew what hit them."

"Guilty as charged. But not really guilty, more that one of us was in the wrong place at the wrong time. The one of us being me. And I'm going to have to take it on the chin. I'm just not ready to, uh, deal with it yet."

"The longer you wait ..." Cruz intoned.

"Really? You're going to give me relationship advice?"

"Kid's right. It's time to face the lion, my friend. Leslie deserves no less."

Jack had no desire to do that. "We're not done here."

He grabbed his cell phone and stormed out the door. Tommy glanced at Cruz. "He's emotionally stunted. Brilliant man, but clams up when he's squeezed by the opposite sex."

Jack walked down the Ritz-Carlton's walkway along the marina.

The early lunch crowd had already filled the hotel's al fresco patio. The sound of laughter, light conversation, silverware being set, food delivered, and wine corks popping lent a festive air. All of it lost on Jack as he tapped in a number and put the cell to his ear. Leslie picked up on the fourth, excruciating ring.

"I didn't expect to hear from you," Leslie said. "I mean, so soon."

She didn't sound too upset, Jack thought, but he knew she was a good actor. "Does everybody know me better than I know myself?"

"That's an easy one, Jack. Of course."

"Huh. This is going to sound like a cliché, but it wasn't what it seemed. If I'd picked up the text, I would've told you to come on by. Angelica was afraid for her personal safety, and I gave her a bed for the night."

"Saint Jack," Leslie said, letting some attitude enter the conversation.

"Well, we know that's not true," he said, attempting to lighten the mood some. Leslie's silence let him know he'd failed.

"Don't take this the wrong way, Jack, but you're in over your head with Angelica. If you get in any deeper, your sterling reputation will be destroyed. Everything the Mafia touches turns to shit, Jack. Total shit. And you're too stupid or naïve to see that simple truth. It's a Mafia thing, not a Bertolino thing. And you're so stubborn, my guess is you'll dig your heels in until there's nothing left of you to salvage."

Jack had nothing.

"Look, I've got a case to prepare. I was just stopping by to congratulate you on the arrests. Let's chalk it up to wrong place, wrong time, and leave it at that. Unless there's something else you want to say."

"No." Jack was in a total shut-down mode. He'd need some time to work through this. "We'll talk later."

"Okay, Jack. Now go and find enough on Brannigan to put him away. The man's dirty."

"Will do."

"And Jack … the DA's office is willing to offer Donny Rice a deal if he turns state's evidence on the entire criminal conspiracy."

"That's good news. Did you hear the tape? A damn good piece of police work by Nick."

"We did ask Nick why Donny thanked him when he first entered the hospital room. Nick said he looked parched and handed Rice a cup of water."

"Okay."

"That's some potent H2O, is all I'm saying."

"Like I said, a damn good piece of police work."

"Okay, Jack … later."

Jack stepped back into the suite, shaking his head. "Okay, that went well."

"I told you," Cruz said.

"*Not.*" Jack sucked in a breath. "Can we stop talking about this already?"

Cruz's head nodded. "Sure. How about we talk about the background search you requested on Chip Boyd?"

"What have you got?"

"Chip Franklin Boyd. You already covered his address and employment history. Boyd was married once, divorced. Marriage lasted nine years. Irreconcilable differences. No arrests for domestic abuse. One arrest for disorderly conduct, charges were later dropped. It was a barroom scuffle. The vic refused to press charges. You already pulled up his service record. Not exemplary, but no red flags.

"You already knew he drove an SUV. No other vehicles registered to his name at the DMV. No outstanding tickets, no DUIs, no liens against his property, no dings on his credit. A pretty average life, from what I can tell. Single for six years now. I can put in a call to his ex if you want. Try and find out what the irreconcilable differences were?"

"Do it."

Cruz nodded and continued. "He has a license to carry, passed a background check before he was hired at the casino. He owns three 9mms and has a deer hunting license, so we can surmise the man has rifles, not registered, number unknown. All reasonable for a man living in Reno who told you he enjoyed four-wheeling in the back country."

"Okay, I'd love to find out where he was the day my rental car was shot to hell and back." Jack reflexively rubbed the stitches on his shoulder and triceps. "He called in sick, but showed up for work the next night. Plenty of time to fly down, shoot up my car, and get out of Dodge. He also could've driven down. I think it's about a seven-and-a-half-hour trip."

"That would mean he's connected to the SWAT team," Tommy said doubtfully. "What are the chances?"

"I know," Jack said. "The only connection to the original case is Brannigan. It's not working for me."

Cruz's Facetime trilled on his laptop. The image of Professor Anderson filled the screen. He didn't look happy. "I can see the gang's all there. Good."

"What's up, Prof?" Cruz said.

"Bad news. No DNA hits on the Sex Offenders Database or VICAP."

"What about CODIS and NDIS?" Jack asked.

"Next on my list. Sorry, guys. I'll stay on it until we score. Oh, great job yesterday, Jack. I think you've got them on the ropes."

"We have to wipe 'em out. Nothing short of that."

CHAPTER 41

Frankie-the-Man opened the heavy Chop House door for Angelica, who planned on picking up her keys, driving to her Hollywood apartment, and taking a shower. As she crossed the threshold, she heard muffled voices emanating from the upstairs dining room. Her back straightened as she recognized the voices.

Angelica sucked in a breath as she strode up the carpeted stairs and cut past the silent white grand piano. Her face a tight mask. Frankie was close on her heels, his hand on his 9mm.

Peter Maniacci sat at the bar and flashed Angelica a my-hands-were-tied expression.

Uncle Mickey Razzano sat at the main table. His piercing eyes appraised his niece as she stepped close. A smug John Franco and two more of Mickey's soldiers he'd flown in for the meeting made it a foursome. Angelica knew she was in for a battle.

"What, no phone call?" she said, trying to tamp down her rage.

"Is that a proper hello?" Mickey said with a chilly smile. "I called the only number I have for you. You weren't home, so I left a message."

Franco chimed in, "She was probably with lover boy."

"Put your dog on a chain, Uncle," she snapped with a power that silenced the room. "He's persona non grata, not to mention bad for business. Boot him out. This is between you and me. It's a family matter."

"Stuff it," Franco hissed.

Angelica's hand lashed out like a cobra, batting the man's New York steak and fries off the table onto the floor. "A little respect, you're in my house now."

Franco jumped to his feet, his chair flying backwards, and drew his piece. It was met with Frankie-the-Man's cannon trained on his kill zone. Peter jumped to his feet with his 9mm that had been snugged beneath the *LA Times* he'd been pretending to read.

"Calm the fuck down, all of you," Mickey ordered.

The men stood down.

Angelica was so outraged at the surprise attack her uncle orchestrated that her heart pounded in her chest. She had to fight for control of the tremor that threatened to creep into her voice. She could not show weakness or the New York family would take over her father's restaurant. "Your boy's been causing trouble here. As I said, he's bad for business, I want him out, now."

"She's got a mouth on her," Franco said.

"She's got more balls than two of you," Mickey said. "Wait outside. All of you. You heard the woman: this is a family thing."

Mickey's men holstered their guns and started for the stairs.

Angelica nodded to Frankie and Peter, who reluctantly followed in their wake.

Angelica walked to the kitchen, pushed open the door and asked one of the kitchen staff to clean up the mess and bring her some coffee, black. It was done on the instant. Her pulse rate ticked back toward normal. There was no question who was boss at the Chop House, and Mickey took note.

Angelica took a seat across the table from her uncle and poured a cup.

"All right now, let's start again. You're full of surprises, Uncle."

"Me?" he said, genuinely smiling. "You've got your father's blood. How's he holding up?"

"Making the best of a bad situation. His lawyers are working on an appeal. They're optimistic. They're paid to be. But Dad thinks they've got a few tricks up their sleeves."

"They better be magicians."

"Rusty turned, and that cemented the conspiracy charge. We've got information that can refute his testimony."

Mickey's dark, unblinking eyes gave away nothing. He sat lizard still, took a sip of espresso, and yielded the floor to Angelica. She had one chance to win him over.

"You need anything else to eat?"

"No, the flight gave me agita. How are you doing? I'm getting reports things aren't going so well."

"With respect, Uncle Mickey, next time, send a man to do a man's job. Someone with an eye for business so he knows what's what. Franco doesn't have the skill set. He's ready to put a bronze plaque with his name on it at his favorite booth, and he makes the regulars nervous." Angelica made a wave to indicate the entire space. "I stand by our bottom line. I've upped sales the past two months, and you can't argue with the overall consistency of the restaurant's revenue stream. It's not an easy feat with the federal regulators looking over my shoulder."

Angelica blew steam off the hot coffee and took a careful, deliberate sip.

"We're a well-oiled machine, and the only problem we've suffered in the past month was Franco. I don't want him in my face. And when I said he's bad for business, it was an understatement."

"I'm getting pressure from some of the other families," he said without judgment. "They've not sold on a woman helming the ship."

"It wouldn't be the first time. I looked it up. Fanny Peluso ran the south side of Brooklyn back in the sixties. Made everybody wealthy. Uncle, I have faith in you. You can still the loose lips and appease them with the bottom line I deliver."

"Times change."

"But success doesn't. My father has always been a great earner for the New York families, and now I've taken charge until he gets out. Give us room to do what we do best. If you want, I'll bring you up to speed at the end of each week, or pay cycle. Your call. But don't kill the cash cow by sending in fools, or a sham corporate entity that will destroy twenty years of hard work. This place is one of the jewels in your crown. Why don't you sit back, enjoy your life, and let me handle the details on the West Coast?"

Mickey seemed to be giving her plea some serious thought. He opened a pack of sugar, and all Angelica could hear was the sound of her own breathing, and his demi spoon clicking against the china cup as he stirred.

Angelica knew better than to jump to conclusions. It wasn't over until the New York capo, her uncle by marriage, who had the power over life and death, gave her the nod.

"This is what you want ...?" he said finally. "Think before answering. You're a young woman. This is the life you really want?"

Angelica locked eyes with Mickey, taking his measure, unblinking. "Yes. I was raised at my father's side. I learned from the best. I love the work, and the people of Beverly Hills love me. They trust me and will support me and our endeavor. I engender respect from my father's men. It's a natural fit. This restaurant will not fail as long as you give me autonomy."

Mickey took a sip of his espresso and hummed in appreciation of the rich brew. His eyes raked the entire room, which would be filled with patrons in a few hours.

"You will never regret supporting me," Angelica said. "And in return, I will never disrespect or turn my back on you."

Mickey answered by standing up. Working a kink out of his back, the crack pierced the hushed room. "Getting old isn't for the weak."

"You've got the countenance of a young man, Uncle."

"Okay," he said finally, pursing his lips. "You've got six months. Then we'll revisit and see what's what. I'll run interference in New York. Don't let me down."

"Thank you," Angelica said, leaning in and giving her uncle a warm kiss on the cheek. A sign of respect.

Mickey Razzano walked past Angelica and turned when he reached the white grand piano. "Send my best to Vincent. Let him know the family stands by him, and that you have made him proud."

Angelica waited until she heard the front door whoosh closed.

Then she walked behind the bar, slammed a shot glass onto the burnished wooden surface, filled it with bourbon and tossed it back. As Frankie-the-Man and Peter ascended the steps and walked across the floor smiling, she set two more glasses down and poured bourbon for her men and a second shot for herself. "Salute," she said. As glasses clinked and the shots were downed, she could read the pride in her men's faces.

Angelica wasn't sure what she had just talked herself into, and what it would mean for her relationship with Jack. But one thing was clear. If she let her father down and lost the Chop House, they would kill him.

CHAPTER 42

Jack was back on the boat, going over his notes. Starting at the beginning. He was frustrated by the amount of time the accountants were taking with Triolo's files. He had Brannigan on the timing of the phone calls surrounding Cheryl Lee's murder, but needed hard evidence that the money paid to Cheryl Lee was generated from Brannigan's accounts. And he still wasn't any closer to discovering the identity of the sniper.

Was Brannigan the man who stabbed and raped Shelley Goldstein? It was possible, he thought. Maybe the body count, the attempt to derail the investigation, wasn't just a ploy to keep his reputation clean enough to be anointed the next LAPD chief of police. It was well documented in the Pitchess motion that the man was prone to physical violence. Maybe there was something darker at play. There were no statutes of limitation on murder.

He also considered Councilman Corcoran. If he killed Shelley Goldstein twenty-three years ago, he'd have every reason in the world to disrupt the investigation. And what was his connection to Brannigan, the arresting officer back at the time of the murder? Until Brannigan's bid for chief blew up in his face, Corcoran was his biggest supporter on the City Council. Favors owed? For what? Strange bedfellows, Jack thought. Maybe just a relationship born of political expediency. Whatever it was, it wouldn't help them now.

Moran and Donny Rice were both tied to the attempt on Jack's life. But even if Moran could also be prosecuted for conspiracy to commit murder in Triolo's death, it didn't come close to tying him to the death of Gloria Millhouse, or the exoneration of Carl Forbes.

Jack needed the forensic accountants to discover the trail that led to Brannigan, or a DNA match to open a door, or Detective Rice to turn against his comrades. The chances of that happening were fifty-fifty. The possibility of walking free, weighed against spending the best years of his life behind bars where his badge was definitely not a friend.

It was time to clear his mind and let the case roll around in his subconscious, see what emerged. Sometimes it worked, Jack thought, taking a sip of wine. If it didn't, he'd just keep gutting out the clues, use shoe leather to knock on doors and ask questions until he found an answer. A gull cried overhead and seemed to be laughing. Jack didn't take it personally.

In the morning, Jack's eyes blinked open and he grabbed a yellow pad. He penned, "Department of Defense database." Somewhere in his dream state he'd put together an event that tied at least three of his principals together.

It brought to mind an article he'd read in *Wired* magazine a few years back about DNA databases. A disturbing notion at the time. During the Gulf War the Department of Defense had trouble obtaining reliable DNA samples for the positive ID of soldiers' wartime remains. And so the DOD began a program to collect and store specimens of DNA from active and reserve force members when they enlisted, or reenlisted, or were preparing to deploy oversees. Jack understood the need, but wondered what the young recruits thought about giving a sample. It felt like bad luck.

Brannigan, Moran, and Boyd had all served in the military. Jack checked his background notes and discovered Brannigan was in the

Marine Reserves back in '91 when the program was first initiated. He decided to run the idea past the professor. It was worth a try. Worst-case scenario, he'd cross Brannigan off Shelley Goldstein's list. Victim number one.

But first he decided to pay Lieutenant Gallina and Tompkins a visit downtown, see how the interrogation of Moran was going. He'd also goose them to stay on top of the forensic accountants.

Then he'd check in with Nick. As the arresting officer of record, he would get first shot at trying to flip Rice. Leslie said the stage was set for a deal that could save the young detective from serious prison time. He just hoped Nick was up to working his magic. Without the morphine to make Rice stupid, Nick was going to need all the help he could get.

Brannigan had been duly warned by Gallina and the DA's office to stay away from his two men since he was a part of the ongoing investigation. With all of Donny's and Moran's cell phones and burners in police custody, the multiple attempts of Brannigan to disobey those orders telephonically and connect with his men was one more count on the prosecution's list when his case went to trial. Jack knew Brannigan was twisting in the wind and his obvious discomfort put a dark smile on Jack's face.

It was a typical Los Angeles winter day. Seventy degrees at the coast, and eighty by the time he arrived downtown. Clear blue skies and not a cloud in sight. It hadn't rained since Vincent Cardona had summoned him to the prison, and there was no precipitation forecast for the foreseeable future. Just the way Jack liked it.

Detective Donny Rice had been wheeled into the interrogation room at LAPD Headquarters on a gurney. The room had a mirrored window, a camera, and a speaker, allowing other law enforcement working the case to listen in on the proceedings. His leg, confined by a full hip cast, was elevated with multiple pillows; his blue eyes, angry. Donny's lawyer was seated by his side while Nick Aprea stood at the foot of his bed. Having dispensed with the preliminaries, he began the interview.

"Let's start with the lie that was signed off on by your Commander Brannigan," Nick said with an air of calm certainty. "You were supposed to be taking a bereavement leave to bury your mother."

No response from Donny.

"I spoke with your mother yesterday, and I have no talent communicating with the dead. Go figure. Although your boss bragged he could beat a confession out of a dead man. Maybe he's got a skill set I'm not aware of. But I digress.

"Your mother sent you a message."

Still no response from Donny who looked bored but the throbbing vein on his temple gave him away.

Nick went on, "I don't get paid as a go-between, but the pain in her eyes when she heard what you stood accused of, the tears she spilled," Nick lowered his voice some, "moved me. She said, tell my boy to do the right thing. Don't let him shame himself or the family. We've always been so proud, she said, and then, I don't know, she was overwhelmed, couldn't talk for a bit. She finally gathered herself and said, 'Tell him," Nick seemed to be taken with emotion and raised his voice, "'don't be stupid and take the rap for your boss. He wouldn't do it for you.'"

Nick walked over to the sliding cart and poured a glass of water. Instead of handing it to the detective, he downed it in one gulp. "All we need is corroboration."

Donny licked dry lips, but he wasn't about to show weakness.

"What we know is, Brannigan ordered the hit on Gloria Millhouse. We know he ordered the hit on Cheryl Lee Williams, and I have you on tape saying you had nothing to do with that chick in Arizona. You hear what I'm saying? You denied any involvement in a murder before I brought it up, and so obviously you were aware of it. Not reporting your knowledge of a murder about to take place ties you to the conspiracy." Nick kept on adding up Rice's problems. "We know Brannigan ordered the hit on his accountant and investment counselor Freddie Triolo, to keep him from testifying against him. We also know that through Triolo, he ordered the hit on Carl Forbes, an innocent man taking the full ride for a killer you're protecting."

Nick summed up, acting like it was one sorry mess: "We have you in an iron-clad, open-and-shut-case for the attempted murder of Jack Bertolino. But here's the kicker. You will take the ride for the entire body count, being a party to, and participating in, the conspiracy to shut down the Carl Forbes case," he said. "Ask your lawyer to tally up the years you'll be spending behind bars as somebody's butt boy."

No response but Donny reached for a cup. His lawyer jumped to his feet and tried to pour, but spilled water down Donny's hospital gown. Rice muttered something unintelligible and drank thirstily.

Nick tamped down the grin that was forming. He glanced through the window at Jack, Leslie, Gallina and Tompkins, who he knew were watching the proceedings.

Nick locked eyes with Donny. Most men blinked first. "Give me the name of the sniper who was on the ridge at Vasquez Rocks when you hit the pavement. I also need your statement that Brannigan was the man. The mastermind who created the plot, and gave the orders."

Rice seemed to be digging deep, looking for the best way out of a losing proposition.

"What was it that sucked you in, Donny? Greed?" Nick asked, keeping the energy up in the room. "When Brannigan became chief you'd all hit paydirt? Step over dead bodies to race up the political ladder in the LAPD. Become players?"

Nick scoffed at that idea. "You're gonna find out the only thing money can't buy is freedom. Somebody's gonna be in your face now for the rest of your life. To tell you when to rise, shit, shower, eat and sleep. Your cellmate's gonna tell you when to suck his cock. Good-looking kid like you should listen to his mother."

Donny turned away from Nick and looked at his lawyer, who remained silent but gestured for him not to speak.

"Again," Nick continued, trying to bring it home. "All I need is the name of the sniper, and the name of who was calling the shots."

"We gotta talk," Donny said, referring to his lawyer. His voice had the kind of dry husk water wouldn't cure.

Nick signed off on the digital recording and started for the door to give the two some privacy. Then he turned on his heel.

"The DA's offer is time sensitive, Donny. The longer you wait, the longer you spend in the hoosegow. And something to think about – as if you don't have enough on your plate – but your reputation was destroyed the moment you gave up your partner in the Bertolino hit. So don't stand on ceremony. You already blew it with your brothers in blue. You're on their hit list."

"If you recall, I was on pain meds. Probably said some things that weren't true."

"Good try, Donny. But we've got you dead to rights. It's time to listen to your mother and do the right thing. You've got ten minutes." Nick walked out of the room and let the door slam shut behind him.

"You're smarter than you look," Gallina said, impressed.

"Wish I could return the sentiment," Nick shot back. "The mirror isn't your friend." He fist-bumped Jack, eliciting a choked laugh from Tompkins.

"Do you think he'll flip?" Leslie asked.

Gallina answered, trying to save face, "We might have to bring in his mother. She sounded persuasive."

"Never spoke to the woman," Nick said, a grin forming.

Tompkins said, "Damn, man."

Jack said, "That's police work."

"Fingers crossed," Nick said. "I think he's smart enough to know his life isn't worth shit at this point. I'm hitting the head, and we'll see what we'll see." Then he remembered about the other interview. "How did it go with Moran?"

"A big nothing," Tompkins said. "He didn't blink when we let him know Rice implicated him in the Bertolino hit."

"Hey, I'm standing here," Jack said. "Attempted hit. Now when Donny flips, we divide and conquer. Play one man against the other, and the rest of Brannigan's team will turn. They know their boss would kill to protect himself. They're his soldiers. Soldiers are expendable. It's going to be one hell of a takedown." Jack kept on thinking ahead and added, "Until that happens, we'll need men on Rice and Moran twenty-four/seven."

"Jack," Gallina said, exasperated. "Badge," he said, pointing to his. "I didn't fall off the back of a turnip truck, you know."

"No," Nick said. "But are you sure your mother didn't drop you on your head during childbirth? Turnip truck? Is that even a thing?"

When Nick walked back into the interrogation room, Donny looked pale, his face a mask of pain. His lawyer sat with his arms crossed, as if he were holding himself together. Nick started the digital recorder and started the proceedings. "What have you got for me, gentlemen?"

The lawyer cleared his throat. "My client is willing to consider turning state's evidence."

"I'll need protection."

He glared at his client. "But in doing so, it will put my client at great personal risk. We would need guarantees of protection, before and after we go to trial, and of course immunity from prosecution. Mr. Rice was not personally involved in any of the murders. He was peripherally involved, but fully briefed by all of the principals. We'll need assurances in writing that the DA's offer is binding."

Nick's eyes probed both men as if he were making a decision. It was a done deal. He paused for dramatic effect, to stick it to the bad cop. Donny squirmed in his hospital bed, trying to get comfortable, and failed.

"Done, and done," Nick said with more force than necessary. "You made the right choice. ADA Leslie Sager is waiting outside. I'll call her in, and you can make a preliminary statement. If Leslie's satisfied with your veracity and your value as a witness, she's authorized to extend the district attorney's guarantee. Don't hold back, Donny, don't lie, or the deal will disappear faster than your cherry when you're set loose in Victorville's general population."

Nick clicked off the recorder, glanced at the two-way mirror and exited the room clenching his fist in triumph.

Jack powered out of the downtown parking structure next to City Hall in his black Camaro. He was headed for the marina, and Tommy's suite, to bring the men up to speed.

He passed a beat-up green Prius with dark tinted windows, parked across the street with a clear view of the garage exit, but paid it no mind. Inside the Prius, the red-haired man peered over the steering wheel and snapped off a series of photos of Jack's new ride before putting the car in gear and following behind at a discreet distance. The morning traffic on the I-10 heading toward the marina made it a piece of cake.

CHAPTER 43

The next day, the crew hit the ground running trying to sustain the momentum created by Nick. A conference call was underway in Tommy's suite at the Ritz Carlton. A few uneaten bagels languished on a silver tray along with a ramekin of decimated cream cheese, a few odd bits of smoked salmon, capers, and squeezed lemon wedges. Cruz had his phone set on speaker and wiped cream cheese off his hands onto his jeans. Tommy was notating on a yellow pad, and Jack had his phone in one hand and a cup of coffee in the other.

Lieutenant Gallina and Tompkins were at Police Headquarters, having just been briefed by the forensic accountants.

"It was all boilerplate bullshit," Gallina said with a cynical grin. "The guy wasn't a financial genius. Brannigan's money was filtered through Triolo's offshore accounts. Two fake entities, bogus corporations located in the Caymans. Twenty percent of Brannigan's paychecks over the last twenty-three years were funneled directly into one of Triolo's investment funds. Triolo used that money to buy shares in the bogus corporations.

He went on to tell Jack that the arrangement was set up so that Cheryl Lee Williams, a stock holder of record, would receive a dividend check every month, deposited into her Wells Fargo account. It was all done electronically and small enough potatoes that it never raised any red flags. "The board of directors of Tri-Term Investments and Mirror Corp. consisted of Terry Brannigan, Freddie Triolo, and Brannigan's partner, Kevin Cook, until the day he died."

"Okay," Jack said." We've got him connected financially to Cheryl Lee, and Triolo, you could pick him up today, but I'm not feeling that move."

"For once we're on the same page," Gallina said. "Let's let him be, think he's still running things. One step ahead. As for Rice and Moran, we'll keep them on ice. When Donny flips, which is in process as we speak, we'll take Brannigan down without a skirmish. Last thing we need is a SWAT team bloodbath."

"I thought Donny was giving up the sniper," Jack said, not pleased.

"He has enough on Brannigan to take him down, but the lieutenant never divulged the identity of the shooter. Nobody on the SWAT team questioned the boss, and he wasn't forthcoming. Donny chalked it up to the less he knew, the less culpable he'd be. Not the sharpest tack."

"We're only halfway home," Jack said without emotion.

"We've done good," Gallina said in a rare glass-half-full moment. "Keep working it from your end, we'll take care of business here and finish this off. Jack, good effing work."

"All right, Lieutenant," he said, deflecting the compliment. "Let's connect later in the day."

The men hung up and took a moment to process the new information.

"What am I missing here?" Cruz said, picking up on Jack's mood swing. "What I heard was good news, no? If Donny can deliver Brannigan, then we've got the man responsible for at least three murders and two attempted murders."

"Without the shooter, who I'm almost certain now is the same man who pushed Gloria off the cliff, we might not find the killer of Shelley Goldstein. Without that information, Carl Forbes's exoneration is nobody's slam-dunk."

It was turning into another day that came and went. Nothing completed in a timely fashion. Frustrating. The DA's office needed another day with Donny Rice before signing off on the deal. Leslie assured Jack there were no real sticking points. The prosecution was just being sure they had an airtight case.

Nick was pissed about Donny not knowing the shooter's ID, and Jack got pissed off all over again.

He still hadn't heard from Angelica, and thought he'd leave well enough alone. The woman wasn't shy about reaching out.

Instead of waiting in a holding pattern, getting more worked up, Jack decided to drop in on Councilman Corcoran and rattle his cage. Corcoran was a loose end, and Jack wouldn't be satisfied until he uncovered the whole story.

Jack made a tire-squealing exit from the Ritz Carlton onto Admiralty Way. He was doing sixty and blew through two yellow lights before the red-haired man in the green Prius realized his mistake and pulled out of the Killer Shrimp lot, where he sat waiting.

By the time he made it to Mindanao Way, the black Camaro was nowhere in sight.

Jack found himself in typical afternoon traffic on the I-10, heading downtown toward City Hall. He made a short stop at Philippe's and wolfed down a lamb dip sandwich. He slathered on enough hot mustard to open his sinuses, and his mind, as he strategized an approach to the prickly politician.

When he arrived, Corcoran's secretary was thankfully away from her desk, but Jack could hear the councilman glad-handing a donor on the telephone. He was fast-talking someone as Jack stepped through his doorway. Abruptly, the politician's smiling voice went brittle, and his face turned. Corcoran excused himself and hung up the phone.

"Get the hell out of here, Jack. Now! I told you to call first. I'm working."

Jack ignored Corcoran and pulled a chair up in front of his desk. He grabbed his cell phone and pulled up the photographs Cruz had taken inside the El Compadre restaurant.

"Do I have to call the police, Jack?"

"I wish you would," he said, enjoying the moment. "Here's a photo of you, thick as thieves at the El Compadre." Jack turned his cell phone toward Corcoran." That's Joe Moran on your right, and three other members of Brannigan's SWAT team. I have photos of you pulling up in the Town Car, witnessing Brannigan being escorted out of the restaurant by the police, and then you entering." Corcoran was looking pale, and Jack pointed out, "Joe Moran and Donny Rice are both in police custody, which I'm sure you've already been briefed on."

"You just don't quit, do you?" he almost hissed. Jack witnessed Corcoran's veneer crack, his public persona gone.

"Not in my nature."

"And so?" he said with self-righteous indignation. "I'm not sure what you're inferring. Why is having lunch with detectives who work in my district somehow open to criticism?"

"I'm going to give you one shot at this, Corcoran. One shot to come clean. If you think Brannigan is going to the mat for you, you're in the wrong business. I want you to take some time, think about the lifeline I'm offering."

"Get the fuck out of my office."

"Explain what Brannigan has hanging over your head," Jack said, pressing. "I think I know, and I can help you. If you're honest. If not, you're going down with the rest of his team. And you won't end up at a country club facility. Murder and conspiracy to commit murder will send you to a federal pen."

"You're not making any sense, Bertolino. None whatsoever. And if you don't leave now, I will dial 911."

"You were what? Eighteen when Shelley Goldstein was murdered. If you unburden yourself of the secret you've been carrying around for twenty-three years, people might understand. You were young, impetuous. You either killed her yourself, or you were there and know who did. And that's why Brannigan owns you."

Corcoran's blush started at his neck and rose to his forehead. The fast talker was at a momentary loss for words.

"And by not coming clean," Jack hammered, "all those years ago, you railroaded an innocent man, while you climbed the political ladder. That's why you stonewalled Gloria Millhouse the day she was run off Malibu Canyon Road. Jesus Christ, man, how do you sleep at night? Even for a politician you're scum."

The councilman was too tongue-tied with guilt to protest. "Fill in the blanks for me, Corcoran, and the DA's office might offer you a deal. They're in a giving mood. I think you understand the implications. There are leaks in all organizations. The rats are biting each other's backs to get off the burning ship. If Brannigan confided to just one of his trusted men, you are already on the DA's short list."

Corcoran picked up his phone and dialed a number. "Yes, this is Councilman Corcoran. Could you please send up security? I'm afraid for my life."

"You got that right, bucko. Your life won't be worth shit once I'm done with you. I gave you a chance. Next time I see you, you better have a lawyer. And I'd get my financials in order or you won't make bail."

Jack stood as two security guards ran into the offices. Jack met them in the antechamber and said, "I was just leaving, gentlemen." Jack flashed his credentials. "I'll put in a word with the mayor for doing such a good job."

One of the guards looked confused as he pushed past Jack into Corcoran's room. "Are you okay, sir?"

"Never better," Corcoran said. "I'm sorry, there was a misunderstanding. Mr. Bertolino was just leaving. I'm okay. Thank you, Charles."

Jack walked out with the guards and thanked them again for doing their job. "You can never be too safe, gentleman."

CHAPTER 44

It was standing room only in Tommy's suite. A little too tight. Jack had pulled the meeting together, and Professor Anderson, who'd been stuck in traffic, was due to arrive directly.

Nick Aprea, Gallina and Tompkins, Tommy, Cruz, and Leslie were all chowing down, making short work of a tray of fruit, pastries, croissants, and bagels, and working on their second urn of hot coffee.

"This is high-end," Tompkins said to Tommy, referring to the food and the killer view of the marina. "I think I'm in the wrong game."

"If this works out, you may be moving up a pay grade."

"Your lips to God."

The door to the suite banged open and the professor stepped in. He seemed preoccupied and nervous as Jack made the introductions. The room went silent as Anderson burned his lip on the steaming java he grabbed.

"Sorry for the delay. Jack wanted me to share my information with all the principals in a one-off." He pulled a handful of documents out of his satchel, skimmed the salient points, and started talking from memory.

"We were coming up empty on the DNA search. All I can say is it was maddening. Jack called the other day advising me to run the DNA over to the Department of Defense's database." The professor smiled. "It appears it was a good move. Not a direct link, but definitely a positive move."

"What the hell does that mean?" Nick said.

"Have some more caffeine, Nick," Jack chided.

"Sorry," Anderson said, not taking offense. "So, here's the deal. We got a partial hit on the DNA at DOD. Not enough to satisfy the courts. Not enough to indict. But enough to continue the search."

"Prof, move it along. Please," Gallina added as an afterthought.

"Right. The partial DNA match belonged to Commander Terry Brannigan."

Silence in the room as everybody processed that explosive bit of information. No one was quite sure what it meant.

"So the deal is," Anderson explained. "There's something called a familial DNA search. It's hard to get the courts to approve the procedure. It's only used as a last resort in extreme cold cases. Only sexual assaults and homicides merit using the familial search in California because it's personally invasive and rife with false positives."

Murmurs started up in the room, and Anderson cut them off. "Suspects who don't have DNA in any of the law enforcement databases, but whose close relatives have had their DNA profiles catalogued, can be looked at. With Jack's help and my team at Project for the Innocent, and the intel you all provided, I made the case and the courts agreed. Shelley Goldstein's murder fit the criterion."

"What happened?" Cruz asked excitedly.

Professor Anderson got swept up in Cruz's enthusiasm and his face brightened. "The familial search gave us a hit. It matched thirty-three of thirty-five alleles on the original DNA sample."

"In English, Professor," Gallina barked.

Anderson took another sip of coffee and said: "The DNA led us to someone else in Brannigan's genetic tree. The man's name is Chip Boyd. He's Brannigan's nephew. His sister's son. The DNA from Shelley Goldstein's rape kit was a positive match for Chip Boyd."

'Holy shit," Cruz said. "He's on our list of possible shooters."

Jack took the floor. "His sister moved the family to Reno back in 2000 before the original case went to court. Brannigan interviewed and cleared Boyd, beat a confession out of Carl Forbes, and used Cheryl Lee Williams as his eyewitness to convict and sentence Carl to twenty-five to life. We all got pulled into the case after Brannigan ordered Gloria Millhouse's death in an attempt to quash Project for the Innocent's case to exonerate Carl."

"Why wasn't Boyd flagged on the DOD database? He was in the army," Tommy said.

"He left a sample," the professor said, "but it wasn't his."

"Someone carrying around that kind of secret," Jack said, "operating under the protective arm of Brannigan, would've been smart enough to job the system. And when we get our hands on Boyd, I'm willing to bet the farm Councilman Corcoran was involved. As a participant in Shelley's rape and murder, or as a witness to her death."

"So you think that's the hook Brannigan used on Corcoran," Leslie said. "The political leverage in his bid for police chief."

"It looks that way." And then to Professor Anderson, "Explain to the group if Boyd's real DNA wasn't in the DOD's database, where you got the hit."

The professor was enjoying himself now. "It appears when he was married, he and his wife went on Ancestry.com. Boyd discovered he was three percent Navaho, and we now have definitive proof tying him to the rape and murder of Shelley Goldstein, our first victim."

"All right, kids," Gallina said. "We have our answers. Let's not squander the opportunity. From here on in, it's all about making our case stand up in court. Let's do this by the numbers and stay healthy. Jack, I won't keep you from the arrest. You've earned it, but no weapons."

The professor handed out tear sheets with the salient facts regarding the DNA results.

"Where's Brannigan?" Tommy asked.

Nick answered. "Doing exercises with what's left of his team up at the G. Dawson Training Center."

"Son of a bitch," Tompkins said. "Let's grab him."

"What about Boyd?" Gallina asked.

"I'll find out if he's in Reno," Jack said. "If we can take Brannigan down before he makes the call to his nephew, it'll save lives."

Leslie came forward and handed Jack a package. "Open this when you're alone," she said, sotto voce. "I thought it might come in handy. And watch yourself, Bertolino."

Leslie didn't wait for a reply. She had to make her pitch to the district attorney, and get the paperwork in the pipeline for search warrants for not only Brannigan's residence but the residences of his remaining eight SWAT team members.

Gallina and Tompkins drove to headquarters to get their paperwork squared away. The chief approved extra manpower to execute the search warrants as well as the takedown at the training center in the foothills of the San Bernardino Mountains.

As Gallina and Tompkins were assembling their crew of uniformed officers who would serve as backup during the arrests, an undercover cop with wild red hair entered the hallway and cornered one of the cops.

"Hey, Red, what's happening?" the young officer asked.

"Same old, same old," Red said, pushing his unruly hair back off his face. "Doing surveillance. You?"

"Can you keep this on the QT?"

"It's already in the vault."

"We're picking up the commander."

"No shit, again?"

"Don't have the particulars, but Brannigan's gonna be pissed."

"Where's he at?"

"Training center. We're taking off in fifteen."

"Watch your back, son. You're heading into a shit storm."

Lieutenant Gallina angrily waved the young cop over.

"Later." And the officer joined his group, waiting for orders to deploy.

Red changed course, walked out of the building, jogged across the street. He jumped into his illegally parked green Prius, grabbed his cell phone and texted a message before pulling away from the curb.

Jack was at the loft, gearing up. He spoke with Duke at the Eldorado Resort and Casino in Reno and was told Chip Boyd had taken a bereavement leave of absence three days earlier to bury his mother. It was the same lie Donny Rice had used as cover while he convalesced. Brannigan was getting sloppy. Making mistakes.

Jack called Cruz at Tommy's suite and had him track down Mrs. Boyd. The woman miraculously answered her telephone and assured Cruz she wasn't in need of any construction work on her house. The very much alive Mrs. Boyd politely asked Cruz to please take her off of his list.

If Boyd wasn't in Reno, Jack knew, there was a good chance he was already in Los Angeles doing cleanup for Brannigan.

He didn't get any argument from Cruz or Tommy when he suggested they hold down the fort in the marina.

Jack opened the package Leslie had mysteriously handed off, and grinned before the surprise was out of the bag. It was a black, lightweight, ballistic-level bulletproof vest. Five and a half pounds of Kevlar designed to be worn covertly under clothing. Jack strapped it on and pulled a black T-shirt over it. He pulled out his Glock, slammed home a full clip, and slid it into his shoulder rig. He added two more clips into the zippered pockets of his black leather jacket. He grabbed his throw-down and strapped it to his ankle. There was a lot at stake for all the players, and Jack didn't expect Brannigan or his team to go down without a fight.

CHAPTER 45

Jack drove the Camaro with Nick riding shotgun toward the G. Dawson Center. The plan was to meet the arrest team in the large parking area below the training grounds, protected from view by thickly forested hills. They were going to appear unannounced, disarm Brannigan and his crew, and escort the men to the waiting police van for transport back to police headquarters and the beginning of their interrogations.

Brannigan was the only player who was under indictment at this point. Gallina was confident more arrests would be forthcoming after the search warrants were served. There was no way a team as tightly knit as these men would be unaware of what Brannigan, Moran, and Rice had been up to.

Gallina's plan was to divide and conquer. Play one detective against the others, using Rice who'd already flipped, until they had gathered enough intel to indict the entire team. Giving them a seamless arrest, the end of a bloodbath, four murders solved, and the exoneration of Carl Forbes.

"You're not carrying, are you?" Nick asked, throwing Jack a knowing smirk.

"No, you heard Gallina."

"Hah! Good." Nick's face split into a tight grin. "I had you covered in case you needed."

"I'm good to go."

"Let's take down these pricks. Above the law cocksuckers."

"You're a wordsmith, Nick."

"Fuckin' A."

Commander Brannigan clicked off the call from Red. He spoke confidently to his men, who were geared like combat soldiers, wearing camo, helmets, and boots. "It's time to stow your laser guns and grab your 9mm's. We're using live ammunition for the rest of the exercise. Trammel, you're in charge of the tear gas. Strap gas masks onto your utility belts. There's enough ambient light in the apartment complex that night vision goggles won't be in play."

A chill entered his voice as he added, "And gentlemen, we may be having visitors. You don't take orders from anyone but me. You keep working the exercise, stay alert with the live rounds, stay safe, and don't stop shooting until I give the order."

"Yes, sir!" the men shouted in unison.

"Take fifteen, and we'll start the hostage extraction."

He tapped a number into his cell, and had a brief conversation as his team changed gear, hit the head, and got ready for simulated battle.

Gallina, Tompkins, Nick, and Jack walked single file up the narrow path through the forested area into what sounded like wartime combat. Ten uniformed officers followed close behind. The men made their way toward a clearing. A mock-up apartment complex was used for live-round exercises where SWAT teams prepared for active shooters, barricaded subjects, realistic building entry, and room-to-room clearing exercises.

Lieutenant Gallina turned to the uniforms. "As I said in the TAC meeting, I want you all to stay in cover until you're told otherwise. No talking, stay invisible. I don't want to exacerbate what should be a by-the-books arrest. Are we clear?"

The men nodded along with a few muffled yes sirs. To Tompkins, Nick, and Jack, he said, "Let's do this. No weapons unless the shit hits the fan."

The team walked shoulder to shoulder out of the protection of the forest. Thirty yards away they saw Commander Brannigan.

Brannigan stood in front of the series of buildings, hand-held walkie-talkie to his ear, watching the action inside the live round apartment complex on a computer screen that was perched on a wooden stand.

The bleed from other law enforcement teams training on the three-hundred-yard rifle range and the fifty-yard small arms range beyond the tree line created a cacophony of deafening, explosive sounds. Brannigan felt the intrusion before he heard his name being shouted over the fray.

"Brannigan. We need to talk."

Brannigan flashed dead eyes but made no attempt to respond to Lieutenant Gallina's order. "Come back when you have an arrest warrant," he hollered back. "And get that civilian off my set. We're using live rounds. It would be a shame if someone got hurt." His admonition came off more as a threat than a warning.

Gallina, Tompkins, Jack, and Nick kept walking, closing the distance to the commander.

Rounds could be heard pinging off the cement walls inside the complex. An occasional shadow would pass the open windows and then disappear, shouting and firing against life-sized targets that appeared to be live shooters facing off against Brannigan's team.

"Tell your men to put down their weapons, Commander," Gallina ordered.

"You got one part of it right. I'm a commander, you're not. I don't take orders from underlings." Brannigan shouted into his walkie-talkie, "Keep shooting."

"Do it," Gallina said to his partner as he pulled his 9mm from his hip holster.

Tompkins texted a predetermined code into his cell phone and then looked back toward the set. A shrill Klaxon screamed through the forested area. A disembodied voice bellowed over a loudspeaker, "All training exercises must come to a halt. Weapons down, gentlemen. That means now." The sound of rounds exploding slowly diminished in the surrounding training areas.

"Keep shooting!" Brannigan shouted again into his handset.

The loudspeaker blared. "Weapons down. That means now."

Everyone stopped shooting except Brannigan's men. Brannigan spoke into his walkie-talkie. Trammel appeared in the window, appraised the situation. A *whump* sounded as he fired a teargas grenade from inside the apartment complex and exploded at the feet of the arresting officers. The men fanned out, choking, eyes watering. Weapons drawn.

Brannigan turned to run, but Jack charged. He threw a punch from the heels and knocked the commander off his boots into the computer setup, sending the equipment flying.

Brannigan had zero body fat but years of scar tissue. Lean, mean, and fighting for his life, he leapt to his feet like a young warrior and led with his fist, snapping Jack's head back. "You're not walking out of here alive, Bertolino."

"In your dreams," Jack said. thundering a punch that Brannigan evaded. He returned a stinging left hook that clipped Jack above his eye. It split his brow and the flowing blood, and caustic smoke, momentarily blinded him.

Brannigan stepped forward, coming in for the kill. Instead of retreating, Jack sprang forward and head butted Brannigan. The blow caught the warrior off guard and staggered him. He tried to shake it off, but his eyes tearing from the gas that swirled around the combatants gave Jack an opening.

The sound of gunfire continued inside the complex.

Jack's big fist scored a solid right that flattened the cartilage in Brannigan's nose. As blood spurted out, Brannigan's head lowered, and he charged like a bull.

Jack sidestepped and rocketed an elbow to the back of Brannigan's head, knocking the commander to the ground. He dropped a heavy knee onto Brannigan's back, pinning him down as he cuffed him.

Jack yanked the killer to his feet, spun him around and shoved him toward Tompkins.

Brannigan lost his footing, but his eyes glanced up the hill in a question. The last thing Brannigan saw was a flash of light reflected off a long-distance scope.

He stumbled, fighting to stay upright.

A high-powered round ripped through Brannigan's chest, knocking him down. He was dead before he hit the ground.

Jack took off running. "Boyd!" he yelled over his shoulder. Nick wiped the chemical tears from his eyes and followed in his wake. Jack moved like a jackal running past the clearing, into the thick forest, up the incline toward the shooter. He knew the sniper's shot came from the hillside above, and the only way out was down toward the parking lot below. Jack signaled Nick and the two men separated. Each made a steady, metered climb up the steep hill.

A chopper thundered overhead, ordering all gunfire to stop. As it circled the scene and banked up and over the canopy of trees, searching for the sniper, the gunfire at the G. Dawson Training Center diminished.

Gallina deployed the uniformed officers, who quickly surrounded the training complex. "Drop your weapons in place," Gallina shouted. "Exit the building with your hands above your head."

Brannigan's men stopped firing. Shocked by the death of their leader, the SWAT team instantly complied. They slowly exited the building, hands held high. Disbelieving eyes trained on their leader, who lay dead and bleeding out on the ground.

Gallina and Tompkins took charge of the arrests. They corralled Brannigan's crew and ordered the men to drop to the ground and assume the position. The uniformed officers cuffed the prone cops, taking all eight of them into custody.

Chip Boyd had been breaking down his rifle, but with the helicopter's appearance he cut and ran, pounding down the hill toward his ride.

He pulled out his Ruger SR9 and headed deeper into the forest, trying for an end run around the action below.

Boyd had mixed feelings about killing his uncle. His target had been Jack Bertolino, but hell, if he had to face the lion, he decided to take down the only man who could pin him for four murders.

He knew Councilman Corcoran wouldn't talk, or it would destroy his career. Boyd had done the stabbing, but Corcoran was there in the room, all those years ago. He was the one who had started the sexual skirmish that led to Shelley Goldstein's death.

When the hysterical woman began screaming, Boyd pushed Corcoran off her body and slammed a pillow over her mouth. Her eyes locked on Corcoran's, begging for help, but he didn't respond. He stood mute as Boyd raped, and then in a moment of extreme panic that was escalating out of control, killed Shelley Goldstein.

Corcoran helped transfer her body to the back seat of Boyd's beat-up Ford Taurus. It was his idea to drop her into the storm drain a quarter mile from their neighborhood.

Brannigan was the only man who knew Chip Boyd had also killed the other three victims. Under his orders.

Jack and Nick were breathing hard, making their way up the steep terrain. Leading with their weapons, running from one copse of trees to the next. The helicopter's rotors created a wind tunnel of detritus and dead pine needles as it circled overhead. A thousand-watt light from the body of the beast crisscrossed the side of the mountain, looking for the shooter but coming up empty. Jack had one mission. Take Chip Boyd alive.

Boyd's legs burned as he pounded down the slope. Suddenly his feet hit loose shale and he slipped into a wild slide, madly digging in his heels before stopping short. He stilled his breathing and listened over the pounding of his heart. He thought he heard labored breathing to his left, and then a twig snap. He moved silently on the blanket of pine needles, cutting hard to the right, and froze in place, weapon raised. He could hear muted shouting in the distance, the roar of the chopper, and an approaching siren as an EMT vehicle arrived on scene. Too little too late, Boyd thought. If he could just make it to his car…

Jack ran from behind a copse of trees.

Boyd fired twice. Two hits. Two rounds to Jack's chest.

Jack's gun flew out of his hand and he dropped hard, rolling down the incline until his body banged up against an old growth pine.

Boyd charged down the slope, stepped in close to put a third bullet between Jack's eyes.

Jack's boots exploded between Boyd's legs. A thundering heel kick to his groin. The man screamed in pain, involuntarily doubling over, dropping his gun. Jack threw a sweeping sidekick, hitting Boyd at the ankles, knocking the killer to the ground.

Jack grimaced as he rolled over and planted a solid punch to Chip Boyd's face. He smashed him again and felt the killer's cheekbone crack. He hit him again for the death of Shelley Goldstein, for the death of Gloria Millhouse, for the death of Cheryl Lee Williams, and for the death of Freddie Triolo.

Nick ran over, gasping for breath, weapon aimed. "Cuff him," Jack croaked as he rolled onto his back and grabbed his chest.

"Are you shot?"

"Shit yeah. But the vest, God damn, Nick, the vest worked."

Nick's face was a mask of worry as he cuffed Boyd and rolled him over onto his back. On second thought he dropped to one knee and nailed him in the gut. Boyd's head lolled to one side and he puked. Big mistake trying to kill the only real friend Nick had.

Nick felt a wave of relief as he reached a hand down and pulled Jack to his unsteady feet.

Tompkins appeared out of a thicket, sucking wind, "You guys okay?"

"Better than Boyd," Jack said. "Better than Brannigan."

Tompkins roughly yanked the prisoner to his feet. Nick picked up Boyd's 9mm with a broken branch, dropped it into a plastic evidence bag, and pocketed it.

Jack grabbed his Glock off the pine needles and slid it into his shoulder rig.

The four men started down the hill toward base camp. The killing was at an end.

Jack made two calls before getting checked out by the EMT crew. He got Ward on the horn and gave him his location and instructions to bring his camera, keep his mouth shut, and he'd have the exclusive on the crime scene mop-up.

Brannigan wasn't going anywhere soon. His body would be left in place until the crime-scene folks arrived. They would pick apart the sniper's nest up the hill and find the rifle used to kill Brannigan. They'd also seize the weapon used to shoot the teargas grenades, along with Brannigan's electronics, phones, weapons, and all of the SWAT team's personal items and vehicles.

Jack promised Ward he'd fill in the details when the dust settled.

The second call he placed was to Leslie, who was nervously waiting at the DA's office for word. She picked up on the first ring.

"Jack."

"How does it feel to save a life? Because you saved mine today."

"Are you hurt?"

"I'm alive. Wouldn't be if I wasn't wearing your gift. Hadn't worn one in years. Wore it today."

"Damn, I'm good," she said.

"Thank you," Jack said sincerely. And then back to business: "Brannigan's dead, shot by his nephew. Boyd is under arrest. I've got hours of cleanup to do before I can leave. I'll call later in the day and fill you in on the rest."

"I'm so relieved, Jack."

"You and me both."

Jack wasn't clear how he felt about their relationship, and he hoped he sounded grateful. He also wanted to hear his son's voice, and made a mental note to call him on the drive home.

It turned out that Jack's chest was a tangled mass of broken capillaries where the two bullets had impacted the Kevlar vest. Both hits were turning his chest a dark shade of purple. His back was seizing, making it hard to turn or even breathe without pain shooting down his spine. The stitches in his arm had torn open, and blood was seeping out. He'd need more stitches over his eye.

The EMT clucked, "You're lucky to be alive." She got no argument from Jack. She was fast and thorough, slapping medicated bandages over the wounds to dissipate the pain, a suture over his eye to stop the bleeding, and then two Vicodin to finish the job.

Jack swallowed the pills with a huge gulp of water. Then he finished the entire bottle when he realized how dry his throat was. The EMT handed him a second bottle, which he gladly accepted. Nick would definitely be driving home.

CHAPTER 46

Carl Forbes was seated at the same metal table in the same claustrophobic jailhouse interview room where Jack was first introduced to him. His head was propped in his hands, elbows on the table, and his rolled sleeves revealed the scars of the failed suicide attempt. He didn't acknowledge Jack or the professor when they first entered the room. Just a glance, then he lowered his head just as quickly.

Jack gave him a moment to gather himself.

"I'm just lettin' you know," Carl finally said. "Being honest here … you're scaring me. Both of you together looking all serious and such. Scaring me. Why do you need two men unless to deliver bad news?"

Jack turned to the professor, whose eyes started to fill and couldn't speak.

"Sweet Jesus," Carl said. "Is it over? Did we lose?"

The professor sucked in a breath, fighting for control. "No, quite the opposite. You're going home, Carl."

Carl's eyes filled in disbelief. He shook his head no as tears streamed down his freckled cheeks.

"You're going home," the professor repeated, all he could muster.

Jack got caught in the maelstrom of emotion, his voice thick as he explained.

"Item A. DNA from Brannigan's nephew, Chip Boyd, matched the sample from Shelley Goldstein's rape kit. Item B. We found microscopic paint slivers, the color of a pistachio, on the bumper of the SUV Boyd used to run Gloria off the cliff on Malibu Canyon Road. Item C. The rifling on the assault weapon he used to kill Brannigan matched the markings on the bullet that killed Cheryl Lee Williams."

Carl trained his eyes on Jack who let that information sink in before continuing. "Item D. Fibers found in the rear compartment of the SUV matched the manila rope used to strangle and hang Freddie Triolo, Brannigan's money man."

Carl rubbed his eyes, trying for clarity of thought. He felt as if he were dreaming, and he was reticent to believe the full implication of the information he just heard. "So, this Boyd character, yeah, I knew Chip from back in the day. Didn't know he was a relative of Brannigan."

"No one did. His sister's boy," Jack explained. "He rolled over on Councilman Corcoran. Placed him at the murder scene of Shelly Goldstein. Said Corcoran started the forced sex play, and Boyd killed her when it went south on them."

"Boyd ... he's one bad man."

Jack nodded his head, "But Carl ... he's not breathing your air. Not anymore. You're the one going home."

Carl smiled and the professor openly wept.

"There's someone who wants to share the good news," Jack said, walking to the metal door and knocking lightly.

The guard nodded through the glass window, unlocked the door and pulled it open. In walked Carl's mother, Eunice.

Mother and son locked in a ferocious embrace.

The energy in the room filled with love, and tears, and pain, and forgiveness, and years lost, and life yet to live. Mother and son, whose bond was stronger than prison walls and a steel jail cell.

Jack tapped the professor on the shoulder, and led him to the door, giving the family privacy. His visit to Victorville wasn't over.

Jack and Vincent Cardona were strolling in the open air under the watchful eye of the gun tower.

"So, you got lucky?" Cardona said.

"Some might say."

"So good. Maybe you could do the same for me."

"My guy was innocent."

The spark of anger from Vincent Cardona was instantaneous. But then his bloodshot eyes crinkled into a sly smile. He brought his meaty fist to his mouth, trying to mute a belch, but fell short. Vincent took a labored breath and continued walking around the caged field, surrounded by double electrified sixteen-foot chain-link fencing covered in waves of barbed wire. "The mouth on you."

Jack didn't think a response was necessary.

"I'm guessing you heard?" Cardona said.

"You'd be wrong. I've been up to my neck in alligators. We haven't spoken in a few days," Jack said, knowing Cardona was referring to Angelica.

"Well, the fuckin' swamp's spreading, then. Fuckin' Razzano. Took a midnight flight a few days ago and had a surprise sit-down with my daughter."

"You don't say," Jack said, not liking the picture Cardona was painting.

"Oh, but I do. From what I hear, she gave my brother-in-law shit right back. Kicked that asshole John Franco out of my joint and got a six-month reprieve from a hostile takeover. She's got balls, I'll say that much."

"She's in over her head."

"You should tell her that. She might listen. Comin' from you."

"What's the end game here? Bottom line, Vincent." Jack couldn't hide his concern.

"I give them the Chop House in exchange for my life. I'm looking at eight years, maybe six for being an upstanding prisoner. And some palms being greased on the outside."

"They'll say yes ..."

"I know. And then try and punch my ticket. But I've got support inside. Major muscle on both sides of the bars, as it were."

Jack knew Cardona was paying off guards and inmates. But he didn't think he stood a chance in hell.

Cardona wasn't done. "And I'll give you the keys to the castle. Where the gold is buried. You deliver it to my girl in a timely fashion, and keep an eye out."

"You're asking a lot."

"Of the only man I trust to do this particular job. You keep enough to make it worth your while. You won't cheat Angelica."

Jack checked his watch and locked eyes with Cardona. "I've got to sleep on this. We'll talk again."

"Whatever. You know where to find me. Do the right thing, Bertolino."

The big man walked back across the field toward the gun tower. Jack knocked on the thick metal door and glanced back at the lone figure, who looked diminished in size. Prison could do that to a man, Jack thought as he turned and disappeared inside the bowels of the beast.

CHAPTER 47

The winter sky was ice blue, the sun more white than orange. Not a wisp of a cloud. The welcome home party in the modest back yard of Eunice Forbes home was underway, and a love fest. Stevie Wonder's *Innervisions* played on the stereo, the sound mingled with the raised voices and laughter. Carl was seated at a long card table looking a bit lost, but happy beyond belief. Family and friends took turns stopping by, shaking his hand, and wishing him well.

Carl sat in disbelief. Eyes wide, taking mental pictures, not wanting to miss a moment of this surreal event. His eyes fell on his mother's white rose bushes that surrounded the back yard. When he was a boy, it was his job to deadhead the roses that were past bloom and turning brown, to keep the plants strong. He looked forward to doing it again. Catching up. Little things. He knew it would take time to come to grips with his new reality. But felt confident, Project for the Innocent would help him make the transition back into a world that hadn't slowed pace while he was imprisoned. He was entering a strange new world.

An air of excitement filled the proceedings. The table was laden with food, and his cousin stood at the grill barbequing chicken and hamburgers. The scent from the smoking grill, mixing with the music, and the laughter, was almost too much to bear. Carl watched as satisfied faces walked in and out of the kitchen with bowls of shrimp gumbo as the screen door slammed behind them. An ice filled corrugated metal tub contained, beer, soda, and bottled water.

Eunice would occasionally stick her head out of the kitchen door, looking for her son. When she was sure he was okay, her eyes would tear up and she'd retreat back to the safety of her stove.

Jack, and Tommy stood with Professor Anderson and a few of his students from LMU. They all had paper plates filled with food. Cruz stepped out of the house with a plate overflowing with Eunice's famous cherry cobbler.

"You know, you could've gone in for seconds," Jack said, amused at the sheer size of Cruz's plate.

"Oh, I will," Cruz assured. And nobody doubted him.

Keith Millhouse walked over to the iced tub to grab a beer and then joined Carl. The two men toasted and stood in silence, taking in the party.

"I just wanted to say congratulations," Keith said.

Carl nodded his head. "Thank you for coming, sir, it means a lot."

"Carl, I can't even fathom what your life will be like the next few months. But I want to offer you my help, in any way I can."

"That's very kind."

"When you've had time to settle in—no pressure, now—but I'd like you to stop by the office. I've seen the files you created, the letters you wrote. Your work that sold Gloria on your innocence. The case you built was solid. Our firm is always scouting for smart researchers. I've already run it by my partners, and we'd like to offer you a job." He clasped Carl by the elbow. "And if you had any thoughts about going back to school, our firm will support you and your aspirations. It's the very least I can do."

Carl was unable to comprehend the turn his life had taken. Not sure what to say. Not wanting to let loose with the roiling sensations that threatened to overwhelm him. "Thank you," he finally said, his voice getting thick. He took a swig of beer to clear his throat. "I'll surely take you up on that kind offer."

"And Carl, I want to thank *you*."

"For what, sir?"

"You helped give Gloria's life meaning."

Carl couldn't speak at first, stymied by the raw emotion he felt. "She was the one … she kept me strong when I was losing my way. I owe your daughter my life."

"Gloria would be pleased." The lawyer was growing misty-eyed himself. "I'll let you get back to it. I don't want to monopolize the man of honor." Keith walked into the kitchen, leaving Carl stunned by the gracious offer.

Jack walked up and grabbed a brew. "How're you holding up?"

"It's a lot."

"Nothing you can't handle. You're a winner, Carl."

"That's a new one, but I'm surely grateful." Carl glanced past Jack and raised his eyebrows. "Somebody's staring your way."

Jack saw Leslie standing in the kitchen doorway. "You need anything, Carl, you know where to find me."

"Thanks, Jack. Now, don't let me keep you."

The men shook hands, and Jack walked into the house. Leslie was finishing a small bowl of gumbo. "This should be illegal, it's so good."

"I had two bowls."

Eunice came up and gave Jack a big hug. "This is the man that saved my boy," she whispered, her eyes shining with tears of joy. "Don't let me interrupt you two."

The kitchen started to fill, and Jack and Leslie eased through the crowd and stepped out onto the front porch.

"What a day," Jack said.

"Good work, Mr. Bertolino."

"A team effort," Jack said, deflecting the praise. "I'm pleased it all worked out."

"So is the mayor. He's offering you a place on his team if you get tired of freelancing. There are worse people to hitch your wagon to."

"You going cowgirl on me?"

"Only if you're fond of leather boots," she joked. "How are you feeling?"

"Grateful to be alive. Thank you for that. You know, you have me for life now. Anything you need. Anytime."

"Well, I think we'll table that offer for now. You have some unfinished business. Let's talk when you come up for air."

"Deal."

"I've got to run, I just wanted to pay my respects." Leslie stepped close to Jack and put her hand on his cheek. "For once in your life you listened to me. Thank God, Jack." Leslie bussed Jack's lips, and Jack watched her leave. He felt something dislodge in his chest, and wasn't sure what it meant.

CHAPTER 48

Jack had his first dinner at the Chop House since the beginning of the Gloria Millhouse case. It had been a rough ride, but the case ended better than expected.

Nobody cried over the death of Terry Brannigan, a dirty cop who had beaten, tortured, and murdered his way to the top of a storied law enforcement career.

Chip Boyd was up on multiple murder charges, and the only good thing he'd done in recent memory was rolling over on his childhood friend, Mark Corcoran.

Corcoran had been immediately ousted from the City Council while awaiting trial for complicity in the murder of Shelley Goldstein. A unanimous request for censure of Corcoran had been submitted and approved by the ad hoc committee of the council. Corcoran wisely chose not to show up for his hearing.

Since there were no statutes of limitations on murder, the dishonorable councilman was going down in disgrace and looking forward to spending the latter part of his years behind bars.

In the end, Boyd was indicted on five murder charges and two attempted. His thinking was he might take the stainless-steel ride, but he wasn't going down alone. He flipped on the entire SWAT team. His only regret was that he couldn't kill his uncle a second time.

Brannigan's men were all indicted on multiple counts of conspiracy to commit murder. It was a black eye for the LAPD that would take time to heal.

Nick, Gallina, and Tompkins, on the other hand, were held up as prime examples of what the LAPD stood for. They all moved up pay grades and received promotions.

Ward had his own photographer now, along with bragging rights, having scooped the rest of the town on the latest breaking story. It moved him up the food chain at the *LA Times,* and he was a happy camper.

Tommy was already winging his way back to Long Island with promises he'd open an office in Century City. Jack was not holding his breath.

Jack's dinner was an aged New York steak, cooked medium-rare. His martini, Stoli with a twist of lemon. The wine, Benziger. Caesar salad was made table-side.

His date, although the meet had been advertised as a business dinner, was perfect.

Angelica Cardona was resplendent. When Jack delivered her father's request to trade the Chop House for his life, the young woman was visibly moved, agreeing to her father's terms. Angelica understood, and was grateful her father was willing to give up his life's work so that she might have a life for herself.

Jack maybe bought into the idea that good things could happen to good people. The old neighborhood twist on the phrase was that bad things happened to bad people. He pushed all his Staten Island superstitions aside and gave himself fully to the wonderful company.

Angelica and Jack had an espresso as the piano man belted out a Sinatra medley.

Beverly Hills was quiet at one o'clock in the morning. The only thing the least bit distracting was the hulk walking in front of them. Frankie-the-Man couldn't be dissuaded from his role as bodyguard, and Jack didn't argue the point.

The odd threesome made their way left off Canyon Drive. The night-blooming jasmine scented the cool air. The lit storefronts dazzled as they turned onto Beverly Drive.

Angelica stopped in her tracks and pulled Jack close, creating some distance between themselves and Frankie. She leaned up and they kissed. They pulled apart, lost in the moment, and then kissed lightly again.

Frankie wasn't born yesterday. He saw what was happening in the reflection of a storefront window. He instinctively turned on swollen feet, it had been a long day, and headed back toward the couple. His eyes flashed across the street and picked up on a man walking at a good clip. His radar went off.

It was John Franco.

"Jack!" Frankie shouted, pounding the pavement as John Franco pulled his weapon and strode across Beverly, his 9mm leading the way.

"Bertolino," Franco hissed.

Jack spun and drew the Glock from his shoulder rig.

Frankie-the-Man fumbled for his gun as he bounded protectively in front of Jack and Angelica. Covering them with his body. He aimed…

Franco fired first.

Frankie took the bullet in the shoulder, and the force jolted the big man back, blocking Jack's shot.

Angelica took a lightning step to the right, pulled a snub-nose .38 from her Gucci bag and squeezed the trigger.

A blood red dot appeared between Franco's eyes like a Hindu bindi. But it wasn't a religious symbol, it was death calling him home. Franco looked startled, surprised by the bullet. His pistol clattered to the curb as he dropped to his knees and fell face first in the gutter.

Frankie-the-Man collapsed heavily onto the sidewalk and landed in a seated position. He reached up with his good arm and grabbed Angelica's pistol, gripping the stock with his meaty fingers. Trading his fingerprints for hers. She didn't fight him.

"Get her out of here, Jack, I've got this covered," he said, wincing as he stanched the blood flowing from his shoulder wound. "I'm good," he growled, "get the fuck out!"

Jack locked eyes with Frankie who nodded assurance, and then turned toward Angelica. Jack knew there were no good moves to play here. Leslie had said as much. Warned Jack he was in over his head. That Mafia business would take him down.

A distant siren pierced the still night. Jack read the resolve in Angelica's eyes. This young woman had just saved his life. It was a pure act. Simple as that.

Jack grabbed Angelica's hand and together they walked past Frankie and John Franco, who lay dead in the gutter. They didn't have to call 911. This was a Beverly Hills Code 3.

The sirens grew louder as Jack and Angelica headed west. They picked up their pace when they hit Rodeo Drive and disappeared into the night.

ACKNOWLEDGMENTS

Many thanks to Leslie S. Klinger for opening the door for me at Project for the Innocent. I started this book three years ago, and it's their life-saving work that kept me writing. Thanks to Sue Trowbridge for making it happen and keeping the ball rolling. And Karen Phillips for the great cover art. Thanks to John Paine for another brilliant edit, my lawyer, Les Abell, my manager, Murray Weiss, and Kathy Solorzano for her knowledge of criminal law.

A heartfelt thanks to Vida Spears. Her constant support and perceptive notes through every permutation made this the best book possible. And my wonderful group of readers, Diane Lansing, Annie George, Phil Casnoff, Bruce Cervi, and Deb Schwab, who lent their time, support, and friendship. And a special thank you to Gordon Dawson, whose insightful ideas and love of writing took me to the finish line. Gordy, my mentor and dear friend, passed away this year and will be sorely missed.

www.ingramcontent.com/pod-product-compliance
Lightning Source LLC
LaVergne TN
LVHW090556110826
845146LV00001B/154

9798988516613